The Kinetic

Alterealm Series

Book 9

By J. Risk

Whitham Royal Family Tree

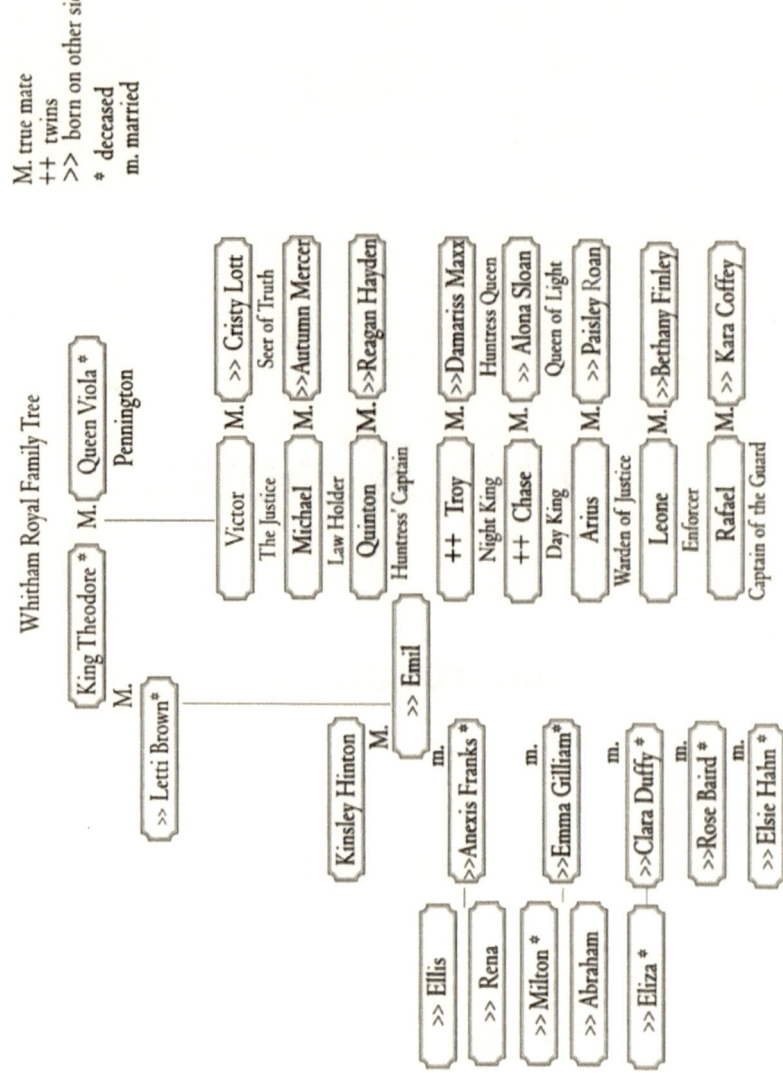

M. true mate
++ twins
>> born on other side
* deceased
m. married

King Theodore *
M.
Queen Viola *
Pennington

>> Letti Brown *

Victor — M. — >> Cristy Lott
The Justice — Seer of Truth

Michael — M. — >>Autumn Mercer
Law Holder

Quinton — M. — >>Reagan Hayden
Huntress' Captain

++ Troy — M. — >>Damariss Maxx
Night King — Huntress Queen

++ Chase — M. — >> Alona Sloan
Day King — Queen of Light

Arius — M. — >> Paisley Roan
Warden of Justice

Leone — M. — >>Bethany Finley
Enforcer

Rafael — M. — >> Kara Coffey
Captain of the Guard

Kinsley Hinton — M. — >> Emil

m. — >>Anexis Franks *

m. — >>Emma Gilliam*

m. — >>Clara Duffy *

m. — >>Rose Baird *

m. — >> Elsie Hahn *

>> Ellis

>> Rena

>> Milton *

>> Abraham

>> Eliza *

She didn't smile or bother with a greeting. "Why is your father being called back?" She glared at the others. "He's retired."

I nodded.

"He's being reinstated as an advisor." Emil said calmly. "To oversee the new rehabilitation facility."

She stared at him for a moment, then bowed her head respectfully. "I'm sorry, Prince, I didn't notice it was you."

Emil offered her a polite smile. "That's fine." He motioned to Nyle. "Nyle will be staying here for the foreseeable future, as will another guard when his shift is over."

My mother frowned. "We need a guard?" She looked at my father.

I watched dad heave a sigh. "Yes, as a precaution."

"Where are you going to be working that we need a guard?" She looked from him to Gudrun.

Gudrun straightened, then bowed his head. "Gudrun Dalston, 'mam."

"Are you staying too?" She put her hands on her hips.

I wanted to back out the door and hide.

"No ma'am. I'm Kinsley's guard."

I was sure the whole realm went silent in that moment.

"Why does my daughter need a guard?" She gave me her accusatory look that she should trademark. "What have you done?"

I opened my mouth, but before I could say anything, Emil stepped forward.

"She hasn't done anything, Mrs. Hinton." He cleared his throat, "she's my mate." He took a deep breath, "and as part of the royal family, she must have a guard."

I dropped my head forward and squeezed my eyes shut tight for a second before straightening again. I looked at my mother. Standing in front of me was a creature I'd never seen. In my life. Just like that, the woman that had hounded me over every detail of my life was smiling and glowing like a flower opening in the bright sunlight.

DEDICATION

This one is for all of the kickass women that get up each day and keep going despite the overwhelming tasks that await them. You are the strings that bind everything together in so many lives, each and every day. ♥

ACKNOWLEDGMENTS

I need to thank my editor and beta/proofreaders. Honestly, without all of you I would probably curl up in the corner and cry. As the writer, I'm obligated to read and re-read and keep reading the same story over and over—the amount of times you go through my work is amazing and the fact you are entertained by the same story each time makes it all worth it.

Thank you and I hope I can entertain you with each one I write.

.

Author's note:

I can't believe we're at book 9! The time flew by as I was lost in the world of Alterealm.

While this is the last book (at this time) in the Alterealm Series, it is not the last time we will see these characters— they will be showing up in the Solrelm Series. I'm already working out the details for Bastian's story in the first book, *Concealed* ... I hope to meet you in Solrelm soon.

xox

Prologue

She looked over her shoulder to be sure the guards weren't paying attention. They didn't notice her; and she kept her head down and never gave them a hard time. A few others wore the same color wristband and were sitting close enough to watch her movements. She gnawed on her lip, not sure if she could trust them. If she was caught—well, she didn't want to think of what would happen.

Kinsley looked at the band around her wrist. As far as she could tell it was used just for sorting purposes. In her case, it meant her eyes changed color. Little did they know she was a full-blood Alterealm resident. She glanced to the other women again, wondering how much Alterealm DNA they had. Some of the women that slept on the main floor wore bands as well, but theirs were ability blockers. That brought her back to the reason she was thinking about all of this in the first place. They *couldn't* find out she had an ability. More importantly, they couldn't discover that she was working undercover for the Alterealm royal family.

She watched as a woman wandered close to the barrier and stopped. That would get all of them in trouble. No one wanted to be on this island, but she was making her escape attempts too obvious. She turned to see if the guard was watching and blew out a breath of relief to see he wasn't.

Her gaze landed on another woman, or more specifically, the bruising on her face. Kinsley's heartbeat sped up, she felt like she was failing. There was only so much interference she could create to keep the men away from the women. She was just as much at risk, with the sheer number of men that came and went from this hunk of land in the middle of the water. Twice now, she'd had to fight to prevent unwanted advances. She almost felt physical pain in knowing that she couldn't always protect the rest of the women. She'd barely slept since arriving: the cries that echoed through the building wouldn't allow her to sleep. She didn't know what the royal family had done on their end, but the security and visits from the higher-ups in this crazy place had increased tenfold.

Okay, she put her hand out and touched the tall weeds growing beside where she stood, *now or never. You can't get caught with the phone.* With her other hand, she reached into her top and pulled out a small phone. Quickly she opened the message function and hit send. *Hurry, hurry,* she chanted in her mind. It vanished from the screen. *Check your messages, Justice.* Clutching the phone against her chest, she turned to be certain no one was looking her way. Taking a quick breath, she backed up a few steps to see a rotted-out knot in the tree. Taking a deep breath, she opened her hand and watched the phone move carefully toward the tree and didn't take another breath until it was tucked inside the knot of the tree, out of sight.

"Hey."

Startled, she turned to see one of the guards scowling at her. With a fake yawn, she stretched her arms over her head and gave him a sweet smile. He watched her for a moment more, then turned away.

Let the cavalry come soon was her only thought as she slowly wandered back to the others.

Chapter One

I stood there looking at all the things I'd tossed on the bed. There was no way it would all fit into one duffle bag. I had no idea what I would or wouldn't need from this point forward. Did royal guards even get days off? I didn't know. They had to, right? The other personal guards spent a lot of time in the yard, so they must have free time.

I looked at my new porter. It had three locations programmed in: the underground chambers, the palace, and the guard's yard. Only the high ranking and personal royal guards had this elite porter, so I shouldn't complain that home was a long way away. I had no idea when I'd be back to even visit.

Sighing dramatically, I went to my closet and dug around for another bag. Finding one that was long discarded, I tossed it on the bed. I needed to pick up the pace. I didn't want to keep Captain Rafael waiting downstairs and alone with my family too long.

My family. They were exhausting. Of course, my father understood what an honor my achieving the placement was as he'd been a royal guard for over a hundred years. His father and also my great-grandfather before him were guards. My mother was not so understanding. I often wondered if it was because my brother had dropped out of the training, or that I, her daughter had passed. Her daughter should be delicate and spend all her time in a dress, doing womanly things. I didn't fit into her belief of what a daughter was. I was petite, a whole five foot three, but that was my only quality that fit her definition of a daughter. I could take down three quarters of the other guards in a practice skirmish, *without* using my ability. For the others I did need the occasional assist, but Captain Rafael and Prince Michael laughed when I used it. As far as I was concerned, using my ability was more than acceptable to defend myself.

Stuffing the last of my things into the smaller bag, I quickly closed it, picked up my bags and went to the door. I paused to look around my room. Truth be told, I wouldn't be heartbroken if I never had to sleep here again.

I walked back into the kitchen and cringed. My mother was hovering over the captain with that look on her face. The look that meant she was trashing my profession again.

"...her best friend's father died on that island rescue." My mother's tone was hostile.

Rafael glanced at me and stood up. "I'm aware, Mrs. Hinton." He inclined his head, "we are doing everything we can to help his family."

My mother scoffed. "That won't bring him back." She pointed to me, "I don't want my daughter to end up the same way."

Rafael cleared his throat. "Kinsley is a *very* skilled warrior. You should be proud of her."

I watched my mother's shoulders rise and fall. I glanced at my father; his expression mirrored my thoughts. I needed to get out of here. "I hope this isn't too much to port back."

Rafael gave me a quick look. "As long as it's not a car, I can manage."

My father chuckled. "I wouldn't say that, Captain, she'll be running back up to get her weights."

Rafael grinned. "She has access to the family's gym now, so hopefully they won't be needed."

"Who is she guarding?" My mother blurted out.

I wanted to melt into an invisible puddle.

"My niece." Rafael said calmly.

I watched my mother process that. "So, she won't be in fights anymore? Will just be spending her time hanging around the palace? You know she hurt her arm not long ago doing *something* for the guard?"

My father interrupted before Rafael could answer. "It's an honor for her to get this posting."

I picked up one of the bags. "We should get going. I want to be there before Rena arrives."

Rafael came over and took the bag from my hand. "It's going to be an adventure." He smirked and gave me a quick wink.

When we stepped outside, I glanced to make sure my mother hadn't followed. "I'm so sorry." I whispered.

"Don't be." He stopped and looked down at me. "It's not the first time as a royal, or captain of the guard, I've dealt with hostile mothers." He grinned.

I blew out a breath. "I like to think any other mother in this realm would be thrilled her daughter was selected out of several hundred to be a part of the royal guard." I shrugged, "but *no*, she'd rather I'd be in a frilly dress drinking tea."

He laughed. "If you prefer, we can get you a frilly uniform to wear."

I cringed. "No. Thanks." I smiled. Hopefully the rest of the family was as easygoing as he seemed to be.

Chapter Two

"Absolutely not."

Prince Emil stomped past, slamming a door as he left the room. Rafael turned and watched him head toward the stairs, then turned to Prince Leone. "What's that about?"

Prince Leone smirked. "I asked him if he wanted a porter for Rena, programmed to a few different locations."

Rafael rubbed the back of his neck. "He does know she's a few centuries old, right?"

"Yeah." Leone looked at me. "All settled in your room?"

I nodded. "I didn't realize my room would be here in the palace."

Leone shrugged, "the other guards are still in quarters for downtime, but we thought having you closer would be easier."

I looked back to the stairs. "To escape the overprotective father, or to be close to my charge?"

Leone laughed, "maybe a bit of both."

Princess Autumn came out from a door down the hall. "Oh great, you're here." She gave me a big smile. "Rena's arrival has been postponed until tomorrow." She motioned to the room we stood outside, "because they moved the wrong bed in." She rolled her eyes, "Alona had a minor meltdown."

She shrugged, "You can hang out with the rest of us if you want."

Both Rafael's and Leone's phones went off. Leone looked at his phone, then to Rafael. "We've been summoned."

"Oh?" Princess Autumn looked from one to the other.

"By Kara." Rafael stated with a smirk. "She wants all brothers to try archery, at least once."

She shrugged, "makes sense I guess."

"Does it?" Leone tucked the phone in his pocket. "I don't ever recall a time lately where I'd be able to pause, aim, and shoot an arrow at someone."

Princess Autumn looked at me, an amused look on her face. "I wonder which brother will be the best?"

Both men frowned at her.

"Well now we have to try." Leone mumbled.

Rafael smirked at him. "I already know I suck."

We watched them both go down the stairs.

"Princess…"

She gave me a hard look. "Don't be calling us all princess and prince. Call me Autumn." She shook her head, "Daxx will throw a fit if you call her queen, oh and *don't* bow to her."

I gave her a puzzled look.

She motioned to the stairs, "You'll see. Let's go watch."

I stayed back with the other personal guards. I was comfortable with these men, as we all watched the royal family. Prince Emil wasn't with them. I still had to meet him. I'd seen him in passing a few times, but was never introduced to him. I wanted to assure him that I would give my life to protect his daughter, if it ever came to that. I'd heard plenty of talk about him in the last few months. I still had trouble believing that he was part human. It must be a small part, because he looked just like the warden, and to my knowledge was three hundred years old. Humans didn't live that long, as far as I knew. I didn't know a great deal about them but now I was surrounded by many of the royal's mates that were part human.

"Relax." Bronx looked at me. "This is the best and occasionally the most exasperating post you'll ever have."

"Exasperating?" I frowned.

Sith chortled from where he stood behind me. "What he means is the kings and princes give us one order and the queens and princesses have something else in mind."

I opened my mouth for a moment, then closed it. "What are we to do?"

Tim shrugged, "go with what the women want." He turned and looked at Felix, "because they're going to go forward with or without us."

"So," I swallowed, "not following orders is the better option?"

"No." Mac said quietly, "but not being with our charges when the kings find out is by far the worst option."

I blew out a breath. "My ward is pregnant and not part of the immediate royalty."

One of the men chuckled, I turned to see it was Woods.

"You're going to get dragged into it." He stated with an amused look.

I turned to look at the royal family as they harassed each other for failed shots. "Just in case that happens, what can I expect from our princesses?"

"You were on the island, so you know what some of the women can do." Sith answered slowly.

I nodded, "Yes, Princess Paisley is a chronos." I watched the dark-haired princess laugh at something Prince Arius said. I turned and looked at Felix, he grinned. "And I saw Princess Bethany's skills in action too." Glancing over I studied Princess Bethany, she looked human but the color arcs she was threatening Prince Leone with matched her fiery red hair.

"First," Tim leaned closer, "drop the princess part," he grinned, "trust me you won't have time to be tossing titles out."

"Not to mention the huntress might stab you for saying it." Bart added.

"Noted." I looked back to see Autumn take the bow

from Michael and shove him out of the way. "I still can't believe all the mates for our royals are human." Autumn didn't look like a warrior, with her petite form and blond hair, but her attitude screamed it.

"Sort of." Bronx stated. "They're not now with the bond, but Reagan is something else."

I looked at him, "Something else?" I glanced at our newest princess, she looked just human to me. She was even wearing a ball cap backwards. Not at all the image of a princess I had in my head. I turned back to Bronx.

He nodded. "Her father was from Solrelm." He put his finger to his lips. "Don't ever share that information."

I scowled at him. "I know not to repeat anything that I see or hear, Bronx." I looked at Reagan. "Does she have an ability?"

Derian snorted, "and then some." He motioned with his head to her, "she can heal with a touch and," he glanced around at the others, "can become invisible."

I waited for him to crack a smile and say he was kidding.

"He's not joking." Bart said.

I watched Reagan take her turn with the bow. She hit the target. "Well crap. Okay, fill me in on the rest of them."

The other guards turned to look at Tim.

He sighed, "I guess I've been around the longest. Okay. Daxx is immune to magic."

"That's handy." Our Huntress Queen was beautiful with her long blonde hair, but I'd heard her speak and there wasn't a single ounce of posh to her. I liked that she was down to earth.

He nodded, "yeah it has been."

"Our other queen is an empath." Sith said quietly.

I looked at Queen Alona, she was laughing and was so graceful all the time. She moved like a queen in my opinion, her long black locks hanging down her back, swaying with each movement.

"And she's lethal with nun-chucks so steer clear in any fights." Sith said with a serious look.

I shrugged. "I doubt I'll be in any fights."

There were several chuckles.

"You can only hope." Bart stated.

"Crissy has visions." Bronx said, "and her mind moves faster than a rocket."

"She fights as well?" I studied the princess. She was sitting away from the others with a notebook in her lap. There was something different about her, not her looks, they seemed normal, but she spent a lot of time off by herself.

"Not as much, she will defend others, but she's the lookout in most cases because she can climb anything." Bronx stated. "And I mean *anything*."

"Autumn has no special ability but fights like no one I've ever seen." Woods said with a proud note to his voice.

I nodded. "I've heard. I still can't believe she got Eunice Bosworth."

"I've lost count of how many they've brought in the past few months. It's in the hundreds though." Tim sat down and leaned back. "It's been a hell of a ride working with the royals."

"I don't know who is guarding who half the time." Mac grinned. "Bethany, when she gets those fire balls flying, I just want to stand back and watch." He nodded his head slowly, "and now that she's learning other magic," he shrugged, "there's not much for me to do."

"I could only stand there with my gob hanging open when she bounced the warden and his mate out over the water on the island." I told them.

"Scariest time of my life." Mac said in a hushed tone.

I watched Crissy jump up and run over for her turn with the bow. The Justice stood there with an encouraging look on his face as Princess Kara was instructing her. "Does Princess Kara have any abilities? Other than rocking that bow like nothing I've ever seen."

"She can hear thoughts." Bart said in a nonchalant tone.

I turned to him. "Like anyone's thoughts?"

He nodded. "Even mages."

My mouth dropped open.

He smirked. "She keeps it on lockdown most of the time, but if you see her fidget with that bracelet she wears, clear your mind."

I nodded. "Good to know." I turned back to the royals to see most of them looking our way.

"Oh shit." Mac mumbled. "I knew they were going to make us take a turn."

"Archery?" I got up as well.

"Yeah. The bow." Felix said quietly as he walked by me.

I looked at them watching us, then to the bow Kara held. "I wouldn't mind giving it a try." I whispered more to myself than anyone else.

Chapter Three

I walked out and checked the balcony area. Like everything else it was huge. My parent's whole house could probably fit on the balcony. Okay, maybe not the entire thing, but it was still a large area. I looked over the railing, the view was amazing. I was on the balcony of the palace. I laughed quietly. When I'd joined the guards, I'd hoped for an assignment in the underground chambers, where all the important positions would be. Now, here I was working at the palace. As far as jobs went, this was my dream job.

If I could shake this nagging feeling in my gut, everything would be perfect. I kept telling myself it was just excitement and my new position, but I didn't convince myself. It wasn't a morbid feeling, but I was tense. The tension that signals from this point forward, everything was going to change.

Before I changed my mind and went home, I turned to look back into Rena's room, boxes were piled everywhere. I wondered if I should move them all to one side, so Rena would have more space. I gnawed on my lip, not wanting to overstep. Not only was I guarding the kings' niece, but she was pregnant. I'd learned the hard way that pregnant women were often moody. Hopefully I didn't do anything to upset her. I stood there with my hands on my hips, trying not to blame myself for the millionth time. She'd gotten pregnant while trapped on the island, when I'd been there.

"Are you the guard?"

I jolted and looked to see Prince Emil standing in the doorway. "Yes." I bowed my head respectfully, "Kinsley Hinton, Prince Emil." I looked back up at him. I was told by some of the guards that he'd been born on the other side, to a human mother with Alterealm blood. He didn't look human—whatever that looked like. His eyes were almost the same as our warden's, only bluer whereas Prince Arius' were grey. They were pretty eyes, but something in them told me he hadn't had an easy life. I supposed that set him apart from his brothers. He was still looking at me. I cleared my throat. "I was waiting for Rena to get here."

He nodded slowly, his short black hair falling across his brow as he did. "She'll be here shortly." With his hands on his hips he continued to assess me. "How old are you?"

I was a bit taken back by his question. "Forty, sir."

He made an odd sound, "don't call me sir—or prince." He scowled at me, "How long have you been a guard?"

I wanted to say long enough, but then remembered he was one of the royal family—regardless of where he was born. "I started training when I was twenty-five." I inhaled a sharp breath, "a-a bit older than most but I had to learn to control my," his gaze stayed locked on my eyes, "ability." I nodded. "I was in the guard program in the North for ten years before I transferred to the royal guard. I've been a full-time guard for five years now." Normally I'd be offended by the questions, but it was his daughter I was to watch over.

Emil's expression didn't change, it was one of complete distain. "Full disclosure, I didn't want you to be my daughter's personal guard," he frowned, "not because you're a woman." He added quickly. "I worry that seeing you will be a constant reminder of her time on the island."

I sucked in a breath through my nose. "I was worried about that too, but she chose me, not any of the others that were candidates."

With an abrupt nod, he crossed his arms over his chest. "I know." The scrutiny on his face as he looked at me was nerve wrecking. "What type of feeder are you?"

I couldn't hide the shocked expression, "essence." I said slowly, not even sure where he could be going with this line of questioning.

"Rena is as well." He said in a hard tone.

"I'm aware." I glanced at the door, hoping anyone would walk in. Anyone that would mean I wasn't in here alone with him.

"She has to feed more often." He stated.

"Sir—" I stepped closer, "Emil," I waited to see if he objected to me using his name. "I was born in Alterealm, my entire family before me, I understand how," I motioned in the air, "things work."

His eyes darkened. I couldn't interpret the look he was giving me. Had I offended him by stating the obvious? His expression changed and was even less pleasant than before.

There was no reason to look at me that way. I inhaled deeply to calm myself before I spoke. Thoughts of reaching out and punching him in the face flew into my mind. Concealing my shock at the thought wasn't easy. I stood straighter and held his stare. The next insane thing to cross my mind was a desire to stretch up and kiss him. I turned away and motioned to the boxes, "I think we should move these to the wall, so your daughter has more room." I didn't care if he was listening. "We wouldn't want her to trip or try to lift them by herself." He grunted then went to pick up one of the boxes.

I held my breath, trying to force my heart to slow down before I blew an artery. My aunt had been right. Why now? How could this happen? Fate was a ridiculous prankster that just shoved things in your direction then laughed her butt off watching for your reaction. I'd found my true mate and he was a prince. *A prince.* Right, because royalty had no problems with commoners or guards for mates. I laughed quietly, then shook my head when Emil glanced at me. "Sorry, I just had and obscure thought." I moved to the boxes furthest from him and picked one up.

How was this possible? To find my mate at only forty. Most were closer to a hundred before they came across theirs. I'd never craved a mate, like most did. I was a guard, it was dangerous. Many guards didn't take the chance of binding in case something happened. I thought of my friend's mother—how hollow she was now without her mate.

Shifting another box, I tried to ignore the man working in the same room with me. I could *smell* him. What was I, some sort of animal? It was like I couldn't not glance at him every few seconds either. What was I going to do? My charge was his daughter, there was no way I could avoid him forever.

"Are you all right?"

I turned to see him watching me. "I'm—I'm fine."

"You've sighed about thirty times in five minutes." His eyes were assessing me slowly, searching.

I hadn't even noticed I was doing that. "Just going over all the protocol and the layout of the palace in my mind while we move this." I lied, but there was no way I'd confess any of the thoughts in my head.

"The women have made a map for the phone of the underground chambers, if you need it." He scowled. "I don't want Rena going there, but if you must."

I nodded. "It will be good to have."

He nodded. "I'll tell them to get it to you."

We stood there in an awkward silence, just looking at each other. Did he feel it too, I had to wonder. Was it obvious to him or would the human part not realize?

Taking a deep breath, he gave me an abrupt nod. "I'm going to go find out what's taking Rena so long."

I bobbed my head with a little too much enthusiasm. "I'll finish this." I motioned to the boxes; then saw he'd already left. I blew out a breath, dropping my shoulders until they slumped. This is not what I signed up for. I took another deep breath and held it. It whooshed out all at once. This was going to be impossible to ignore. I bit my lip. What was I going to do? What could I do? My only course of action was to avoid him as much as inhumanly possible.

Chapter Four

I stood outside the door and watched as Rena opened another box and looked in. I'd never been a personal guard, so I wasn't sure if I should offer to help, just stand here—or what I should be doing. In truth, I felt a bit unnecessary standing outside a door in a palace that was both heavily guarded and warded against unlawful entry. I wasn't going to complain. I still couldn't believe I'd been posted here. I would do whatever it took to protect her, but what dangers were really in here?

She stopped and looked at me. "This room is bigger than Alona's apartment." She glanced around, "and yet I still feel like the walls are closing in on me." She touched her rounded stomach briefly. "I need something to take my mind off—" she waved her hand in the air, "everything."

I wasn't sure if I was meant to reply or just listen.

"Do you know where my office will be?" Flipping her long pale hair over her shoulder, she came over and stood in the doorway.

I nodded, "I was shown it, yes." I motioned to the stairs, "It's on the main floor." I looked at the floor in front of me for a moment, "until you're settled, then you can have it moved to the underground chambers if you like." I glanced up to gauge her reaction.

Rena bit her lip, "I think I'll stay above ground for now."

I nodded. "Would you like to go to your office?"

Looking around the room, she nodded, "yes, please." She quickly moved to grab her phone off the bed. "I'm honored to be asked to help."

I motioned for her to go first. "I'm not exactly sure what you're going to be doing."

She grinned at me over her shoulder. "According to Daxx and Alona, I'm going to be weeding out the garbage that ends up on the Kings' desks."

We went down the stairs slowly. I wondered if I should lead in case she slipped. Annoyed at second-guessing myself, I stepped quickly to walk beside her on the wide staircase. "I personally don't know how they find time to govern and fight the war."

Rena smiled at me, "I think it's wonderful that the royal family aren't afraid to get their hands dirty."

I recalled some of the battles I'd been at, particularly the old quarry that was now simply a pit of mud. It felt like it had taken a week to get all the mud off. I remembered how covered all the royals had been as well. "No, they're not." I smiled.

Rena paused for a second. "Finding out I'm part of the royal family was a bit of a shock, but now that I know them and everything they do, I'm so proud to be here."

I cleared my throat, "I didn't ask if I'm to address you as princess, lady or..."

She shook her head. "I don't want a title." She nodded, "I just want a family." She grimaced, "I've been stuck with two over-bearing brothers and, well, you met my dad—*other* family is wonderful, and the best part is they know I don't age and why." She paused in step, "I have distant relatives out there and I can never meet them." A look of sadness briefly appeared before she stared walking again.

I hadn't thought of what it would mean to live on the other side and not age like a normal human. I frowned. What she had gone through was so far beyond my imagination or knowledge.

We walked in silence until we reached the door to her office. I motioned to the door across the hall, "that's the kitchen," I pointed a door further down, "my room is there."

Straightening her shoulders, she opened the door and stepped inside. "It's almost as big as my room."

I watched her walk along and touch the ornate filing cabinets and then walk over to the large table in the middle of the room. With a grin, she went over to the big desk with the computer sitting on it. "Now," she looked back to me, "how do I go about getting this process started?"

"Oh," I hurried over to point at a list I'd been shown on her desk. "All the department supervisors are listed right there." I shrugged, "call them, I guess?"

She nodded slowly, "easy enough." She went around the desk and sat down. "I was told only important reports and issues are to be brought to the kings, everything else I'm to set up a committee to decide a direction, or designate who is to deal with any pertinent issues." She looked at the list for a moment, "I suppose I should start with the office director." She smirked at me, "I don't know what that is." Blowing out a breath, she nodded again. "This is what I needed. Something to do."

I watched her for a moment, then went back over to stand outside the open door. Now what?

Three hours later I was sitting in a chair outside the door, watching people come and go. Rena had brought me the chair, and to be honest, if I sat here doing nothing for much longer, I was going to fall asleep.

"Well, that looks like a hard gig."

I looked up from the floor to see Princess Paisley and Princess Autumn standing in front of me. I got up and motioned in the room. "Rena has been getting the ball rolling."

Queen Daxx came up behind them. "Good. The crap that lands on Troy's desk is ridiculous."

I glanced in the room again. "She seems quite excited to be doing it."

Autumn snorted, "after being stuck in an apartment this long, I'm not surprised." She looked behind her to see Princess Bethany and Princess Kara coming to them.

I noticed all of them were dressed for battle and wondered if they just wandered around dressed like that. So far being a palace guard was nothing like I'd imagined it would be. The same went for the royals. They were not the typical *royal* family I'd pictured for most of my life.

Princess Paisley looked in the room and watched Rena talk on the phone and nod, while looking through a stack of papers. "You should come with us." She looked at me and then turned to the Huntress, "she should come with us," she shrugged, "one more guard can't hurt."

The Huntress nodded slowly while looking me up and down. "I like that she's our size and a guard."

Queen Alona and Princess Bethany came down the hall.

"Kinsley is coming with us." Daxx told them.

Queen Alona smiled, "The more the merrier." She gave me a smile and stepped inside Rena's office. "Do you have plans for the next few hours?"

Rena motioned to the piles of papers spread around the large table, "only to figure out what all of that is, and how I can prevent all the trees in Alterealm from being cut down to print it."

"I am thrilled you're going to simplify my king's office work."

Rena grimaced. "I hope I can."

"We're going to borrow your guard." The Queen gave me a quick look.

"Oh. Yes, I don't think I need a guard unless I leave the palace—considering these piles, it may not be for a week." She went over and picked up one of the piles.

"Make sure you take breaks and eat."

Rena nodded, "I don't think I have a choice, Mitz has been in here three times already." She started looking through the pages she held.

"I'll let you get back to it." Queen Alona inclined her head and came back out. "Shall we?" She motioned down the hall.

"Criss and Reagan are meeting us with the guards out back." The Huntress said.

I cleared my throat, "Where are we going?"

"To look for portals." Princess Kara told me. She stopped and looked at me, "please don't call us princess constantly."

The Huntress laughed, "told you it got annoying."

"Portals?" I glanced from her to the—Daxx.

She nodded, "Rea can see where the mages—or more importantly where Arwan has used magic."

I adjusted the strap holding the case for my blade on my back. "You have an idea where to look?"

Paisley glanced back at me. "No, but we seem to find something every time we go looking."

I didn't know what that meant, but I followed them.

Chapter Five

I looked back to the palace that was at the top of the road. If anyone had told me I'd be out on a stroll with Alterealm's princesses a week ago, I would have sent them to medical to have a brain scan.

"At least the weather is nice." Bethany said.

Daxx stopped and looked back at Tim. "Is it ever not here?"

He grinned. "You've been here since spring."

Daxx nodded. "This is fall now?" She turned to Alona, "how long have we been here?"

Alona hesitated for a moment. "I have no idea. It feels like a minute some days, then eons the next."

"Does it snow here?" Kara turned around to look at her guard.

Bart nodded. "It does snow in Alterealm." He motioned around us. "Not in this area though."

"I can't wait to see snow." Crissy sounded excited. "Vic said we would go to the cabin when it does."

"There's a cabin?" Paisley snapped another picture of the view, then tucked her phone away.

"It's called the cabin, but it's more of an estate in the northern mountains." Felix said.

"An estate." Daxx looked at Alona.

"Who do we speak with to find out what the family owns, I wonder." Alona mused quietly.

"I've barely adjusted to a palace. I don't know if I can digest anymore." Reagan said with a grin.

"There's a path this way." Autumn stopped walking.

"Is there a shortcut down?" Daxx looked from the path to the road. "This feels like it could take all day on this road."

"If I were on team bad, I would use a path and stay off the road." Bethany said as she nodded.

"Makes sense." Autumn started walking down the path.

I looked up at Woods, wondering if the guards should go first. He gave a brief shake of his head. Sighing, I continued to follow without comment.

"That is a pretty lake." Paisley took a picture.

"It's a bit swampy in that area, princess." Felix said loud enough she'd hear.

Her shoulders slumped. "That's too bad, it looks so nice from up here."

"We are not going near *any* water." Kara said looking at Crissy.

Crissy nodded. "Water and floating rocks."

"That." Kara pointed at her then looked around slowly.

"Maybe the floating rocks were the portal markers Arwan was using?" Reagan offered.

Crissy stopped and looked at the ground. "I don't think those were it." She looked back to her, "the markers. They weren't big enough."

"How big are these floating rocks, Criss?" Daxx didn't look happy.

"Big." Crissy nodded and started walking again.

"Oh jeeze." Daxx hissed out a breath and followed.

I looked at Bronx. "Floating rocks?" I kept my voice down.

He nodded. "Her latest visions are of bad water and floating rocks."

I opened my mouth to comment, then realized there was

nothing I could really say. "Got it." I said softly, then stared at a boulder as we went past. I was beginning to second guess my decision to tag along. Standing around the palace in case Rena wanted to go somewhere was mind numbing, but at least I didn't have to worry about bad water and floating rocks—whatever that was.

"It's like a stream used to run here." Reagan stopped and looked down at the rut we were standing in. She turned to Derian.

He shrugged, "I don't know, I was never stationed up here."

"Is that a cave entrance?" Autumn pointed.

"They love the caves." Daxx went past her and walked off the path.

I hurried to follow the guards as they rushed to see what they were talking about. My gut was starting to turn into a tight knot. I wasn't sure why, but something was not right with this whole scene.

"It is another cave." Kara pulled the case off her back and made fast work of assembling her bow.

I watched the other women get various weapons out, but noted none of the guards were, so I left the blade on my back.

Reagan went over and looked in the cave.

"What do you see?" Daxx watched her intently.

"Green." Reagan said in an exasperated tone.

"Crap." Daxx looked at Bethany. "Think you can take a look?"

Bethany nodded, then turned to Reagan. "Can you make yourself invisible and come with me?" She gave her a wide-eyed look. "It freaked me out last time, going in alone."

Reagan nodded and blew out a breath. "I can only do it for about a minute before I lose focus." She rubbed her hands together. "Prince Bastian says it's all about holding the thought in the mind, but apparently my mind is scattered and short term." She grinned.

I moved away from the guards to stand closer to the

women. They may have seen all this before, but it was new for me and more than a little exhilarating. Reagan pulled a surijin from a pouch on her belt. She held the handle in one hand and the weighted end in the other. When she nodded to Bethany, she slowly disappeared. Bethany moved her hand down her own body and vanished as well. Everyone stood silently watching the entrance to the cave. I'd seen a lot in my years, but nothing like that. I glanced around at the other princesses and none of them seemed awed. I lived in a realm where our people could do things that were considered amazing and impossible and now, I was learning that our once human princesses were probably more powerful than my own people. I frowned, I needed to rethink my whole belief about these women—and possibly humans in general.

Bethany appeared first, then Reagan right behind her.

"There's nothing in there. It's a long tunnel." Bethany looked at Reagan. "Was there more haze?"

Reagan nodded. "Yeah. It got thicker as it went down."

"The tunnel goes down?" Daxx asked, then looked at Tim. "Are the caves in this area mapped out somewhere?"

Tim pulled out his phone, "I can ask." He tapped the screen, then put the phone to his ear as he stepped away from the group.

"Do we call the guys?" Paisley asked.

Alona tucked her nun-chucks under her arm and hugged her waist. "They're currently taking turns trying to get more information from Willis and his top people."

Kara nodded, "Izzy is helping with that. She's listening in, trying to hear anything useful."

Daxx put her hands on her hips and looked at the ground. "I don't want to pull them away from that."

"We could give them a heads up." Paisley said. "We have eight," she looked at me, "nine guards with us, surely that counts for something." Her look wasn't as hopeful as her words implied.

Alona nodded slowly. "Who do we call?"

"Neither king." Daxx said quickly.

"Definitely not Arius." Paisley added.

"Or Michael." Autumn looked unamused. "He'll start talking variables and all that stuff."

"I'll call Vic." Crissy nodded as she pulled out her phone. "He's the most reasonable one of the brothers."

Daxx laughed quietly. "Maybe to you."

"It's true." Alona smiled, "he will see the whole picture and has lately been coming to our defense."

Daxx nodded slowly, then turned back to Crissy. "Okay, Criss. Give it a shot."

Crissy nodded and started typing on her phone. "I always message first because calling at the wrong time could get his head chopped off." She glanced up from the phone. "If he's being justice." She nodded. "Oh." She smiled and taped the screen again.

"Heart, what is it?"

She had the phone on speaker. It was strange to hear the justice's tone so soft.

"Vic, we went for a walk." She nodded.

"Are you well?"

She nodded. "Yes. I am well." She said slowly enunciating each word.

"Where are you?"

"We went down the road from the palace toward," she closed her eyes for a second, "Valena— that little town."

"Have you found something?" His tone was still soft, but I could hear the concern.

"I think we did." She looked at the cave entrance. "It's a cave," she looked at Bethany, "or could be," she paused, "Beth and Reagan went in and looked it's a tunnel leading down." Daxx pointed to Reagan, "oh and Reagan sees green haze."

"I see." The Justice's tone was harder now.

"We want to go in and look." Crissy nodded again. "We have nine guards with us and all of our weapons." She gave Daxx a serious look.

"Am I on speaker?" That tone I knew.

"Yes." Crissy held the phone up higher.

"Bronx, you are to dial in immediately and keep me posted with each step taken."

Bronx straightened. "I will."

"I am going to mute the call on my end. Be aware if anything happens my brothers are not going to be as agreeable as I am." There was no mistaking the seriousness of his words or tone. "I will inform them when they aren't otherwise occupied."

"How's it going there?" Daxx asked.

"We are getting some viable leads—for the first time." Victor informed her. "There is still no movement from the tracker placed at the asylum, so that is a small comfort."

Daxx grinned. "Great. We'll shout if this turns into anything."

"Before you get yourselves into a situation would be preferable, Daxx." He answered.

"Absolutely." She nodded. "We just can't sit around doing nothing."

"I understand. Have care." The background noise was gone.

Daxx nodded and looked from the phone to Bethany, "how cramped is this tunnel?"

Bethany shrugged, "It's pretty narrow."

Daxx nodded, "Okay, lets stagger going in, so we're not all smushed in a small space."

I stepped forward, "I think a guard should go first."

Daxx smirked, then motioned to the entrance. "After you, *guard.*"

I hadn't expected her to pick me but wasn't going to pass the chance to be chosen first. As one of the few female guards, it never happened. Everyone always went with the large men. I pulled the blade from my back and went in. Bethany was right behind me, the sparks arcing from her hands serving to light the way.

I glanced back at her, she smiled, "no flashlight necessary." She turned, "Rea, you come in behind me, we need to know if the haze gets worse or vanishes."

"Do we have a game plan if we find Arwan?" Paisley asked softly.

I stopped and glanced behind to see the women come in one after the other. It was too dark to see how far back the rest of the guards were. I sucked in a deep breath, preparing myself to do whatever it took to protect the queens and princesses.

"The green continues." I heard Reagan say.

I continued down the tunnel. I was no expert, but the walls looked like nature had carved them out, not a man. When my heart wasn't pounding in my chest, I'd decide if that was a good thing or not. A few steps later I noticed the tunnel was starting to get wider and blew out a quick breath of relief. The worst-case scenario had this tunnel narrowing into a dead end.

"It's like the walls are coated in green." Reagan said from behind me.

I breathed another sigh of relief as we entered a small cavern, there was a little more breathing room now. I moved into it, checking as best I could with the low light to make sure we were alone. There was a tunnel leading out the other side, so no dead end.

"What does that mean?" Paisley turned in a circle and looked around the space.

"Maybe this space is protected?" Bethany walked over to the wall and touched it. "Or not." She whispered.

"Great." Daxx huffed out a loud breath. "A dead end."

I frowned and looked from her to the opening on the other side. "Are we following the…" The slate beneath my feet shook as a loud rumbling filled the cavern. I stumbled sideways, trying to keep my balance. Large rocks and stone scattered around my feet. The dust made it hard to see anyone. I stepped back a few steps and after a near miss with one that went past my foot.

When it stopped, I tried to see.

"Hold on." Bethany coughed, "I'll give us some light."

Chapter Six

I put the blade back in the case on my back and pulled out my phone. As I hit the flashlight on the screen, the whole cave was illuminated with a bright orange light. Bethany was lighting it up. I turned and aimed the light toward the opening on the other side. It was gone. "The tunnel is gone."

Daxx pulled Crissy to stand again. "There was no tunnel over there, Kinsley."

Alona turned to look at her. "There wasn't?"

Daxx shook her head and shone the light from her phone around at the others, quickly assessing everyone was all right. "No, just a pile of stones."

"It was an illusion." Bethany whispered. "I saw a tunnel entrance too."

"How's the haze now?" Kara turned to look at Reagan.

"There's still a lot of it here." Reagan turned slowly. "Like, *a lot*." There was a nervous edge to her voice.

"Shit." Daxx turned to look at the area we'd come in. "The guards are on the other side of that." She pointed.

We all turned to see the rocks covering the opening where we'd come from.

"This was a trap." Reagan stated in a quiet voice.

"Well if you're still seeing green, it's not finished." Daxx put her katana in the case and turned slowly. "Do we have phone signal?"

Crissy's phone started blaring loud music.

"That would be a yes."

"Vic…"

"Cristy. What has happened?" Victor didn't sound happy on the other end.

"Is everyone okay?" That was Rafael.

"We're fine." Kara said loudly.

"We're also trapped." Alona went over and stood beside Crissy.

"We're on our way there." Arius sounded like he was running.

"Are the guards okay?" Paisley asked.

"They're all right." Quinton said in a gruff tone.

"It was an illusion." Bethany said, "all of us but Daxx saw an opening on the other side when we came in. Reagan says there's still a lot of green haze."

"Port out. *Now*." Arius said bluntly.

Paisley nodded and closed her eyes. "Just need to settle my heart down." She opened them. "Okay." She continued to stand there. Frowning, she squeezed her eyes shut again. "It's not working."

"Try your porter." Rafael said.

"Right." Blowing out a quick breath, Paisley pushed her sleeve back and opened her porter. She frowned again. "Not working."

"I can't port either." Daxx said.

"So they've taken our option to leave." Bethany said in a whisper. She gave Paisley a quick look, "but my magic works. I don't understand what's happening."

"Check the exit you all thought you saw, maybe it's an illusion too." Michael's tone was calm and even.

I went over and shone my light where it had been. "It's filled in now. I mean we can *see* it is." I carefully climbed up a few of the rocks to look at the top of the pile of stone. "And very real. We can probably dig our way out though."

"Uh, I hate to say this," Paisley sounded scared, "but it's filling with water."

"Bad water." Crissy whispered.

"Stay clear of where you came in." King Chase said, sounding like he was in a hurry. "The guards are moving the boulders and it may cause them to fall toward you."

The women moved as far away from the collapsed rock pile as they could.

"What do you mean it's filling with water?" Leone asked in a strained voice.

I climbed back down off the rocks and was standing in ankle deep water. "It was dry when we entered and now it's over my boots." I told them in a loud voice.

"Where is it coming from?" King troy asked.

All of us began shining the lights on our phones around the cave.

"I can't see anywhere it could come from." Paisley said in a hushed voice.

Autumn went over and shoved against the area we'd all seen a tunnel. "How's that digging going?" Standing back, she kicked the pile, it didn't move.

"Not great." Michael stated in a flat tone. "It's like the stones are replacing themselves as fast as we're moving them."

Autumn stopped and shone the light on the rising water. "Maybe send someone to see if there's another tunnel." She turned and looked at me. "We're going to try to move things on this side."

"I've already sent three of the guards to look around the other side of this area, for possible exits." Arius said in a low tone.

Paisley nodded and rubbed her hands over her arms. "A mage wouldn't hurt."

"Rafael has gone to get Romulus." Arius told her.

"Get Clairee." Bethany said quickly, "I don't know how to break this spell." She lifted her arms and then opened them above her head. The arc of light grew between her hands.

"Get back."

Autumn and I moved away from the pile.

Bethany inhaled slowly, then flung her arms toward the blocked exit. The sound of the magic hitting the stones echoed through the cavern. A few smaller rocks bounced from the pile to land in the water below. "It's breakable." She said in an anxious tone.

"Cristy, check the upper part of the cave. Look for light from outside." Victor's tone didn't reflect any emotion.

"Okay, Vic." Crissy handed Alona her phone and walked over to the wall and looked up, she continued along the edge slowly, running her hands along it as she did. "The walls feel slimy."

"Water still coming in?" Rafael asked.

"It's almost to our knees now." Kara told him.

"Bethany. Put in your earpiece, Clairee is going to call you." Leone said quickly.

The princess nodded and reached into her pocket. "Okay." She put it in her ear and then stared at her phone. "Clairee. Can I break this with a spell?" She turned and looked at the pile of stones. Nodding, she glanced down at the water, "I moved a few, but I don't think I have enough power to clear it."

"If any of you are in your leather jackets, take them off so you're not weighted down." Troy said.

I took off the case for my sword and shrugged out of mine without second guessing his order. Putting the case back on, I stood there holding my jacket, unsure of where to put it.

Daxx dropped hers. "Done." She crossed her arms over her chest and stared at the area we'd come in. "Any luck on your side?"

"Okay, yeah I'll try." Bethany backed up, then slipped, almost landing in the water. "Hold on, I need to lose this coat." She glanced around, then held her phone out to me.

Dropping my uniform jacket, I moved over quickly and took it. Shrugging out of her coat, she tossed it behind her and nodded. "Okay." She blew out a breath. Taking the phone back, she tucked it in her back pocket.

"What?" Quinton growled. "The other tunnel that you thought you saw is running with water." He said, then there were some mumbled voices, "it goes down the into the lake by the marsh."

Reagan turned in a circle, "so without the spell this cavern is filled with water normally?" her voice squeaked at the end.

"It appears that way." Troy said calmly. "Mac, Bronx and Derian are trying to get to it on the other side, but the water is moving fast."

There was complete silence for several tense seconds.

"Okay." Bethany nodded, "so if I break this barrier we'll be pushed out with the water?" She looked at the water at her feet, "and if it's not moving fast enough, we drown."

"It's possible." Michael stated.

"To hell with that." Autumn shook her head, looking around quickly. She pointed, "We'll stand there," everyone turned to see where she was pointing, "and hang onto those rocks until Beth breaks this."

The area she pointed to was close enough to where the blockage was, and we shouldn't be washed out in a rush of water. I nodded. "It could work."

Everyone moved over to where there were large spaces jutting out of the stone wall.

I continued to stand in the open, if I had to save one of them, I wanted to be ready.

"Stay clear." Bethany said in a quiet voice. She closed her eyes and raised her arms slowly, the cavern filled with bright light from the arc running between her hands. Opening her eyes again, she visibly inhaled a deep breath and then hurled the energy at the stones. Some shifted, then echoed as they bounced down the wall. She shook her head, "it's not enough." She looked behind her, "I can't get enough distance to get the force I need."

"Miss Hinton," Victor's voice had me straighten, "can you move the stones with your ability?"

I jolted. I hadn't even thought of that. I nodded and moved over to stand in front of the stones. "I'll give it a try." I ignored how deep and cold the water was, and how it impeded the speed I could move. I blew out a breath. "Shine some light. I need to see them."

Several lights hit the pile in front of me. I nodded slowly and focused on one of the medium sized stones near the top of the pile. I didn't need to use my hands, but I found it helped me focus if I held them out toward my target. Right now, I needed the extra help focusing. It took a lot to get the stone to move at first, it was wedged between others. I gritted my teeth and stared at it. It had been a long time since I'd moved something of this size.

"It's working." Kara whispered.

The stone finally came free. I moved it so it would set down in the water, well away from the space we were trying to clear.

"Did you see that?" Reagan shone the light on the wall. "It was an open space for a second and then another stone filled it."

"Bastard wants to drown us." Daxx was not happy at all.

"Can you move them faster?" Autumn asked.

My heart was pounding so fast, panicky, and didn't want to let it show.

"Ladies, the tunnel you entered is becoming unstable, we're going to the other side." Troy informed us.

"What do you mean unstable?" Daxx put her hands in the air and stared at the water that covered her waist.

"When Beth hit it and Kinsley moved that rock, the walls here crumbled a bit." Rafael reported.

Autumn growled, "When we find that no good mage, I'm going to…"

"Kinsley, think you can hold a rock in the air, and I'll smack it with energy?" Bethany was giving me a hopeful look.

I nodded, "I can, but I think we need to hit it multiple times as fast as we can to break this." I turned and looked at the pile of stones. The water was past my knees now. My shins were aching from the cold.

"Oh." Paisley stumbled through the water until she was beside us. "I can hold the stones that Kinsley lifts and you can keep smacking them, Beth." She gave me a wide-eyed look, "while you're picking up the next one."

I bit my lip and turned to look at the amount of stones we needed to move. "If we do it fast enough, a few of you can get out before it fills in." I was cold, but the royal women in here were far more important than I was.

"But that leaves you three behind." Daxx didn't sound pleased.

Beth put her hand up to her ear. "Clairee thinks if we move enough of them, his spell won't work." She nodded, "he's using a lot of power to maintain the spell."

Autumn snorted, "good, I hope it sucks up all the energy he stole to look young."

Paisley looked at her, then the wall. Nodding she turned to Alona, "You and Daxx get out first."

"I think…"

Paisley shook her head to cut off Daxx. "The queens need to get out first." She gave me a look, before turning back to her queen, "if anything happens to either of you, that gives them an advantage."

"Kitten, just for once go with it." King Chase pleaded.

"Daxx." King Troy added softly.

Daxx heaved a sigh. "Fine. We're first." She held out her hand to Alona.

Alona went and stood with her, beside the wall out of the way. "Tell us when." She said in a quiet tone.

I turned back to the stones. "Let me lift one for you to hold, then I'll get another one ready, so we can do this as fast as possible."

Paisley nodded and stepped back.

"Just keep the second one out of my path." Bethany backed up a few steps and raised her hands.

I studied the pile, trying to find the ones that would open

the most space. "I'm going for the bottom ones." I glanced at our royal witch, "you hit it near the middle."

She nodded, "and hopefully weakening two places at once…"

"We'll get us out of here." Paisley said her expression determined.

Bethany gave her a look. "As the shortest here, I'm running out of body to keep out of the water."

"Same." Paisley said and looked down to see the water was reaching her waist.

"You've got this, ladies." Arius said in a breathless voice. "We're almost to the other side now."

"Some of us are at the bottom by the lake." Rafael stated.

"See you soon." I said in a determined voice. "Lifting the first one. Tell me when you have it." I looked at the rock, it was bigger than the last. If this was to work, I needed to start with the largest I could get free. It started to move, carefully I lifted it in the air, so it was lined up with the center of the pile.

"Got it." Paisley said.

I didn't look to check, just focused on the bottom of the pile again.

"On three." Bethany whispered. "One."

I freed the next one and held it in place until they had the last one out of the way.

"Two."

"Stay clear." Paisley said.

"Three." The rock hit the wall with such a force, that it broke several free.

I lifted the stone.

"Got it." Paisley said quickly.

"One."

I dragged another one out.

"Two."

"The magic is faltering." Kara said quietly.

"Three."

Stones flew far enough that water splashed me as I lifted

another one.

"Got it."

I quickly glanced to the center. "Two more, then rush out the hole."

"One." Bethany said loudly.

I lifted the next one.

"It's not filling back up hardly at all." Reagan told us.

"Two."

I moved the next one up so I could grab another as fast as possible.

"Three."

The sound of falling rocks followed by splashes yielded a few excited gasps in the cavern.

"Got it." Paisley's voice was louder now as well.

"One."

"After this one, my queens." I said through grit teeth as I pulled another stone.

"Two."

"We're ready." Daxx replied.

"Three."

I focused on nothing but the next stone.

"They're out." Kara said quickly.

"Got it." Paisley sounded breathless.

"One." Bethany sounded more determined.

"We're ready to go." Kara told us.

"Two."

I pulled the largest one I could and held it.

"Three."

Water splashed my face. I vaguely realized how high it was but couldn't stop.

"Got it." Paisley sounded like she was right beside me now.

"One."

"After this one." Kara told whoever was going with her.

"Two."

I focused on a stone in the side of the pile this time.

"The opening isn't closing." Autumn said.

"Three."

This time the sound of stone bouncing off stone echoed through the cave.

"Got it."

"We have the queens." Arius' voice came through Crissy's phone.

I lifted the next stone.

"Cristy, put your phone away, we'll stay in touch through Bethany's call to Clairee." Victor's tone was quiet.

"Ok, Vic, I'm going with Autumn next." Crissy answered.

"One." Beth's voice was quiet.

I held the next stone up and ready.

"Two." She sounded breathless.

"Three."

Water splashes was all that I heard, moving to hold the next stone up. I paused long enough to realize I could see outside. "You two go right after this next one."

I moved the stone up.

"What about you?" Bethany asked.

"Got it." Paisley sounded distracted.

"I'm a guard, I'll follow." I said as I moved back out of their way.

"Okay." Paisley answered.

"One," Beth whispered, "Two." The water was to her chest as she held her arms above her head. "Three."

I watched her magic knock the stone into the side of the pile and more rocks fell. They both moved quickly to the opening and then vanished from my sight. I turned and double checked all the others had gotten out. When I turned back there was water all around me. I choked and then took a deep breath, holding it. I couldn't get my footing; I was being pushed toward the opening. The rushing water covered my head as it shoved me out the opening. I was sliding along slick stone. I held my arms in against my body and tried to breathe when air touched my face.

When daylight hit my face, I barely had time to see one of the guards holding out his hand as I plunged downward. I looked below me and was thankful to see there was water. I had enough time to catch my breath before hitting the water. My back hit the bottom of the shallow lake, spurring me to push to the surface.

It was over my waist when I stood up, but after expending all my energy, I barely had the strength to make it to a large rock in the middle. Leaning in, I rested my arms on it, then put my head down to rest.

"She's here." Someone shouted.

I looked up to see three of the guards with Captain Rafael standing in the swampy growth about twenty feet from me.

"Are you okay?" Rafael started into the water.

I nodded, too breathless to speak.

Emil appeared beside the guards and ran into the water. He went past Rafael and reached me quickly.

I blew out a breath. Despite my revelations about him, I was happy he was here. I was very happy I was here. This was so far from any scenario I could have ever pictured when I agreed to accompany the royal women on their exploration.

"Are you all right?" He leaned down and grasped me around the waist to help me get to my feet.

I nodded, "I think so. My back hit the bottom when I landed." With weak knees I stood, gripping his arm to steady myself. "How are the others?" I glanced down and wanted to groan out loud when I remembered I was wearing a tank top that was not standard guard issue. My strap and weapon were also missing.

His expression was hard as he glanced behind me. "You have some scrapes. The others are okay, a little shaken." He glanced to Rafael, "we caught them before they went over."

I glanced up at the distance I'd fallen, my stomach clenched when I noticed everything I could have hit instead of the water. I nodded. "I think the magic let out just as I went to leave, the force of the water shoved me out." I took a few steps in the squishy muck at the bottom. Stopping, I looked from one brother to the other. "Can we find a temporary guard for your daughter?"

Emil frowned, "I thought you said you were all right."

"I am." I turned to my captain, "but I want to be there when we find the jerk that did that." I pointed up to where the water flowed off the mountain. "I don't take kindly to someone trying to drown me."

Rafael smirked, "I'm sure we can arrange something."

Chapter Seven

I was still cold, despite a long, hot shower. I held my hands clasped behind my back and stood at the side of room with the other guards. A shiver went through me. I hadn't bothered to go feed when Sith had knocked on my door and told me the family was meeting and we were to attend.

I'd taken too long in the shower, but it had felt so good I hadn't wanted to get out. As I'd stood in the warmth of the water, I could only think about my conversation with the captain. I know his reaction had been favorable, but now I was second-guessing my choice to resign as Rena's personal guard.

I forced myself to stand straighter. What if I was just sent back to the yard to await a new assignment?

"Kin."

I looked up to see Felix looking down at me.

"You need to feed and lay off the thousand emotions you're feeling right now." He smirked.

I'd forgotten he was an emotion feeder. I blew out a breath. "I didn't want to be late." I whispered.

Mac leaned forward and looked around him. "Not everyone is here yet, there's time."

"We could be rushing off with a minute's notice, you need

to make sure you're right." Sith added.

I groaned to myself. I was failing so badly. "I know." I watched the princes huddle together in the corner, talking quietly. "I don't want to take a chance there's a lineup and be late."

Woods grunted, annoyed. "Normally I can't pick up your emotions, but you're playing havoc with my focus right now."

I sighed. I hated being a weak link.

"Come on." Mac motioned with his head to the door. "I'll help you out."

It wasn't unusual for fellow guards to help with feeding when time didn't allow otherwise. I'd never had to rely on any of them before. I'd worked too hard to get here. I didn't want to be 'that woman' who couldn't stand on her own. I watched a few of the princesses come in. They looked fine. I nodded. "Okay." I turned and followed him quickly into the hallway.

He continued until we were well out of sight of those in the room. Stopping, he looked down and me before bending his knees and leaning down to my level.

I rolled my eyes, "not a word about tiny people. We all can't be giants."

Mac grinned wide but made no comment. Tilting his head to the side, he looked down at the floor.

There was no need for any preamble, this was part of our lives. I bit into his large muscled neck. For a brief second, I appreciated that heavily muscled guys weren't volunteers at the feeding bank.

Licking over the punctures, I straightened away. I looked up at Mac to say thanks only to see him looking elsewhere as he straightened slowly.

I turned around to see Prince Emil standing a few feet from us. His eyes were red. I figured his human side didn't allow him to control his feeding urges. Then I noticed the anger in his expression.

"I don't think this is the place for *that*." he bit out between clenched fangs. Giving me a cold look, he motioned to the stairs and glared at Mac. "Go check on my daughter, her new guard has been detained."

Mac didn't even pause. "Yes, sir."

I watched the gentle giant walk away with long strides and then turned to the prince. "Sorry, I didn"t have time to..."

"I care not for your habits." With another brief, hard appraisal, he turned on his heel and went into the solarium.

I blew out a breath and looked at the floor. Great. One more reason I was going to be posted to an empty forest on the outskirts of civilization.

"What's wrong?"

I looked up to see Prince Leone looking concerned. I blew out a defeated breath. "I think I just got myself reassigned to the furthest post from the palace."

His expression became serious. "What?"

I motioned to the room Emil had gone in. "I didn't have time to feed after," I waved my hand in the air, "using so much energy earlier."

"It's amazing what you did. Thank you." He nodded.

"You know I'd do anything to protect the royal family." I felt I needed to say it out loud.

"Of course." He glanced toward the room. "What happened?"

"Mac offered to help me, so I didn't have to leave the palace and Prince Emil walked up on us," I grasped my hands so I wouldn't wave them around like a frantic lunatic, "I think he thought something else was happening."

"Oh." Leone smirked, then sobered quickly. "Don't worry about it. I'll talk to Raf, all guard assignments go through him."

I nodded. "Thank you." Taking a deep breath, I tried to compose myself. "I think—" I slumped my shoulders forward, "I'm not sure if there's a protocol or anything, but I think I need a meeting with the captain—at least I think this would fall under the full disclosure policy."

"For?" He stepped closer. "Is something else going on?"

I opened my mouth, then snapped it shut, only to open it

right after. "Prince Emil is my mate." I blurted out. His eyes widened. "I don't know if he knows—but I won't let it affect my job—" My heart was beating frantically. "I know a prince doesn't mate a guard..."

Leone chuckled. "You need to talk to Mitz, not Raf." He grinned at me. "This is going to be interesting" he commented, chuckling to himself. He patted my shoulder, then motioned to the door. "Let's go. I don't know about you, but my main desire right now is to find Arwan and end his miserable existence."

I bobbed my head quickly. "Bastard tried to drown us."

"Exactly." He started walking. "Karma owes him a beating." He grinned down at me. "And today, *I'm* karma."

I laughed softly. "Then I volunteer to be karma's backup."

Chapter Eight

I was standing with the guards when Mac returned. He gave me a quick glance, but I couldn't tell if he blamed me or not for the scene in the hall.

Prince Leone stood off to the side with the Captain. I couldn't see their faces at this point, so I wasn't sure what about me they were discussing. Could they prevent me from being sent away to a doldrum post? Had sharing that my mate was one of their brothers helped or hindered the verdict? Both turned to look at Emil in unison. Well, at least I knew what they were talking about. Emil didn't notice, he was too busy sending scathing looks at me.

I blew out a breath and glanced to the Captain and our Enforcer. They were both looking at me now. They looked amused. Someday, when my head wasn't still reeling, I might find it amusing that a lowly guard was the fated mate of a Prince. I wasn't there yet.

The Captain motioned for me to come over.

Felix looked down at me, one eyebrow raised.

"Nice working with you." I mumbled and headed to face Captain Rafael. He jerked his head toward the door. I went without comment, trying not do something girly and juvenile like throw myself at his feet and beg to keep my assignment.

Once outside I noticed Prince Leone had come with us.

"First," the Captain cleared his throat, "you are not being reassigned."

I struggled to maintain my erect posture and not slump in relief. "Thank you."

"Actually," he rubbed the back of his neck, "I'm wondering if we need a guard for you now."

He turned to his brother, who shrugged.

"I don't understand." My heart started skipping inside my chest.

"You're my brothers' mate." He stated simply.

Protocol went out the window, I started waving my hands around. "That doesn't change my job. I'm here to protect the royal family."

He considered my words for a moment and nodded his head slowly. "That doesn't change the fact that if they got to you, it would affect this family."

I looked from him to Leone. "It's not like we're mated..."

Rafael laughed quietly, "I've learned that doesn't matter." He glanced into the room on the other side of the glass. "Judging by Emil's reaction earlier, he's aware, or will be soon."

"I'm pretty sure the only thing he feels for me at this point is distain." I cleared my throat,

"Sir, if we could keep this between ourselves for now..."

This time Leone chuckled, "it's a hard secret to contain."

I took a deep breath, not sure where to go from here. "I understand." I didn't, but I needed to respond.

"Okay," Rafael nodded, "we'll keep it between us for now." He glanced in the room again, "and for now no guard, but you are not to go wandering alone from now on."

I frowned, "I'm not?"

"You have experienced how far Arwan is willing to go to get rid of our mates."

I nodded slowly, "Yeah. Okay. I get it."

"Good. Now let's go in there and see what the next step is." Rafael motioned to the door.

"Better be food, I'm starving." Leone said as he went past us and back into the solarium.

I went back in and took my place with the guards. A few of them gave me curious side eye. I shook my head letting them know it wasn't of importance. That was a lie, but I was not ready to explain. I watched the royal family moving around the room, all while processing what had just happened. *I was a guard.* I didn't *need* to be guarded.

Rafael went over to Emil and spoke. Emil glanced at me for a half a second then back to his brother. After a moment he inclined his head and then went over and sat in a chair in the far corner.

Focusing on the floor for a second, I dug deep to clear my mind. I needed to be present, not pondering things I could do nothing about. I also couldn't give into the urge to levitate something heavy, only to drop it on Prince Emil's head.

Mental lecture completed, I glanced back up to see the remaining family members coming in the door. *Back to business, Kin*, I instructed myself.

Prince Michael came in carrying a small box. He set it on the table and took out a phone. Pausing he checked the screen and held it toward his mate. She went over and took it. He then handed her a porter.

I glanced at my wrist and realized I'd most likely drowned the one I was wearing.

With a jerk of his head, the Captain told me to go over to his brother as well.

I waited until he'd given all the royal women new phones and porters, then took off my old one and held it out to him. "I don't know if you fix these or..."

Captain Rafael came over and leaned closer to his brother. "Does Kinsley's porter have a tracker?"

Michael frowned and looked at him. "Trackers are for..."

Rafael nodded his head quickly, "she needs a tracker."

Moving slowly, Michael looked to me for a second before

looking back at his brother. "She needs a tracker?"

"Yes, a tracker." My captain repeated.

They exchanged another look. "Okay, I'll—uh, get a new one with a tracker." He cleared his throat and handed me the porter. "Use this one for now."

I nodded and took it.

"Here's your phone." He avoided looking directly at me, "the family numbers are in, you will need to add any personal ones."

I hadn't even thought of my phone. I held my hand out, then he pulled it back and looked at Rafael again.

"Does she need anything else?"

"The group call app, an ear bud." Rafael said quietly. "She's going to be working with us going forward. I have a new guard for Rena."

"I see." Michael cleared his throat and handed me the phone. "I will get Paisley to download the app after we've eaten."

I looked at the phone. It was nothing like the one I'd lost. "Thank you." I said quickly, then turned to go back to the group.

"Kinsley."

I turned back to Captain Rafael, wondering what else there could be.

"See Mitz about ordering a good leather set for combat." He held my look, "one with a few more panels for protection." He motioned to the door. "I'll get you a new blade after this."

Leone had been standing close, came over. "You work out in our gym from now on too, not at the yard."

I was beginning to feel a little uncomfortable. "Yes, sir, Prince…"

"Leone." He smirked at me, "I think dropping the titles from here on out is a good idea."

I held my breath for a moment before nodding and going to where the guards were standing.

Felix winked at me. "Welcome to the royal fray." He

grinned, "there's never a dull moment."

I briefly acknowledged him, busying myself putting on the new porter.

"Mitz will be here with the food in a moment." Queen Alona came in. "We had to settle her down after she found out what happened."

King Chase was immediately on his feet. "I thought you were going to rest?"

I clenched my jaw trying to think of these people without their titles. The talk with my Captain—Rafael and Leone could have been a whole lot worse, so I needed to comply with everything they wanted.

Alona gave him a brief hard look. "I am fine. We are all fine. I am also hungry."

"Oh." He cleared his throat. "Then food you shall have."

Alona smiled. "So glad we're on the same page, my king." Lifting her chin, she glanced around the room, "and I have a request—as a Queen."

All eyes were on her.

With a soft smile, she motioned around the room, "not one word will so much as be *thought* about confining us ladies to the palace or closed quarters." She looked to Paisley, then Bethany, "we handled it and are all still here."

Autumn patted Michael's chest and went and sat down, she leaned forward on her knees and looked at me. "None of us would be here right now if it weren't for Kinsley." She pointed to a chair across from her. "She goes where we go from now on." Nodding she pointed to it again. "Sit, you can eat when the food arrives."

I looked from her to the Captain, he shrugged one shoulder slightly, so I took that as a yes and began walking to the chair.

"In fact, all the guards can grab some eats." Autumn nodded and glanced quickly at King Troy, then back to the guards. "Yeah, go get some food. If you want to bring it back here to eat, and listen in, go for it."

I stood beside the chair and watched the guards, my

friends, trying not to smirk as they walked from the room.

"Sit." Autumn shoved the chair out.

I sat down and felt like I was on display as everyone stared at me.

"So, thanks." She leaned on the table and looked at me. "I was pretty close to freaking out in there." She frowned, "I'm not good at swimming."

I tried to shrug it off, even though I'd had my own moments of panic. "I wanted out of there as much as everyone else."

Prince—Victor and Crissy came into the room. Crissy dropped her bag on a chair, then came running over. A few feet from the table, she launched herself at me and all but landed in my lap. The chair slid back with the impact.

"Thank you." She squeezed my neck.

I looked at Autumn to see her smirking.

The Justice came over and gently unwrapped his mate. Enclosing her in his arms, he inclined his head. "I am in your debt." He looked around at a few of his brothers, "we all are in your debt." Then he walked over and deposited Crissy on the chair beside him.

Mitz came in carrying a tray and the room was quieted as they watched. Setting it down, she turned and looked around the room. It wasn't hard to see the affection she had for them all. She paused and looked at me, a gentle smile reflected in her eyes. "I'm brewing some green tea for you, love. I'll bring it along with the rest of the food."

There was no hiding the shock on my face. "Thank you."

She walked out of the room again.

I glanced to Autumn, she grinned at me. "Mitz is a peach."

"All right, everyone, grab your food and sit down." Troy stood in the door. "We have a lot to cover and a date with some unsavory people later on."

"Can't wait." Chase got up and hovered near the table that held the food. "I gather you've processed all you saw?"

His twin nodded slowly, "I was just comparing notes with Elder Udela, confirming a few locations."

"A few?" Autumn looked excited, "that's great."

Queen—Daxx came in carrying a tray. "Is that jerk at any of these locations?" She set the tray down, "the one that tried to drown us." She gave her mate a hard look.

"Pretty sure he knows which jerk you mean." Quinton went over and picked up a plate.

Daxx shrugged, "just making sure, there's a lot of jerks out there."

Autumn stood up. "Come on, let's get some food."

I got up slowly, "I don't mind waiting."

She snorted, "you have to eat when you can around here." She glanced at me over her shoulder, "same goes for sleep."

I nodded, knowing how crazy things had been lately. I felt awkward and a bit overwhelmed. First, the royals all seemed normal, in ways I'd never imagined. In my whole life I'd never thought I'd be sitting down to eat with them. Then, as I noticed Emil scowling at me from his chair was if I should retire now, and go home to wear my mother's frilly clothes.

Chapter Nine

Michael came rushing into the armory. He spotted me and came over. "Here's your new porter." He held it out, "with a tracker."

I took it and replaced the one on my wrist. Holding the other out to him, I gave him a quick glance. "I don't understand the tracker part."

"Well," he looked over at Kara, "we've had a few instances where people have been ported through portals or gotten lost—Arwan and his people take battles to whole new heights…"

I nodded. "Got it." I patted the new leather coat. "Thanks for the gear."

He shrugged, "yours was a little soggy."

I smirked, "just a little." I motioned to the sword on my back, "the upgrade is amazing, lighter than my other…" I stopped speaking when Emil came over. The look he gave me could have soured milk.

Michael gave him an odd look, then inclined his head to me. "See you over there."

I gave him a stiff nod, not taking my eyes off the gorgeous, but indignant, man standing and scowling down at me. I cleared my throat. "About earlier…"

He held up his hand. "I owe you an apology for my reaction." He shook his head slightly, "I have forgotten how often one needs to feed when they're—" he waved his hand up and down at me, "so young." Emil continued to stare at me, then let out a long sigh, "I don't know what the hell is wrong with me…"

"Would you like that list alphabetized or random?" Quinton came up beside him.

Emil sent him a hard look.

Quinton smirked, "if you're done being dramatic, Kinsley's coming over in the first group to set up watch."

Straightening, Emil inclined his head. "I'll see the both of you there." He turned on his heel and stomped to the other side of the room.

Watching him for a moment, Quinton turned back to me. "You'll get used to my brothers, they're all a bit strange."

"Coming from the strangest of us all." Leone grinned at me. "Ready?"

Quinton paused beside Crissy, "any insights into what we're walking into?"

Crissy blew out a breath, "I don't know." She frowned, "there's pieces—so many pieces and I can't…" she looked down at the floor, "it's a broken place," she nodded, "that's all I see." With her eyes wide, she looked back up at him, "I don't see blood, though."

Quinton stared down at her for a moment. "Shout if anything comes to you." He smiled, "a few seconds' warning is better than none."

Crissy nodded, then walked away without a sound.

He turned back to me with a questioning look.

Nodding, I patted my side with the three smaller blades. "I'm as ready as I can be. I don't know the entire strategy though…"

Quinton motioned to a group in the corner, "we'll go over it when we get there."

I didn't even know where 'there' was, I'd missed the meeting while I was getting my new gear. I almost stumbled when I realized who was in the group we were going over with. Aside from a guard I hadn't seen in a while, he'd been on some secret assignment, there were also three of the elders. In battle attire.

Elder Drusla gave me a nod when we joined the group. She was a legendary warrior, and truth be told, the entire reason why I always wanted to be a guard.

I gave her a nod of my own, although it probably wasn't as graceful as hers.

Elder Segos patted Quinton on the shoulder, then made quick work of securing his long white hair.

I had seen him fight in the practice yard a few times, his skill was beyond what I ever could have, or it felt that way.

"Elder Marinus," Quinton didn't hide the surprise in his voice, "it's nice to see you coming with us."

The Elder gave him an amused look. "I couldn't sit on the sidelines." He too secured his black hair back as he continued to speak. "The Captain explained what took place, and I felt I needed to lend a hand."

Quinton nodded, "that's too bad for Arwan's people."

"Do we know if he's going to be there?" Elder Segos asked.

Quinton shrugged, "we don't know who will be there, just that this location was inside many of the heads we have in the cells."

"Good." Elder Drusla nodded, "many should be there, then." She patted her side, "I always wanted my own port box to send criminals back to the cells." She smiled, "only took them fifteen hundred years to give me one."

Quinton chuckled, "I'm hoping it means there are going to be so many, extra port boxes were needed."

The elders nodded in agreement.

Looking around, Quinton paused on Reagan. She immediately looked at him. He patted his heart once and she nodded. I had heard mates could communicate through their bond, but this was the first time I'd seen it with my own eyes.

Ethan cleared his throat. "Is everyone ready?"

"You're taking us over?" Elder Drusla asked.

"Yes." He held up his wrist his porter was on. "They programmed a few extra guards' porters to transport everyone over." He glanced at the Quinton. "It's uh," he shrugged, "well, you'll see."

I didn't like his words at all, or what they implied. A nervous tingle went down my spine. "Let's go." I said abruptly before they dragged the suspense out any longer.

Chapter Ten

I turned slowly and looked at the trees and thick ground growth behind us.

"You've got to be kidding."

At Quinton's tone, I looked to see what the others were looking at. "What is this?" I grimaced, "or was this?"

Ethan cleared his throat, "an amusement park."

Elder Drusla glanced around, "in the middle of a forest?"

"I don't think it was always this way." Elder Marinus pointed, "there's a badly neglected roadway."

Quinton pulled out his phone. "Connect the group call, the other teams are coming over in different locations."

I took out my phone and connected through this app. Putting the earbud in place, I pushed the small button and turned it on.

"This is a first." That sounded like Prince Arius.

"I've always wanted to go to a big park." Bethany said.

"I don't think the rides are running today." Chase's tone was filled with amusement.

"There are so many high places." There was no mistaking Crissy.

"Road to the south is well used." Leone's voice was quiet. "North road is inaccessible, fallen trees."

"Good, one less place to watch." Michael said.

"Cristy, we need you to climb and point us to which buildings to access." Victor's tone was both commanding and gentle.

"Okay, Vic. I don't think the Ferris wheel is safe, so I'm going to climb the flying tower, it has a ladder."

"Which one is the flying tower?" Daxx sounded stressed.

"The tall one with the cables running down." Paisley informed her.

"I'll cover you while you do." That was Kara, "just let me get up on this platform first."

"Be careful, Kara," That was Rafael, "we don't know if they have scouts."

"Witches and Mages are going to stay cloaked at the West side, until we call for them." Alona's voice was soft.

"Duchess…"

"Relax, Chase, I'm moving now to guard the platform Kara is going to be on." Alona sounded annoyed. "Sith is three inches behind me."

I moved so I could see where the princesses were. I spotted Kara climbing up onto the platform. If I didn't know to look for her, I would have missed her altogether in the vines and growth covering most of the structure. She kept going until she reached the top. Bart was about halfway down the winding stairs, alert and looking around.

"There's movement near the large building at the North side." Kara reported.

"We see them." Emil replied. "Roughly twenty just standing around doing nothing."

"Okay, Crissy, you are clear to go now." Kara told her.

"Okay, I'll be quick." Crissy answered.

It didn't take much searching to find the tall tower with cables running from it. My heartrate rose as I watched the young princess go up the ladder with a sure swiftness. I doubted I could have climbed that fast.

"Almost there." Crissy said, not even out of breath.

I couldn't watch any longer, so I took those few moments

to look around. This was going to be a nightmare. There were too many areas to escape. Aside from the four buildings on the site, there were other structures: the fun house, haunted castle and the gardens were all large enough to hide in. I glanced toward the water slide, as best as I could, overgrowth obstructed my line of sight. I didn't see any functioning watercraft, but it was hard to tell with all of the seemingly abandoned boats just floating there. All were covered in a mossy overgrowth and some looked to be on the verge of sinking.

"This place is huge." Bethany said in a small voice.

"Covering it is going to be a challenge." Autumn sounded exhilarated. "I need the workout."

"If there are stairs, I am calling veto right now." Michael added.

"Does the roller coaster count as stairs?" Rafael asked.

"It's not on *my* side of this park." Michael said quickly.

Leone appeared beside us. He nodded to Quinton, who took his ear bud out and stepped closer. I didn't know if I was invited, but I wouldn't be doing my job if I stood there oblivious.

Taking out the earpiece, I went over to them.

"This is…"

"A strategic nightmare." I finished for Leone.

He nodded. "Michael told me to get you," he looked at me, "over to where Arius and Autumn are." He rubbed the back of his neck, "most of the guards will concentrate on the building breaches, but we'll need more of us spread out here to catch any strays."

I straightened, "where are they?" I glanced back over the long-forgotten park that looked like it had survived an apocalyptic event.

"To the left of the main building," He pointed, "we need to cut them off before they can reach the road or the water."

I nodded. "Got it."

"The elders and I will cover this side." Quinton motioned to the treed area we'd come from.

Elder Segos nodded. "We'll spread out with a fifteen-foot span between us, and keep an eye out for any hoping to vanish into the woods."

Elder Drusla didn't even acknowledge the conversation, she pulled the blade off her back and started to jog in the other direction.

Leone gave Quinton a quick look before giving me a hesitant one, "*your* Captain says you are to stay with Arius and Autumn, no one is to be alone."

I weighed his words for a second, wondering if the order had to do with my confession earlier. Keeping my expression as blank as I could, I nodded. "Understood."

We put the earpieces back in place.

"What do you see, Reagan?" Autumn asked.

"No green," She answered, "well, other than trees and plants." Reagan added.

"No magic works for me." Quinton said tersely.

"They probably never thought they'd need magic wards out here." Leone said as he gave me a look asking if I was ready to port. "It took us four hours to find this place. I have mosquito bites in pretty awkward places."

Someone chuckled, I could only assume it was Bethany.

As soon as we came out on the other side of the park, we both quickly dialed back into the call. Arius gave me a nod, then checked the direction of the road.

"Can we get some witches to place a warning spell on the road?" He asked.

"We'll go do that now." A woman replied.

"Thanks, Clairee." Troy said.

Arius looked to Autumn, she nodded.

She was dancing on the spot, like she was warming up for a big fight.

I turned and realized that I could see more of the park from here. It was spread out and there were so many areas people could hide. I blew out a breath and rolled my shoulders. This was beyond a strategic nightmare. Inhaling slowly, I blew out all the negative thoughts with my breath.

"Everyone get to your positions, we're breaching the three largest buildings in five." That was King Troy.

"Wait, where is everyone? I don't want to waste my time running after someone if they're running right to one of you?" Daxx asked.

"I'm in shock, she's asking for a plan." King Chase said.

"Har-har, Chase." Daxx didn't sound impressed.

"I have a good shot at two of the buildings from here. I can slow down any if they run." Kara informed us.

"Stay there, then." The Captain told her.

"I can shout out where anyone is going." Crissy announced.

"Perfect." Quinton replied, "we don't have a clear view here."

"Sith, another guard and I will cut off anyone heading to the fun house." Alona said, "if it's anything like ones I've seen, finding anyone inside it will be next to impossible."

"Do that." Chase said quickly, "I feel it would be false advertising and not fun at all."

I was busy trying to locate the spots they were mentioning. I knew what the Captain's orders were—but if I had to get somewhere to aid someone, I needed to know where I was racing off to.

"I'm outside the center building." Paisley said. "We're behind it now."

"I'm with her." Bethany added, "haven't spotted anyone yet."

"I'm in the center with Emil and some guards, hopefully we can round up any strays." He gave Arius a quick salute, then ported.

"I'm breaching the largest building." Troy said in a hushed voice.

"Middle building with the tag-team nightmare." Chase whispered.

Arius looked behind us again, where the derelict bumper boats floated. "We have the dock covered."

Autumn nodded while she squatted a few times. "And the

road. We have Kinsley with us and one of the guards is heading here after the breach, so we're better than good here." She gave me a beaming smile.

"We're almost to the group outside the building. Hold position until we dispatch them." Michael spoke so quietly I barely heard him.

"Need a hand brother?" Quinton asked.

Michael made a scoffing noise, "I have Victor and eight guards with me. They're not even armed."

"Hmmm, a light warm up." Chase said.

"I have four guards with me. I'm checking the whole site for portals." Reagan stated.

"Are the guards on the call?" Quinton's light tone was gone.

"Yes." Reagan answered.

"Make sure to shout if you run into problems." There was no mistaking the order hidden in his words.

"They know their job, Quint." She said in a light tone.

"Mmhmm, and Rea—gloves stay on." That order had a softer tone.

"Eyes on a swivel, my dear mate. Try not to get stabbed today." She answered him.

I looked to Arius, who was smiling. Working closely with the royal family was going to take some getting used to.

"I will help breach the largest building, then move about as needed." Victor said calmly. "We're engaging this crew—now."

The line was silent for a few moments, no more questions as we listened to the sounds of a skirmish through our earpieces.

"Okay, let's get this party started. Fight hard, boys." Daxx sounded happy.

"Stay safe, ladies." Emil said in a low tone.

"We'll try the rides after, brothers, try not to get trounced." Chase said.

"Is there any other kind of fighting but hard?" Leone asked, sounding like he was running.

"You were moving in slow motion at the last practice." That was Quinton harassing him.

"Your vision must be failing, old man," Rafael whispered, "we were going full speed."

"Next to Autumn, we were all standing still." Alona added.

I glanced to see Autumn grinning as she flipped the hood off and pushed up her sleeves.

"A little bit of focus might be a good thing right now, my insane family." Emil said, but his tone wasn't as serious as he let on.

I'd fought with the royal family many times since I'd been a guard, but I'd never had the earbud in—I had no idea of what they were saying to each other on the verge of battle. For some reason, I always assumed they were discussing strategy.

"Hey, babe?" That was Paisley.

"Yeah?" Arius looked toward the trees behind the largest structure.

I couldn't see anyone there, but he knew exactly where his mate was.

"Try to stay dry today, no swimming." Paisley said in a whisper.

"I've had all the water I need for a month." Alona said in a flat tone.

"In five…" That was King Troy.

"Ready here." Leone reported.

"On your count, brother." The justice stated.

"Two." Chase said.

Then there was silence. I could make out breathing, and faint sounds, but not enough to know what was happening. Arius was tense and focused as he stared off at nothing. I'd been told they could communicate, the royal family, through a bond and had to wonder if he was focusing on what the others were doing.

There were echoing sounds of doors slamming, at the exact same moments they had breached all three of the biggest structures. It was amazing to witness working with this family.

Chapter Eleven

"What do you see?" Kara asked.

"Shit…" That sounded like Daxx.

"Chaos." Someone said, then a loud squealing sound echoed all around us.

"Damn it." Someone shouted into the mic.

"Where is it coming from?" Alona yelled.

It was echoing though the mics and deafening all of us, the noise was an alarm coming from the large area we had to cover.

"It's on a pole by the garden area." Kara shouted into the mic.

"We're on it." Reagan said.

"So much for the element of surprise." Quinton said loudly.

The noise was cut off and then we could hear fighting in our earbuds.

Arius turned to face the closest building and stood with his swords in his hands.

"Some coming out the back of the middle building." Crissy reported. "They're heading toward you, Quinton."

"We see them." He answered.

"Some went out the back." Chase said sounding out of

breath.

"I'm on it." Kara said in a solemn tone.

"She got two." Crissy said a few moments later. "One is running toward the carousel."

"We see them." Leone replied.

"Arius, a group went out the side entrance." Michael said between grunts.

Arius straightened and zeroed in on those trying to escape. He motioned with his head to Autumn.

She moved quickly to stand behind a small kiosk.

I followed her and ducked down at the opposite end.

"Six." Arius' whispered through the mic. He didn't hide, or attempt to not be seen.

I understood what he was doing. One against six, it would give those trying to escape a false sense of hope. Autumn was watching Arius and looking for the escapees. As a fighter, she knew how to read a person's actions.

"It's under control here. I'm moving to the center building." Victor stated.

"Our idea of under control," Michael grunted, "differs, brother."

"We could use some justice rage in here." Paisley said loudly into the mic.

"It's like they're multiplying." Chase sounded winded.

"Leone, there are four running toward the roller coaster." Kara reported.

Arius straightened, holding his arms open. I looked to see they were ten feet from him. "Leaving so soon?" Arius asked in a flat tone.

"Do you need me to send some guards, Emil?" Reagan asked.

"No." Emil barked, "keep them," he growled low, "with you."

"This guy can run." Leone huffed into the mic.

"Don't let him reach the roller coaster." Emil said hurriedly.

The sound of metal hitting metal came from Arius was

engaging all six that hoped to get away. I glanced to Autumn, she grinned and stood up.

"Tsk tsk. Six on one doesn't seem fair." She hopped over the kiosk counter and landed gracefully in front of two of the men.

I didn't pause to admire her technique, I stood up and intercepted a swing intended for the back of Arius' head. The man on the other end of the sword couldn't hide his shocked expression. It didn't last long as he swung at me, his look quickly replaced with one I was so tired of seeing. That look that telegraphed it's just a tiny woman.

Gritting my teeth, I blocked his swing and kicked him in the chest to give myself more room—and just to let him know I wasn't just a little woman. I didn't want to get in the way of Autumn's or Arius' skirmishes either.

A man dropped on the ground beside me, Autumn advanced on him, a look of intense focus on her face. Reaching behind her, she pulled out a nylon zip tie. With a grin, she grabbed the man's wrist and secured it to his ankle. "Tying them up over here when someone with a box gets a sec."

I barely had time to miss the swing of the man I was fighting. With a move I'd practiced until I could do it in my sleep, I got my blade behind his and reached with my other arm to grab the handle and twist. His blade hit the ground at his feet. My shorter height hadn't always been easy, but I'd spent years finding all the advantages I could.

When he leaned down to grab me, I used the butt of the handle against his throat. As he stumbled back, I chanced a glance. There was a stool lying in the dirt. Switching my sword to my off hand, I used my ability to heft the stool in the air and bounced it against the side of his head.

Autumn landed a spinning kick on her opponent and took a few seconds to toss me a zip tie.

It dropped beside me. Picking it up, I went over to the man lying unconscious on the ground and grabbed his foot. I dragged him close to Autumn's first victim and then secured his foot to the other man's free hand. With a shrug, I turned to see Arius was taking on three as Autumn dealt with one other.

"Where the hell does he think he can go once he climbs it?' Emil's voice registered through the earpiece.

"No idea." That was Leone. "Start climbing, I'm," he grunted, "busy."

I didn't have time to look and see what they were doing when one of the men that had been fighting Arius noticed me. He charged toward me. Shifting the sword to my other hand, I ducked when he swung, again using my size against his. His swing was met with air, momentum throwing off his balance. I was able to trip him completely, using a sweep of my leg against his.

"Alona, they're heading toward you." Kara called out.

"We're ready." She replied.

"Shit."

I spun to see Arius ducking one man's swing, as the other was jumping into one of the bumper boats. Glancing back to the guy at my feet, I kicked the sword from his hand and then kicked my boot against his head. Years ago, I thought a move like that was fighting dirty. I'd since discovered that anything that allowed you to walk away unscathed was fair. He didn't move. "Tie him when you're free, Autumn." I said hurriedly as I ran down the dock. I had no idea what I was going to do to get the man now jumping from boat to boat, but I had to try to catch him. Unless he planned to swim to freedom, I had no idea what his intentions were. Sliding the blade into the strap on my back, I jumped into the first boat. I swayed and almost toppled right out of it. Not pausing long enough to plan this, I stepped and leapt to the next one. "If he makes it to the other side, can you slow him down, Clairee?" I was out of breath as I took the next jump.

"It would be my pleasure." She answered.

The next boat slid sideways across the water when I landed. There were still eight boats between us. Inhaling quickly, I got my balance and jumped to the next one when it rocked toward another boat. The water was green with algae and I did not want to swim today.

"Main building cleared." Michael reported.

"Could use a hand in the fun house." Alona said quickly. "They went in, no one has come out."

"You're up, brother." Rafael piped in. "Our building is almost empty."

I jumped again and knew there was no way I was going to catch him doing it this way. Pausing for a split second, I changed directions and aimed myself to line up with him instead of chasing.

"Two headed toward the garden building, Reagan." Crissy said quickly. "Two going to the castle."

"Haunted castle, great." Leone didn't sound impressed at all.

"Better than dangling off a roller coaster." Emil growled out.

I almost lost my focus wanting to look and see if he was all right. Blinking, I frowned and then focused on the boat I was jumping into. One more and I could try to slow him down. It was like he was running around in circles now, finally realizing there was nowhere to go. I couldn't let him reach the dock again.

When I had my balance, I focused on the boat across from him. It was further than I normally tried, but they were light and floating already, so I hoped. Holding my hand out to increase my concentration, the boat moved without too much trouble at all. With a grin, I used my ability and shoved an empty boat toward him. I shifted my focus to the next, just beside him. I wanted to see his expression as the boats started surrounding him without anyone touching them, but I couldn't give him the chance to come up with a new plan.

He swore and a moment later I heard a splash.

Hopping to the next boat, I focused and moved it in his direction.

"How is everyone?" Troy sounded winded, but still regal in his request.

"We're good." Bethany reported.

I watched the guy trying to swim in the thick, slimy water. He wasn't getting far. I moved the boat closer. Slow and steady, I told myself.

"A dozen or so left here." Daxx called out.

"Kinsley is riding a boat to the last one here." Arius sounded amused.

"Could use a hand in here, brother." Michael said with a tone of annoyance. "All these mirrors…"

"On my way."

"This haunted castle," Leone whispered, "is like all my nightmares rolled into one."

The boat bumped against one closest to the man as he tried to climb out of the filth. I grimaced; I did not want to touch him. Bending down, I grabbed the boat beside us. "Get in." I told him. His frustration turned to defeat as he complied and grabbed the side of the boat. I put one foot on it to hold it steady. Once he was in, I held onto the boat he was in and used my ability to move us across the water. "Coming to you, Autumn."

"I see. I don't want to touch him." She sounded amused.

"I'm on my way there." Victor reported.

By the time the boat bumped against the dock, Victor stood beside Autumn. He looked slightly amused as he leaned forward and held the box up to the slime and algae covered man. With a grin, he held out his hand to assist me onto the dock.

"Need a hand in the gardens." Reagan said quickly. "This is like a jungle," she panted loudly in the mic, "and smells like a swamp."

"On my way." Victor stated. He looked at Autumn then to me, "I believe Emil could use a hand." He motioned in a direction then took off running back toward the park.

"Try to send them back out, Reagan, I'll take them down." Kara said.

"Trying." Was all Reagan said.

"We got the ones heading to the trees." Quinton reported.

"Was like hide and seek."

"Normally I like looking at myself in a mirror," Chase's tone was low, "but this is taking it to the extreme."

Someone chuckled into the mic.

I followed Autumn, trying to see where Emil was as we ran. I spotted him climbing the roller coaster after a man just as we encountered Rafael fighting three guys.

"Go." Autumn said. "I'll lend Raf a hand."

I nodded and took off toward the roller coaster again. I had no idea what I was going to do once I got there. Emil was almost to the top at the highest point. The man he was chasing was slowly making his way down the track. One slip, and either or both would plunge to their death.

I ran faster. As I reached the ride, I climbed up the platform that would have been used to get in the cars for the ride. The rails were rusted, and I had to goad myself into stepping on the track between them. I bounced, giving it a quick test. It seemed strong enough. My legs were too short to take the wide steps to the next brace. Blowing out a quick breath, I started hopping from support to support, climbing the gradual incline.

I made the mistake of glancing toward the ground, it was a lot higher than I thought. I was pretty sure that my heart was beating so hard it would be visible on the outside of my body. I kept going. One of the princes were up there, and it was my duty to come to his aid. I'd sworn an oath that I would always put my life and well-being aside to serve the royal family and the realm.

"Oh my—have a care, Kinsley." That was Alona.

I could only assume if she was watching me, then things were under control with the fun house.

"Emil, start crowding him to move him toward Kinsley." Leone said, short of breath.

"He's carrying a satchel." Emil said in a tense tone. "I don't know what's in it, but he almost plunged to his death to save it." He sounded out of breath. "I wouldn't have followed him if it weren't for *that*."

I glanced up to see how far until I was close to the man. Emil was right, he was clutching the bag against his chest with one arm as he made his way down the bars. I don't think he noticed me, which was good. I still had no idea what I would do once we met up. I paused for a second and examined the rails and metal I was standing on. There was no way to fight up here. I touched my side with the blades and hoped my aim was true today.

"I'm going up with a rope." Leone said in a breathless way.

"I can help." Crissy said.

"Stay where you are, heart, we still need a watch until we sweep the entire site." Victor said.

"Okay, Vic. Be careful, Kinsley, I want you to see the snow." Crissy said.

I frowned and knew I couldn't pause to wonder what she meant.

"Twenty feet." Emil stated.

I glanced from my footing to see how close the man was. "I'm going to try reasoning with him." I told anyone listening. "I don't know what's in the bag, but he's really protecting it, so if he falls, he could destroy whatever it is."

"He doesn't look like a fighter." Emil said.

"An important geek?" Paisley said. "We need him."

I nodded, even though no one could see me. I stopped and braced my legs far enough apart to balance comfortably. I refused to look toward the ground so as not to psych myself out. I looked at the scared man coming toward me. I held up my hand. "We're bringing up a rope to help you get down."

He stopped, panic clear on his face. Slowly, he squatted down closer to the braces.

"Just stay there, like that." I said to him. The expression on his face was filled with so much fear, I didn't know how he was going to react.

"I have to protect it." He finally said.

"Nothing is worth more than your life." I told him.

He shook his head. "You don't understand."

"Almost there." Leone huffed out a breath. "I'll come up just behind him, Kins."

I made no motion to let the man know I had someone else talking in my ear. "You can explain it, once we're down from here."

He hugged the bag tighter.

"Let's do this the safest, easiest way." I said calmly, "for all of us."

"I can't. I have to protect this." His voice cracked, he was in full panic mode now.

I wanted to sit down, standing up and balancing was making the pit of my stomach knot. "I don't care what's in the bag." I lied. I adjusted my footing to keep my balance and he jolted like he was going to run. Stupid man, I thought. There's only one way to go here, and that's down. Pulling one of the blades from my side, I lifted my other hand and used my ability to levitate it from my hand. I let it hover in the air. "As you can see, I could take that bag from you if I wanted to." I made the blade go in his direction. I couldn't look to see his reaction. "But," I brought the blade back to my other hand, then looked at him, "I just want to help you get down from here."

"I'm-I can keep the bag?" He was shivering and wearing only a t-shirt: nerves and the breeze up here was far cooler than on the ground.

I, on the other hand, was soaked in a nervous sweat. "I am not taking the bag." I told him. I could see Emil was only a few feet to go to get to him but didn't allow myself to shift my eyes to give his location away. "First, sit down completely so you can't slip."

The man nodded and quickly sat down on the slats between the rails.

"That's it." I kept my voice calm.

Emil was right behind him now. He leaned down and put his hand on the man's shoulder. The expression on his face said he wanted to throttle him, but he restrained himself. "Now, Leone."

Leone appeared beside the man and climbed the rail. He glanced at me with a quick appraisal, then to the man sitting there holding the bag. He untied the rope from his waist and held it out to Emil. Emil took it. "I'll hold the bag for a second." He held out his hand.

The man looked at the rope Emil held and reluctantly gave Leone the bag. As he started to stand, Leone held his other hand toward him, and the man vanished.

Emil blew out a breath and sat down, still holding the rope.

I put the knife back in the case on my hip and carefully lowered my body to sit down.

"Good job, Kinsley." Rafael said.

Leone opened the bag and looked inside. "I have no idea what this is." He said. "It's a thick rectangular chunk of glass."

"How big? What color is it?" A man asked.

"Uh," Leone squatted and held the bag out to Emil, when he took it Leone carefully pulled out the glass. "It's about eight inches long, three thick and maybe five inches wide." He turned it in his hands, "It's clear, no color."

"That's it." The man sounded excited. "Of course, that's how he's able to do control so much power and cast in different realms..."

"Romulus, don't make me walk all the way over there and smack you." That was Daxx.

"Explain." Troy didn't sound pleased either.

"It's—it is like a computer screen per se, he can bring up a cast and see what needs altering or reinforcing..."

"You're saying we just stopped him." Alona asked.

"He can still do spells where he is, but he now has to physically be there to work them." Romulus explained.

"Finally." Quinton said, "we're going to get him."

"We still have to find him, but we have lots of heads to explore and we've got his toy now." Chase replied.

"You need to get that down here *intact*." Romulus said, "one chip or scratch could destroy it."

Leone glanced at Emil and then slowly lowered it back into the bag. "You can track all the spells and whatever else he has been using it for?"

"With some time, yes, but it has to be intact. I need to see it before it's ported." The mage told him.

Leone nodded. "No pressure. Okay, I'll bring it down." Opening his jacket, he put the bag inside, and held it in place with the straps across his chest from his swords. He blew out a breath, then looked from Emil to me. "I guess you guys get to admire the view until I get back up here with the rope."

Emil looked over the edge. "I'm am not climbing back down." He moved his chin toward me. "We'll go down the way Kinsley came up."

I glanced over my shoulder to see the rails leading down to the platform. I blew out a breath and turned my body around slowly, while still sitting.

Leone pulled the rope up and tied one end through the rails. "The whole site checked yet?"

"Almost finished." Arius reported. "There's a lot of things to go through in the main building…"

"Supplies to port back." Paisley added.

"Eighty-two" Arius stated, "that has to be a record for us."

"Considering the size of this place," Michael sounded winded, "we outdid our old records."

Leone looked at me and rolled his eyes at his brothers' comments. "All right, I'm coming down." He climbed over the outer rail again.

Emil watched until he disappeared, then came toward me. His expression echoed my own thoughts, climbing down was going to suck.

"So, Crissy—snow?" Kara said.

"Oh." Crissy made a strange sound. "Can I come down?"

"Yes, we've cleared the property." Victor answered.

"Okay, good." She made a noise of excitement. "My cable it too short to rappel." She sounded disappointed.

"Just go slowly, everyone that's up high, please." Alona

said.

"Yes, we need warm coats and thick socks." Crissy said as if she had just been asked about the snow. "Maybe we can get some of those insulated things people wear under their clothes."

"You mean long johns?" Bethany didn't sound impressed.

I got turned around and looked at the distance we had to go until our feet were on the ground again. It looked like it was miles to the ground. My heart started pounding as I moved in a slow crab walk down the rails. Normally I didn't have an issue with heights, but everyone has their limits, and the height of a roller coaster was apparently mine.

I glanced behind me to see Emil was doing the same thing, only with his height, he was going to have an easier time. I bit my lip, technically I should be behind him as the guard, in case he slipped. I glanced at his face, judging by the expression of annoyance, mentioning such a thing would just get me barked at.

Chapter Twelve

I started moving slowly, being careful of where I placed my feet. I still had to stretch a lot further than I was comfortable with. I was just starting to get into a rhythm when I did the stupidest thing and looked down. It hadn't seemed this high when I was climbing up it.

"Slow and steady." Emil's voice came through the earpiece.

I forced myself to lift my chin and nod, but I wasn't going to turn around to look at him. I was feeling dizzy now. Later, after my feet were on the ground, I was going to berate myself like no other time before.

Shifting my hands one at a time so I wasn't stretched out, I blew out a breath and moved my foot to the next brace. There had to be a better way to do this. Lifting my other foot, I put in on the same brace and shuffled my hands along the rail.

Before I could settle my weight to move again the sound of creaking metal echoed and I found myself dangling from the rails by my hands. The gasps through the mics barely registered as I fought to keep my grip.

"I've got you." Emil grasped my wrists tight.

I looked up to see him leaning over and holding my wrists.

His jaw was tense with the strain, but his eyes conveyed a calm I needed to see right now.

"When I tell you. Let go." He said softly.

I gave him a nervous nod and held his look. Trust was stressed during guard training. Sometimes you had to put your life in someone else's hands. Emil wasn't a guard, but the look he was giving me told me I could trust him to get me back up.

"Let go, now." He said in a hushed voice.

As he lifted me, I looked for anywhere to brace my feet. When I was high enough, I managed to get one boot on a rail support, relieving some of my weight from him.

I tumbled back into his lap. I closed my eyes and swallowed down the fear stuck in my throat. He made no move to release me, for that brief moment I was glad for it.

"Okay. I was enjoying watching your torment climbing down, brother, but you're not holding that glass thing, so now might be the time to tell you that you could just port the both of you down." Chase's voice broke the silence.

Emil's hold loosened. "You could have reminded me of that *before*, brother."

"I could," Chase said, "but you missed our childhood, so I'm trying to make up for it."

Emil's chest rose and fell. I could feel his breath on my neck. "Hang on." He whispered.

Before I could acknowledge it, I was sitting on the ground at Chase's feet. Emil released me immediately and stood up.

Chase held out his hand to me. "I apologize for not saying it sooner." He inclined his head to me.

Despite how I felt, I shrugged it off. "No biggie." He was a king and I was thrilled to have my feet on the ground again.

Alona came over, giving Chase a hard look. "Are you all right?"

I nodded, then huffed out a quick breath. "Yes." I looked around the park, "I think I've had my fill of adventure parks for today."

She smiled. "I couldn't agree more."

"I'm anxious to get back and see my new guests." Arius came over and gave me a huge grin.

"Where's the glass thing?" Emil looked around, a hard expression on his face.

"Romulus went back with four guards to start analyzing it." Rafael told him.

Emil nodded his head slowly, "and we'll find Arwan with it?"

"He mumbled something about that and shutting down any active spells." Quinton looked around at a few of the others.

"How is he going to know if it's safe to shut them down?" Bethany looked over at Leone, "what if people—good people, end up trapped?"

Leone rubbed the back of his neck and turned to Troy, "I'll go tell him not to shut anything down until we know more."

"Might be best." Troy straightened and glanced around the area we stood in. "We have a lot of work to do with all those prisoners." He motioned to Arius, "we'll meet in the hall once you have the preliminary scans completed."

Arius nodded. "I'll go make sure they're getting it done."

I cleared my throat. "Do you need a hand at the cells, warden?"

Arius looked me up and down but didn't get a chance to speak.

"I think she's pulled her weight enough for today." Paisley said. "Join us at the meeting room after you get back."

I opened my mouth, then closed it and looked at the Captain, he inclined his head. "Okay. I'll see you all shortly." I opened the porter on my wrist and pushed the first button my fingers connected with. I didn't care which location I ended up at. I just needed some time to compose myself after the roller coaster.

I came out at the palace courtyard and blew out a breath of relief. Going to one of the stone benches I sat down. It seemed every step I took, I now needed to rethink. How had

I ended up here? I looked up at the sky, were the gods guiding my lifeline now and purposely testing me? Shaking my head, I looked back to the ground. Since when had I started believing anyone but me steered my path? My mother's nattering was to blame, I was sure of it. You could only listen to the same thing about a billion times before it worked its way into your head.

A low mewling noise caught my attention. I turned to see the cub the guards had told me about. "Tawny, isn't it?" She was beautiful and I was in awe that I was this close to a mountain lion.

She paused in step and gave me a quick appraisal, scenting the air for a moment before bounding over to me.

I ran my hand over her head. "You are going to be gorgeous when you're bigger." And lethal.

She rubbed her head into my hand, then moved so it was running down her back.

"Are you staying out of trouble?" I'd never had a pet of my own. My mother always thought they were a nuisance. There was something invigorating and yet calming just petting her. A wild animal consenting to your touch was the biggest symbol of trust I'd ever experienced.

"There you are."

I turned to see Kara standing in the doorway of the solarium.

"She's like Houdini." Kara came over and squatted down beside the cat. Tawny turned her attention to her, rubbing along her leg. "She has her own room, own yard and still manages to get out."

"Found her?"

The Captain was standing behind us.

Kara nodded, "yes." She gave him an exasperated look. "I don't know how she got over here this time."

He smiled down at her. "She's a wild animal, confining her isn't going to be easy."

I noted the gentle expression on his face when he looked at her. "What about putting a tracker on her," I held up my hand, "like with our porters."

"Your porter has a tracker?" Kara looked from my wrist to her mate.

I nodded, "you could get her a collar and put one in it."

Kara gave Rafael a quick look then clasped her own wrist in her other hand. "I don't want a tight collar." She nodded, "but it's a good idea."

Something Bart had said came back to me. She was fidgeting with her wrist. I cleared my throat and stood up. "I should go get changed." I needed to figure out how to stop failing at my job so badly.

"We'll be meeting shortly." Rafael smirked, "Arius, Troy, Chase, they're all barking orders at different people, to get us the answers fast."

I nodded, still not sure why or how I'd become part of the inner group. I exhaled the breath I hadn't realized I'd been holding. "I'll be happy for a few normal locations and regular battles."

He smirked, "I don't think that wish is going to come true."

Kara stood up, "you're doing great, by the way." She smiled at me with great understanding in her eyes. "The family can be—" she shrugged, "overwhelming at times."

I wasn't sure if I should nod to that or just smile. I chose the latter. "I'll see you shortly." I turned on my heel and made my way into the palace. Had she been listening to my thoughts? How did one even do that? Was it an audible or did my thoughts pop into her head like they were her own? Someday, maybe I'd get up the nerve to ask.

Chapter Thirteen

I was much more composed after an hour of silence and mental coaching. I was probably the only guard in history that second-guessed every second of their day. The only time I felt confident was when I was fighting. All my internal chatter stopped and my body took over.

Kara stood with Bethany talking quietly. Bethany looked surprised with something she said, then they both turned and looked at me.

So much for that internal pep-talk. I was so out of my league being around the royal family.

Emil stopped in the middle of the room and stood there looking at his phone. His expression was filed with sorrow.

"What's wrong?" Arius put his hands on his hips and watched his brother.

Emil cleared his throat, "my great-granddaughter has passed away." He stuffed his phone in his pocket and looked at Arius. "I'm always torn, each time," he shook his head in a sad motion, "is it a blessing they lived a normal existence and weren't tormented as I was, or—?" He shrugged, "It's still a sad moment each time."

I had to look away for a moment, his sadness caused a lump to form in my throat. I'd never stopped to consider what it might be like for him to have to watch from a distance and never know his relatives. I frowned, okay, so some relatives could be a blessing to not know, but still it was hard to grasp.

"You track all your descendants?" Quinton asked him in a soft tone.

Emil took a deep breath and blew it out. "Yes. I hire a new investigator about every five years and have them send photos and inform me of births and deaths." He shrugged, "the photos tell me if they're aging or not."

"How many appear to not be aging?" Troy stood up, then leaned against the table.

Emil closed his eyes, like he had to look at some internal list. "Four great-great-grandchildren and three great-great-great grandchildren, although they're not that old yet, so it's too soon to tell."

Quinton looked over at Chase, "couldn't Bastian take a look and know?"

Chase nodded slowly, "I'd imagine he could. He said they can see even the smallest traces."

Emil looked from one to the other, "what could this tell me?"

Reagan got up and went over to him, a look of understanding on her face. "Whether you need to be interceding in their lives because they're more Alterealm than," she gave him a pained smile, "human."

Putting his hands on his hips, Emil met her eyes, but I don't think he was really seeing her. "It would take a lot off my mind if I knew." He looked at Chase, "so if none have any," he waved his hand in the air, "traces, then I don't have to worry about their offspring?"

Chase picked up his cup and went toward the coffee pot. "We can find out to be certain."

Emil nodded, "let's do that." He took a deep breath and then exhaled, "now if you'll excuse me, I need to go inform Rena that Kimberly has passed." He nodded again, "she keeps the family book now. I'll be back in a few minutes." He walked out.

"I keep forgetting about his life before we found him." Leone looked at Bethany, whose sadness was palpable.

"I can't imagine how trying it's been for him all those years." Alona said softly. "To watch your family die, never being able to know them."

Crissy got up and went over and hugged Victor, "he had to be a different person each time he was married."

Daxx sighed and looked at Troy, "what do you mean, Criss?"

Victor kissed the top of her head before releasing her.

Crissy continued to stand leaning into him, "because he had to keep changing his name, so he wasn't found out." She nodded, then squeezed her eyes shut, "he was Ernest when he was married to Rena's mom."

"I wonder how that conversation went," Rafael crossed his arms over his chest and leaned against the wall, "when he had to explain to Rena why she was different and not aging." He looked at Kara, "Hi, I'm your dad and my name isn't Ernest."

"No one's name should be Ernest." Alona said with a quick shake of her head. She turned to Chase, "contact Bastian and do something about this. *Today.*"

Chase opened his mouth, then looked at Troy.

"He's going to be here tomorrow." Troy said, "checking those we caught at the park to see if any are his."

Chase turned back to Alona, "we'll make it happen, beloved."

I turned and looked out the window, taking time to digest all this information. Of course, I knew Emil had a life before his siblings found him. I just hadn't stopped to think of what that life was like. I understood the need to hide how and who he was, but beyond his children that were now here in Alterealm, I hadn't thought there were more out there. Large families with ages of nieces, nephews, uncles and so on being a confusing mess was something I'd grown up with. It was normal. Here. How had he…

"Kins?"

I jolted and turned to see everyone looking at me. "Sorry." I glanced around trying to figure out what they'd said to me prior to my name.

Rafael grinned and motioned to the table, "Romulus will be here in a minute with his findings on that glass thing."

I nodded and quickly went toward the table. "He's going to explain it too, right?" I sat down, then looked around at a few of the others, "because all that magic stuff is," I shrugged one shoulder, "beyond me."

Quinton laughed, "exactly. I like tangible things I can see and smack."

I smiled at him. "Yes."

Chapter Fourteen

I looked around the table at the royal family while the mage rattled on, endless things I knew nothing about. No one else seemed to have a clue either. The four elders in attendance looked bored, at best. I glanced at Emil, for what had to be the hundredth time, he was distracted and not paying attention to anything that was said.

Leone looked at Romulus, then to Clairee before leaning on the table and giving the mage a hard look. "Now explain all of that, without the side trips—in plain English."

The mage took a deep breath and nodded slowly. "It's very exciting," he waved his hand in the air, "I've never seen one of this magnitude." He looked at the piece of glass sitting on a cloth in front of him. "Arwan is controlling," he shrugged, "at least twenty different casts through this."

"Are you able to pinpoint locations?" Troy held the mages look with a regal focus.

Romulus' head bobbed a few times.

Not enough to move his greased back hair though, I smirked and looked at my lap for a second until that thought cleared my mind. Composed I looked over at him again.

"Not the exact location," he glanced at Clairee, "but with the witches' help we can get close enough to ferret out the spells."

"Good." Quinton pointed to him. "We start there and clear each location."

Troy nodded, then turned to Victor. "I'm more concerned that he can sense this happening while we're doing it."

Victor studied him for a moment, a look of great contemplation on his face. He looked at Romulus. "Can he duplicate this glass tablet? Perhaps move each location?"

Romulus looked at the glass rectangle. "It has to of taken him years, if not decades to get this one tuned," he shook his head and looked back at the justice, "I don't think he'd have the strength to replicate another in such short time."

Clairee sat forward and looked to one of the men, I didn't know, sitting behind Romulus, "he'd have to physically go to each location to redo it?"

The man nodded.

Clairee turned back around and looked to Michael, "if you could send sentries, or," she shrugged, "whatever to each location, you might catch him trying."

Michael sat there for a moment looking at her. He turned to Elder Arian, "the wasteland hasn't moved an inch?"

She nodded, causing her curls to bounce. "Not one. The outer edges seem to be recovering signs of life as well."

"That's great." Paisley looked from the elder to Troy, "that means at some point there will be plants and more than…"

"Dust of nothingness." Daxx finished. She turned her attention to Crissy for a moment, then looked back at Romulus. "Are there any locations in that thing," she pointed to the glass tablet, "with snow. A lot of snow?"

Romulus put his hands on either side of the glass. "I don't have locations, yet, just know the number of spells this is holding."

Daxx nodded her head slowly while turning her head to look at Troy. "We'll give him a team of guards," she looked over at Elder Arian, "and scientists if necessary, to start finding these spots."

Troy gave her a soft look. "Immediately." He glanced

over at Rafael, "call in half the guards stationed around the realm," he connected with Chase for a moment, "we're going to need all hands on this one."

Rafael nodded and picked up his phone. He started typing on it, then paused and looked over at the mage, "Go. Start doing whatever you have to do to give us target sites." The mage jolted and stood up.

"I'm going with him." Elder Arian got up. She turned and smiled at Elder Drusla, "I'll find you battle sites, Enota."

Elder Drusla smiled, "I look forward to it."

The room was quiet as the mages and Elder Arian left the room.

Rafael frowned at his phone, then got up and went over to Quinton, he leaned on the back of his chair and showed him the phone. A look of surprise was on Quinton's face. Rafael shrugged and glanced at me for a brief second, then nodded and went and sat back down.

Chase looked from one brother to the other, "care to share with the class?"

Rafael tucked his phone in his pocket. "An update on Gudrun and Detrick." He looked down the table at Victor, "they're at the yard demanding to be reinstated."

Victor's usual immovable expression faltered for a moment. "I wasn't aware they were out of the hospital." He turned and looked at Alona.

She smirked for a moment, then cleared her throat. "They've both made a remarkable recovery." Her gaze flicked to Reagan for a second before nodding, "and have been deemed fit for duty."

Quinton leaned closer to Reagan, his eyes on the baseball cap she was wearing backwards, "that would explain your new love of hats." He reached over slowly and pulled the hat from her head. Her hair was streaked with lighter shades.

Reagan took the hat out of his hands. "Gudrun is my uncle and Deet, your best friend." She shrugged, "I had to help them."

Quinton studied her for a moment, his expression

changing a few times. He turned and looked to Alona, "she is barred from the medical building."

Alona grinned, "if you say so."

"I for one," Chase smiled at Reagan, "will take the help of two seasoned guards, regardless of how their recoveries came about."

"They're going to be out of shape," Rafael said in a thoughtful tone, "I'll have Ira put them through some drills before we make any decisions."

"Or," Leone leaned forward and gave Rafael a steady stare, "place them with another guard that can keep an eye on them, without damaging their egos."

Rafael glanced to Michael for a second, then turned to look at me. "Kinsley, Gudrun and Detrick are going to be your shadows."

I raised my eyebrows, "aren't they going to be more offended being placed with a guard that's an infant in age compared to them?" I looked around the table slowly, trying to figure out how my opinion was being considered, "and a woman?"

Leone grinned, "not if we tell them they are *your* guards."

Rafael looked to him quickly, a surprised look on his face.

"It could work." Michael said before anyone else could comment.

"Won't they find that odd?" Bethany sat forward, "a guard needing guards?"

Kara turned and gave Rafael a small smile, then looked at Bethany, "will they question that a woman needs guards?"

Bethany took a deep breath and sat back in her seat. "Probably not." She rolled her eyes and turned to me, "us poor, helpless women folk always need watching over."

Chase snorted. "Yes, you are all so helpless, you make us men look inept."

"Speak for yourself, brother." Arius grinned at him. "I'm perfectly happy to be saved by our helpless women." He turned and looked at me, "I think Kinsley can pull it off. Keeping an eye on them."

I sat straighter in the chair and nodded briefly at him. "I will do whatever I can."

"Perfect." Michael rubbed a hand over the side of his face, "one less thing to worry about."

"I trained Gudrun Dalston." Elder Segos lifted his chin and looked to Victor, "he was a stupendous warrior, and I am certain he still is."

Victor inclined his head to him, "I agree." He looked down the tables at me, "Miss Hinton uses a style I believe Gudrun was fond of, distraction."

The elder nodded his head slowly then smiled, "yes, he took using what was around you to a whole new level."

"If I'm not required to be here," Elder Udela stood up, "I'd like to go listen in on some of those brought in earlier." She gave me a big smile, "I'm so enjoying feeling useful again."

Troy motioned to the door, "any help you can give would be appreciated." He glanced to Daxx, "there's a lot of heads to go through, if you can narrow down the field things will be much easier and go faster."

Emil, who had been silent through the whole meeting sat forward. "I actually have my children coming shortly for another meeting." He looked at Troy, then to Chase, "if there's more to go over here, I can postpone it."

Chase and Troy exchanged a look. Chase turned to Emil. "Until we have locations, there's not much to do right now."

"I have to wait for all the guards we called to get back to the yard." Rafael sat back.

"Do you want us at this meeting?" Alona gave Emil a soft look.

"Absolutely," he waved his hand around the table, "it's a family meeting and you're—" he smiled, "family."

"Okay, I suggest a short break before the family meeting." Chase stood up. "I need coffee and want to check on another meeting being planned."

Alona stood up and then looked around, an excited look on her face, "I'm going to meet my father's family." She hugged her waist. "Chase is arranging a meeting that my father can be at."

Arius nodded, "that reminds me, the visitation area is almost finished."

"Visitation area?" Daxx got up.

Arius nodded, "Yeah. Paisley thought a secure room for visitation would be a good idea."

Paisley smiled up at her mate. "That way, Beth can see her friend, Alona, her father—"

"That's amazing." Bethany covered her mouth for a second. "I check in on Erin a lot, she's like herself now that the spells from Marcus have worn off."

"She can never be completely free, you know." Leone reached out and touched the side of her face.

"I know." She whispered.

"I've been working with Ellis for a secluded area at the new facility, for intakes like Erin and Levi." Arius stroked his hand back over Paisley's dark hair. "Like the reform farm, only with fences."

"They can be out of the cells?" Alona put her hand on her chest and turned to Chase. The king immediately pulled her into his arms and hugged her.

"Yeah." Paisley stood up. "They'll have actual rooms, with walls...it was going to be a surprise, but there's been no time."

"It's a wonderful surprise." A tear rolled down Alona's cheek.

Daxx got up. "Moving on." She waved a hand around in a circle, "we don't have time for this emotional *stuff*."

Troy chuckled, and then nodded his head slowly. "We'll take a half hour break before we reconvene for Emil's meeting."

Chapter Fifteen

I sat, silent, as the others chatted. At the other end of the table were Emil's children. The first son was almost a mirror image of our law, Prince Michael. Abraham looked like him, minus the scar. I studied Ellis and Rena and decided they must have resembled their mother, with their pale hair. Emil came into the room and stood beside Arius. There again, the family resemblance was so strong there was no doubt the Whitham genes were strong.

Was having a beautiful child something women thought about? Not that there would be any of that in my life...I sat straighter and cleared my throat. Why was I thinking about things like that?

Rena glanced over at her father. "I brought the list." She patted the worn leather-bound book in front of her. "Are you going to explain what's happening?"

Ellis nodded, "I had a panic attack when you first called me about this meeting."

Abraham laughed. "Same. Family meetings have usually meant new names and new locations."

Emil shrugged out of his jacket.

I tried to ignore the outline of the muscle under his t-shirt and focus on what people were saying. I looked away. This was getting out of control. My mind never wandered like this.

"No new names or relocating." He sat down where he could see all his offspring.

"Good." Ellis sighed loudly, "I'm out of E names to use."

Rena laughed, "you've picked some doozies over the years." She smiled at him, "Ezra."

Scowling, he glanced to his brother for a second, "not as bad as *Ace* over here."

Abraham shrugged, "It was the sixties, anything went."

Emil laughed and all his children looked at him.

"It's not funny, Dad, or should I say Ernest." Abraham said with a smirk. He turned and looked at Bethany, "Imagine being in your forties and your dead father returns—still looking thirty and tells you he's really Emil and doesn't age."

Bethany opened her mouth then grimaced, "I can't even picture that."

Abraham nodded, then turned back to his father. "Name changes and moving is over?"

Emil clasped his hands on the table in front of him. "Yes." He gave a slight shrug, "except during the odd moments when you check on our properties or investments…"

"We have a guy for that." Chase kissed the top of Alona's head, then sat down beside her. "Or team," he shrugged, "they have a way to keep an eye on things without anyone's identity being compromised."

"Really?" Abraham looked at his father. "I don't even know what I'm going to do now that I don't have to rotate properties for the four of us to stay hidden."

"I'm never going back over." Ellis said in a firm voice. He motioned to Arius, "I like my new job and plan to emulate my uncle in keeping the criminals in hand."

Arius grinned and bowed his head slightly. "The new facility is really coming together. You're doing a great job."

"I'm never going back over again." Rena turned to Abraham. "Sell my cabin."

He opened his mouth, then closed it and gave her an abrupt nod.

Rena cleared her throat and looked around at a few of the others. "I have something to share, before Prince Bastian gets here."

The light teasing mood in the room was gone, just that fast as everyone sat and was silent and looked at her.

"First," She smiled at Autumn, "the ultrasound showed a perfectly healthy baby growing normally."

Autumn reached over and squeezed Michael's hand.

"Do we know if it's a he or a she?" Emil asked.

Rena smiled. "I didn't want to know."

Emil nodded, without comment, accepting her decision.

Rena's happy expression changed quickly, she looked over at Troy. "The doctor thinks it would be prudent to know if there are any genetic issues on the father's side," she looked down at her lap for a moment, nodding as if she was giving herself a mental shake, taking a deep breath, she huffed it out, "I've agreed to let Uncle Troy look to see the father, so they can find out if he's in the cells—so the doctor can check."

The room was silent for what felt like hours, even though it was only a few seconds. I had to work hard to not let the tears hovering under the surface fall. I, more than the others in this room, understood the struggle of being on that island.

Autumn leaned on the table looking at Rena. "You're insanely brave." She bobbed her head once, "and know if we have him, he will be punished." She nodded, then glanced briefly at her mate determination on her face.

"I also," Rena looked over at Michael, a soft look on her face, "have decided that I want to be known as this baby's aunt, not mother." She sniffed, and touched her stomach with both hands, "I love it, I can't not, but I can't raise it." She frowned, and turned to Alona, "does that make me a bad person?"

Alona shook her head, then wiped the tears from her cheeks. "Not at all."

Rena wiped her hand over her eyes, then lifted her chin and looked at Autumn, "Autumn and Uncle Michael will be known as the parents."

Autumn was up out of her chair so fast, no one could have seen it coming. She hopped over the table and landed in the middle of the circle of tables. Dropping to her knees, she reached over it and grabbed Rena's hands. "You will never regret that." She nodded, "I will protect that baby with my life."

Rena smiled at her, letting the tears fall. "I know." She looked over at Michael, "heaven help anyone that does this child wrong."

Michael grinned, "you have no idea." He cleared his throat and stood up, "Autumn," he held his hand over the table.

Autumn looked over her shoulder at him, then stood up slowly. "Thank you," she whispered to Rena.

I glanced to Emil, he looked pleased with all of this. Without warning he turned and looked at me. I sat straighter and wiped the tears from my cheeks.

"Prince Bastian will be here in a few moments." Victor announced, then set his phone back on the table.

"Uh," Alona turned to Paisley, "how much of my makeup is running down my face?"

Paisley smiled and reached over to wipe under Alona's eye. "You look great."

Taking a deep breath, Alona put her hand on her chest and inhaled slowly. "I'm a puddle of weepy inside." She pointed a finger at Rena, a grin on her face "a little notice next time please."

Rena smiled. "Sorry. I wasn't sure I would share until it came out of my mouth." She grimaced, "pregnancy hormones are unpredictable."

"Oh joy, something to look forward to." Alona joked.

"My Kings."

Everyone turned to look at the door. Mac stood there, a serious expression on his face.

"What is it?" Troy asked.

"Prince Bastian is here." Mac continued to stand there with his hand on the door.

"That was fast." Troy nodded, "let him in."

The prince from a different realm came into the room. I had to work hard to contain my surprise. His dark hair was short and looked like he'd hadn't bothered combing it when he woke up. He wore a leather jacket, his expression was anything but serious. He made an elaborate bow, waving his hand in the air. "Royal people. This is becoming a habit." He smirked and sat down. Without warning, his dark eyes locked on me. "Hello…" He raised his eyebrows at me in question.

"Kinsley Hinton." I supplied quickly.

He continued to appraise me for a moment, then turned and smiled at Chase. "Your group is constantly expanding." He winked at Alona. He paused briefly on Emil's children, but made no comment.

"Did you check the prisoners in the cells?" Arius asked, in tone with zero emotion.

"I did." He turned a blank expression to the Warden. "None of mine were there," he shrugged, "but you may want to get in touch with Princess Aireese's people and that other woman," he frowned then looked to Victor, "from Aridon?"

Victor inclined his head, "Empress Ananta."

"Yes. Her." The prince nodded.

"We brought over prisoners from two other realms?" Quinton scowled.

"You did, and thank your lucky stars they're only fledglings, or you could have been cursed or fried," he smirked, "or whatever." Bastian's expression was serious now.

Chase looked at him, "I don't think it's actually fire, is it?"

Troy made hissing sound, "isn't it?"

"There's a book in the library…"

"Heart," Victor interrupted Crissy, "it's not pertinent right now."

"Oh. okay." She leaned back in her chair.

Victor looked at Bastian, "the pertinent issue *is* that there is another realm involved that needs to be informed."

Prince Bastian nodded, "I was hoping you asked for this meeting to tell me you found your mage."

"Not yet." Troy gave him a steady look, "but we do have a device that will help us find him."

"This is good news." The prince leaned on the table, "the information we have says he's the key to it all," he shrugged then sat back, "but if FaTerra and Aridon residents are involved, it's still going to get messy. Messier even." Blowing out a breath, he looked around the table. "Is there any more business speak?"

"There is something else we'd like to ask of you." Victor folded his hands neatly in front of him.

Prince Bastian looked at Reagan, "I owe you, so I'll help if I can."

"It's actually for us." Emil said as he motioned to his children. "My children and I."

Bastian studied Rena and her brothers for a moment. "I find it hard to believe you spawned such a lovely woman, but," he turned back to Emil, "what can I do?"

Emil held his hand out to Rena, who placed a folded piece of paper in it. "These are our descendants," he opened the sheet and looked at it for a moment before offering it to the prince. "We were hoping you could look and see if we need to watch for Alterealm genes passing on."

Bastian nodded his head slowly, "if there's enough of your DNA in them, I will see it." He studied the paper, "let's see who we have. Charles, Katherine, Aaron—and Douglas will be easy enough, they're close to the area where I cross over." He studied the paper a bit more, "the other four are spread out, so it will take me a few days to get to those places," he glanced up, "what with the take-over-the-realms plot absorbing far too much of my free time."

"I would appreciate it." Emil's expression changed to a softer, more emotional one.

"You know the next few generations will still have to be looked in on." Bastian smirked and glanced around the table, "your genes have some powerful mojo to them, they can lie dormant for several generations before they show up again."

Emil nodded. "I will keep checking until the day I die."

"All right then." He looked around at the others, "anything else?"

Troy glanced to his twin, "no, I believe that's it."

"Good then." Bastian looked across the table at Reagan. "I'm narrowing down the culprit," he sighed loudly, "the ones responsible for the hypocrisy my people have been living."

Reagan nodded.

I crossed my arms over my chest and leaned back, looking around. What was he talking about now?

"I can't undo what was done to your father until I know by whom and how." He nodded his head slowly, giving her a serious look.

"I appreciate your efforts." Reagan said and leaned against Quinton's shoulder.

"Can I ask," Bethany waited for the prince to look at her, "if you don't mind, why are you so outraged by Reagan's existing?"

"Why?" His voice was low.

"Because females being born to his realm are rare." Crissy blurted out

Bastian pointed, "that." He nodded, "we've had medical people, science people, history people— all the people trying for several thousand years to figure out why." He turned and looked at Emil, "the male-female ratio is now roughly 101 to 1." Emil looked surprised. "Exactly. A whole realm of unhappy bachelors doesn't make for a fun realm." His expression saddened, "not forgetting that our cherished females feel their only place is for procreation." A look of disgust filled his expression.

"Then you've been told you can't have children with any but from your own realm?" Reagan sat forward and leaned on the table

"Yes." He smirked at her, "which is why I see you as a stunning miracle and symbol of overdue justice. As soon as I find those responsible for spreading the lies…"

"I'll look in the library." Crissy nodded. "Cross reference," she frowned, "go back to the start."

Bastian raised an eyebrow at her, then nodded.

"Don't you need proof?" Paisley gave him a strange look, "I mean that it's not a one-time thing," she cringed and turned to Reagan, "not that you're a thing…"

"I get what you're saying." Reagan smirked.

"Oh, I have it," he looked back to Reagan, "your father isn't the only person to have had his mind scrubbed." He nodded. "I do know that. I found, we—my brother and I found, other inconsistencies where people vanished while on duty but haven't vanished at all." He scowled, "we're trying to find out if children were born from that."

"There are people out there that are part Solrelm and have no idea?" Reagan frowned.

"Yes."

"Hopefully they don't find out by going invisible." Daxx said.

Reagan blew out a breath, "wouldn't that be something."

"Oh." Crissy leaned on the table, an excited look on her face. "I could do a search and help you look for more people like Reagan." She nodded, then her expression sobered, "after we find that mage."

Bastian inclined his head, "all help would be sincerely appreciated."

"You'll keep us apprised of your progress?" Victor asked him

Bastian rolled his eyes. "Yes, aside from my brother and two others, you are the only ones that don't look at me like I'm insane."

"You need to watch out for a woman and a bus." Crissy was on her knees on the chair now giving him a serious look.

"I do?" he glanced beside him to Emil, then Leone on his left.

Crissy nodded. "Yes. What I saw was for you. A woman and a bus."

"Oh good, now I have to be wondering about a woman and a bus as well." He looked at her for a moment. "Is there anything more that goes with that?"

Crissy shook her head, "no," she then nodded, "well, yes, it's bad if you don't find her."

"I see."

"Is she driving the bus?" Daxx asked.

"Is she riding the bus?" Bethany asked

Crissy squinted, "I don't know it doesn't show me, but Prince Bastian has to find her."

Bastian cleared his throat and stood up. He tucked the paper in his jacket pocket, "I will fit bus watching into my other duties." He shook his head. "I've decided I need to vacation with you royals." He smirked, "it's always interesting and entertaining seeing you."

Chapter Sixteen

I stood beside Tim in the family's private workout room. First, it wasn't just a room, it was more stadium sized. I wondered for a moment how they'd managed to build a room this size underground. I'd been told this is where I was to practice and work out from now on. My eyes strayed to the wall of practice weapons; I didn't even know what more than half of those were. I shook the questions off, I was good with the few I preferred to use, so I didn't need to stress about expanding my weaponry skills.

Some of the brothers were going at each other with wooden swords and bos so focused that I wondered if it was practice or they were trying to injure each other. Of course, with their fast healing, I suppose they would recover from any training bouts without issue. Add Reagan's ability, and they could pound on each other with no lasting ill effects. I flexed my hand, remembering my recent injury and how long it had taken to get back to full strength. I hoped working with the royals would have some perks, I hoped for no long recovery time for any injuries sustained.

Other than Tim and I, the guards were working with the women on various techniques or jumping in the fray with the brothers. All of this action was far more entertaining than the guards' yard.

Alona and Crissy looked to be working on evasive maneuvers and excelling. Bronx and Sith were who they were trying to evade or get past. Before that, I'd watched Crissy scale the wall and repel down. She climbed a rope faster than anyone I'd ever seen, and considering that rope climbing was one of the drills we were put through often, and she was better. I hated climbing, and after the roller coaster, was more than happy to keep my feet on the ground.

Kara and Daxx were currently trying to outdo each other with the throwing knives. I was on the other side of the room but could see they were both to be reckoned with, and to never speak out of turn if there was a knife nearby.

Michael, Emil and Quinton seemed to be trying to help Reagan and Bethany learn some offensive moves. Twice Reagan had dropped the small fake katana and used her surijin to trip one of them. Bethany kept bouncing her fire balls off them to knock them back.

It was always good to better oneself. However, watching these women, I didn't think it was necessary. Sticking with what worked for you was often the best plan. Then again, this was a room full of seasoned alpha males and they'd want to protect or shelter their women. That was a situation I was more than sick of being in. When I started my guard training, the men laughed it off. They didn't expect me to last through the first round. Most of the female guards were six foot tall, and much larger than me. When I was still there after the final cuts, the males that had been trying to knock me out of the competition were suddenly trying to protect or assist me. All of it was more than a little annoying, but I kept my head up, my moves fluid and made the list of guards. The trials continued after that, but most of the guards had accepted I was here to stay, and I could handle myself. Shaking off the ghosts of the past, I looked around at the rest of the family.

While Arius and Leone practiced with a lot of vigor, Paisley stood off to the side. She spent most of her time looking down at her phone, but three times now, she'd looked up and then stopped Leone's swing in midair before it connected with Arius' body. It was entertaining to watch.

Victor and Autumn were the most active and created the most noise in the room. They were using practice batons and working to outmaneuver each other. I had to admire their stamina.

"This is how they blow off steam." Tim crossed his arms and nodded while watching.

"This is not what I pictured." I told him truthfully.

He chuckled, "it is ever changing, but I have nothing but admiration for the family."

I nodded slowly, "yeah, I didn't know what I was getting into with so many new princesses, but," I motioned to around the room, "this is nothing close to what I imagined."

The Captain, with a big smile on his face started walking toward us.

"Tag, you're it." Tim said quietly, "I never know whether to try my hardest with the Captain or not." He shrugged, then moved fast in Daxx's direction.

Rafael stopped a few feet in front of me. "How's your arm?"

I rolled my shoulder, "Fine. I was cleared for duty again."

He nodded slowly, "to guard Rena, who is nowhere near any fights." He frowned, "or better not be." Leaning on the bo, he studied me. "I can't send you off to somewhere less," he glanced around to see where everyone else was, "active." He smirked, "but expecting you to sit on the sidelines if we get into something would be stupid because we need all the help we can get." He straightened up again, "so, let's work that arm and make sure you are in top form."

I was trying not to be offended. This was my Captain though, and his commands were my law. I nodded.

With a grin, he motioned to the wall of weapons. "Pick your toy."

I walked toward the wall as my eyes moved over the choices. I wanted to impress him, to show him I was at full strength, but didn't want to choose a weapon I wasn't one hundred percent comfortable with. I wasn't wearing any of my gear, so I had no straps or cases. Stopping in front of the wall, I looked down at the track pants I wore. There would be no tucking a weapon in these. Sighing, I pulled a smaller wooden sword off the wall. I started to turn, then changed my mind and used my ability to float a baton down as well. Catching it in midair I nodded and turned back to the Captain.

Captain? I had to remember I wasn't supposed to use the titles. *Rafael* stood back twenty feet and motioned to the area beside him.

I checked to see that there was enough space for us to move without running into the others. Nodding, I dropped the baton on the edge of the mat. He looked at it then raised an eyebrow. He knew me well enough that he'd have to block my sight from that if he managed to knock the sword from my grasp. I shrugged, then stepped into the starting position.

"Don't let my status affect your decisions." He raised the bo, "but do believe this affects whether you are on the front lines or on clean-up."

"Does it?" I had to know if he was having thoughts of benching me.

He smiled that famous Rafael smile, "yes."

He gave me no pause after that, he advanced on me with lightning fast moves. I'd sparred with him a few times in the yard, but mostly to check form and not to *try* to take him out. It was time to step up and show him what I could do. I ducked his next swing and slid a few paces sideways to come up on his left side. I didn't have the momentum to take his feet out from him, so I went for the bo instead. I managed to displace it from his grip, but he caught it before it hit the floor.

Growling inside my head, I blew out a breath and hoped my anxiousness went with it. I needed cool and calculating right now, not haphazard swinging. I ducked his next few attempts, dropping my sword to the side, hoping to find an opening to get under his elbow as he went for another attempt. He knew my favorite move and was keeping his form tight and close to his body. That left no room to even attempt to unbalance him. I rolled away from another swing, making sure it placed my baton within my sight. I had wanted to do this without using my other skill, but this was the Captain of the guard and he knew all my moves.

When he advanced again, I knocked the bo back with the sword and swooped in for a second move to unhinge his hold with one hand. Ducking down, I got the sword up near his arm and twisted it. It was just strong enough he released it. I backed up quickly and glanced at the baton, and lifting it with great speed, I sent it flying in his direction. It connected with his gut and hit him hard enough that his stance slumped with the force. I moved fast and knocked the bo from his hands, finishing off by holding the wooden tip against his throat.

He lifted his hands out from his body admitting defeat, then rubbed his lower ribs.

That's when I noticed there wasn't another sound in the room. I glanced around to see everyone had been watching us. Alona started clapping, a big smile on her face. Even the guards were smiling and nodding. Had I just passed some sort of test?

"Well done, Miss Hinton." Victor nodded, then wiped the sweat of his brow.

"That was excellent." Autumn came toward me. She held up the baton in her left hand, "I've never thought of chucking it at my opponent."

I shrugged, "sometimes I have no choice."

She nodded, then looked at Rafael and smirked. She held up the baton again. "I can show you some other moves." She nodded then motioned between us, "they always underestimate the little female."

I grinned. "Yes, they do."

Rafael chuckled, "great, that's just what we need, two of you to contend with."

Chatter and motion filled the room again slowly and I was

glad for it. I hated being the center of attention. I turned to speak to Daxx as she came over, but I caught the look on Emil's face. The high from my victory faded. He looked angry. I couldn't even think why.

Arius walked up to Emil and put his hand on his shoulder, leaning in to speak to him. I don't know what he said, but Emil's expression froze for a few seconds. It went completely blank, no emotion whatsoever was left. Rafael went over and nodded in agreement with what Arius was saying. Emil's expression changed to shock. Grinning, Leone added something more, but his brother didn't find it nearly as amusing as he had. Emil scowled at Leone, then at Arius. He shook his head, turned on his heel, and stomped to the door. Once reaching it, he paused and glanced at me. The look I read was one of loathing. I swallowed the lump in my throat. So much for wondering what his reaction would be when he realized our constant clash was because we were true mates.

I blew out a breath.

"So, Michael told me what's going on." Autumn said.

"Yeah, Troy told me." Daxx said.

I looked from one woman to the other, not entirely sure I'd wanted the others to know. The understanding expressions on their face made me feel better. I tried to shrug it off, "nothing is going on. It will go nowhere." I didn't know if I was trying to reassure them that I could do my job, or if I was trying to remind myself.

Daxx smirked, "regardless, your part of this family now."

Autumn nodded, "I didn't think Emil would be a jerk, but," she snorted, "they all have their flaws."

Kara came over. "Are we talking about it now?" She looked from Daxx to me. "I suspected and Rafael confirmed it." She looked around the room. "I don't know if they all know."

Daxx laughed, "they all know. They couldn't keep a secret if their lives depended on it."

Alona and Bethany walked over.

"What's happening?" Alona asked.

"We're going to need girl's time." Kara said.

"Oh." Alona smirked, "hot tub girl meeting?"

Daxx nodded. "Yeah. That works for me."

"No wine." Autumn said abruptly. "We could have to go out without warning."

Alona sighed, "all right then, no wine." She smiled, "fruit trays and cheese."

Autumn paused for a moment and considered that. "I could go for some of that."

Daxx motioned to the door. "We'll give Kinsley two hours, then meet at the hot tub."

I looked over to where she motioned to see Reagan and Quinton talking to two men. One I recognized as a guard that had been part of training us, he'd aged, but it was him.

"I still can't believe they're ready to go so soon." Alona said.

"They look better than when we found them." Autumn stated.

Daxx put her hand on my arm. "We're leaving it up to you to let Rafael know if they're not up to fighting."

I nodded slowly. "I have to do that and pretend they're guarding me at the same time." I had no idea how I was going to do that.

Daxx snorted, "good luck." She pointed to the other door. "I'm going to help Troy go through some heads. Meet you girls at the hot tub."

I watched her walk away. "where is the hot tub?"

Kara smiled, "it's marked on the map we put on your phone."

"See you there." I watched them walk away. I'd never been in a hot tub, but they all seemed excited about it, so why not. I turned to look at the men I was going to have to dupe, somehow. They were both big men, no surprise there. They looked okay, but my knowledge of health ranked right up there with my knowledge of frilly girl things. None. Sighing, I picked up the baton and went over to join them.

Chapter Seventeen

An hour later I was ready for a nap. Tim, Sith, Woods and Derian had stayed behind to help me with Gudrun and Detrick. I looked around, all of us looked ready for a nap.

Detrick was laying on the mat, he lifted his head and looked at me. "You've come a long way, Kinsley."

I grinned, "it's been an uphill battle."

Derian chuckled and slid down the wall to sit. "You're a guard at the palace, I'd say your climb was successful."

I shrugged, "So are all of you."

"I am feeling quite outdated right now." Gudrun sat in the middle of the mat.

I still couldn't get over the fact that, including his confinement he'd been in the royal guard for close to four hundred years. "I think this last hour has aged us all."

He smiled at me. "Nothing is as it was."

Woods sat down as well. "A lot has changed for all of us recently."

Tim nodded, "since the moment *the* Huntress arrived it's been one hell of a ride." He sat down a few feet from Woods.

"I am delighted the royal sons have found their mates." Gudrun nodded his head, "and must admit that they frighten me a bit."

I laughed, "I think it's awesome." I nodded slowly, "that the women are powerful and amazing."

"The things we've seen them do," Sith motioned to Tim, "is crazy, but I wouldn't be anywhere else."

"So," Woods looked around at the others then to me, "I overheard something earlier."

"Yeah?" I wiped the sweat running down my neck.

He nodded, "I heard the Warden tell Prince Emil that you are one of them."

"One of what?" Tim looked confused.

"One of the mates." Woods said in a quiet tone.

I blew out a breath.

"Is it true?" Tim leaned forward, his eyes wide and questioning.

I nodded. "Yeah, but it doesn't change anything. I'm still a guard like…"

"It changes everything." Detrick sat up.

I shook my head. "No, it doesn't. I'm still one of you."

Derian laughed, "not really."

"We'll have to take orders from you." Gudrun gave me a sincere look.

I shook my head again.

"It makes sense now." Detrick looked at Gudrun, who inclined his head in agreement. "We couldn't figure out why we were guarding a guard."

I sighed loud. "You weren't." I looked from one to the other. "They wanted me to keep an eye on you."

Detrick smiled, "well that's a given. I've been out of commission for the last fifteen years."

Gudrun chuckled, "try three hundred and sixty-five."

Everyone looked at him. "You have missed a lot." Woods nodded.

"Yes, and I hope to catch up, quickly." He studied me for a moment. "Are we to bow to you?"

I almost squealed out loud. "What? No." I motioned around the room. "I'm pretty sure Prince Emil thinks me no better than the plague."

"Well, you have to understand how his life has been." Tim said in a quiet tone. "He spent three hundred years over there with no idea what he was, it had to have taken a toll."

"I heard Alona and King Chase discussing that once he thought that he was a vampire until he realized some of his children were like him." Sith told us.

We all sat there for a moment. I cleared my throat, "well, I don't see a time any of you will have to bow to me." I grinned, "princes don't mate guards."

Tim chuckled, "I guess we'll find out."

Gudrun gave me a serious look. "How bad is it?" He lifted a hand, then let it drop, "this war we're fighting."

A few of the others sighed loud enough to be heard. "It's pretty bad." I used my shirtsleeve to mop off my face, "I don't understand all of it, but in summary Willis Hubert..."

"Him again?" Gudrun mumbled.

I nodded, "it's worse. He's been working with Arwan, the mage?"

He gave me a blank look, "I know who Arwan is. That's true then, he's alive?"

"And then some." Tim said.

"He's sucked the life out of the wastelands." Sith told him.

Gudrun nodded, "Our Justice told me of that."

"Well, apparently Arwan is the one in charge, and it now several realms are involved..."

"Which ones?" His look was hard.

"Solrelm, FaTerra and Aridon are all we know of, at this point." I gave him a steady look, "I've never dealt with any of them before." I motioned around the room. "I've only been involved in things in Alterealm—" I shrugged, "until I was sent to that island, I'd never even crossed over to the human side."

"Souls, fae and fire—this could get messy." Detrick mumbled. "No word of Veiltide's involvement?"

I shook my head. "Is that good?"

Detrick shrugged, "they're said to be ruthless warriors."

"Let's hope they're on our side." Tim said hopefully.

I turned to Gudrun, "I still don't understand half of what happened, I just go where I'm told."

"Each realm was given a task." Gudrun said quietly, "ours was to police all the realms, all six." He nodded slowly, "a few thousand years ago the realms voted that each would be responsible for their own—justice, so we were left with just the humans to keep an eye on."

"I have to wonder if this mess we're in would have happened if Alterealm had still been in charge of it all." Sith said.

"Hindsight won't help us here." Detrick said. "It's not a pretty place to get stuck in."

Gudrun nodded his agreement. "It seems we're back just in time." He glanced to Detrick.

Detrick got up slowly. "So, did we pass?"

Gudrun also stood up, "are we fit for duty?" He looked at me.

I got up, every muscle objecting. "Yeah, you guys can watch my back anytime."

"With that new glass thing, your wish may come true ten times time over." Derian motioned to the door, "I'm going to grab a shower and go see what Reagan is up to." He stopped and looked at Gudrun, "I guess you're a part of the royals now too?"

Gudrun shook his head. "I'm her uncle and I'm a guard. Nothing more."

"It's still pretty cool." Derian walked over and put his sword back on the wall. "That you're back *and* related to Prince Quinton."

"I remember when he was a kid." Gudrun smiled, "I'm so glad he's grown up to be less troublesome than he was."

Tim laughed, "oh, wait until you hear them when we're about to step into battle." He grinned at Sith, "you'll be wondering what the hell is going on."

Sith nodded, "it's never a dull moment."

I put the baton back on the wall, then turned, "hey, guys," I glanced around at them, "do I wear a bathing suit to a hot tub meeting?"

The men exchanged looks.

"A hot tub meeting?" Derian asked.

Tim chuckled, "right, you're just one of us, huh? A hot tub meeting is what the queens and princesses do."

"Oh, really?" Derian studied me for a second, then bowed. "See you later Princess-guard."

I scowled at them as they left the room. I had hoped them knowing would make this easier, but clearly, they weren't going to be helpful at all.

I was late meeting the women. I opened the door to see Mitz standing there.

She gave me a gentle smile, "before your confusion grows, let me explain why I'm here."

I stepped back and let her come in the room.

She paused and looked around. "We need to get you moved to a larger room."

I closed the door. "We do?" I looked around it was bigger than my room at my parent's house. Not that I was ever in my room often enough to care.

"Yes." She nodded and went and sat on the end of the bed. "Something more fitting for the mate of one of the princes."

I sunk down in the small chair beside the door. "Oh. That."

She smirked, "Leone said I should speak to you, then explained why."

I slumped back in the chair and blew out a deep breath. "It's not really necessary, I know—Emil knows *now*, and that's about as far as it will ever…"

"Maybe I should introduce myself properly." She lifted her chin, "My name is Mitzine Pennigton." She gave me a brief smile, "I believe you know of my sister Queen Viola."

I know my jaw dropped but I couldn't prevent it. "Your sister was the Queen?"

Mitz nodded, "yes." She chuckled softly, "imagine the scandal when the queen's sister fell in love with her guard."

"Commander Ira was your personal guard?" I sat forward and stared at her.

She nodded. "Yes. We went to a post in the North to distance ourselves from the thrones and not cause a big to-do over it."

I just sat there, trying to puzzle out how that would have been.

"We're not even official mates." She made quotation marks in the air, "but the heart doesn't care when you find the right one."

My shoulders slumped, "I've never really been in the dating scene."

She gave me a sweet smile, "because fate had someone for you." She shrugged, "I'm just happy that for those of us without a true mate, love is still possible." Her expression softened, "having someone at your side through everything is—" She shrugged, "there's nothing that can compare to it."

I blew out a loud breath. "I don't see Emil…"

Mitz laughed and stood up, "Emil is your problem to sort out." She grinned at me, "good luck to you there." Her expression sobered, "I just wanted you to know that a guard mated to a prince, is acceptable in this family—now." She looked around the room, "I'm going to see Alona and tell her we need to find you a better room, and she can decorate it." She paused beside me and patted my shoulder. "I'm sure he'll figure things out, dear." She motioned to the closet. "There's a swimsuit in there."

I stared at the door after she closed it

Chapter Eighteen

I stopped at the corner and looked at the map on my phone. I was suddenly happy I wasn't a guard in the underground chambers. The architects that designed this were aiming for a maze, I was sure of it.

Finding my place on the map, I started a slow jog in that direction. It should be just down here around the next corner. I ran past a door.

"Kinsley."

I stopped abruptly and walked back a few steps and looked in the room. Inside on loveseats and chairs were five of the princes. I glanced at the sign, it said girl cave.

My Captain gave me a don't say it look. "We were notified the girls were having a meeting and not to disturb."

I nodded, not sure if there was more to it.

"But they're not here." Leone stood up.

"Or at the palace." Arius also got up.

"Did you need them?" I glanced down the hallway. "You could call them…"

Quinton shook his head, "no we can't. They'll think we're checking up on them."

I frowned, "and that's bad?"

Michael nodded, "that's *very* bad."

"Do you know where this meeting is?" Arius raised his eyebrows at me.

I nodded slowly, torn between sharing and upsetting one of the princes. "I do." I said slowly. "It's because of me." I cleared my throat, "or for me, I'm not certain."

"The hot tub." Quinton looked at Leone, who nodded his agreement.

"Oh, it's one of *those* meetings." Michael looked relieved.

Leone wiped imaginary sweat off his brow.

I motioned down the hall. "Did you want me to…"

"No." Rafael shook his head. "No, you didn't see us, we weren't here."

I opened my mouth to respond, then closed it an gave an abrupt nod. They ported out one after the other. I stood there for a moment more, then giving my head a quick shake, I rushed down the hall.

I leaned back and closed my eyes. "I think I could sleep here." It felt so good. I opened my eyes again.

Alona chuckled, "it does drain the stress away."

"If only it could fix everything." Daxx said.

The tray with fruit floated in my direction, I took a piece and popped it into my mouth.

"I can't believe you're Emil's mate." Paisley gave the tray a gentle shove in the other direction.

I rolled my eyes. "No one was more shocked than I when I realized it."

"I envy you that." Bethany said with a cringe, "knowing such a thing. The rest of us were clueless." She sighed, "I thought Leone was sending me to the cells for the rest of my life and that's why he was acting so weird."

"Well, you did mindnap him and lock him in a house." Daxx say with a smirk.

I gave her a curious look.

She nodded, "it's true. I did." She smiled.

"I didn't understand the blood bond and thought Arius

was a dirt bag." Paisley shook her head, "that was a rough trip."

"They do suck at explaining." Alona offered.

"That's an understatement." Daxx mumbled while chewing. "The number of things those brothers left out when I landed here," she sighed, "it could have gone better." Waving her hand, she motioned around the room, "I almost went ballistic when I read that prophecy."

"Of the king's nine sons?" I clarified.

"That one." She nodded, then looked at Crissy, "of course if I had Criss' input then, it would have been much easier."

I turned to Crissy. "You understand all that prophecy lingo?"

Crissy nodded. "I must. I read it and it just pops into my head," she motioned to her head, "then mixes with the other stuff and I just know." She nodded.

"What does it say for Emil?" Kara asked.

Crissy closed her eyes.

I sat up, "you know it all by heart?"

"She has a photographic memory." Paisley told me.

My mouth dropped, "wished I had that in school."

Daxx nodded, "right."

"Tell us, Crissy." Alona said softly.

Crissy closed her eyes again, "okay." She looked at me and smiled, "of course it's you." She nodded, then stared at the water in front of her. "A lost brother will claim his place beside the thrones with one that is equal to him in a way no other woman could be, as she has the one thing he has sought through the years."

I continued to sit there and listen to it inside my head a few times.

"So, what does she have?" Reagan asked.

Autumn shrugged.

"Could be that she's not like his wives." Daxx said. "She won't grow old and die on him."

Crissy smiled. "Something like that."

They all turned and looked at me. I held up my hands, "I

have no idea." I blew out a breath, "Until I spoke to Mitz earlier, I didn't think a guard and royalty mixing was a thing."

"But now you do?" Bethany asked.

I leaned back again, giving the tray tap away from me. My appetite was gone again. "I never expected to have a true mate," I looked around at them, "I'm a guard, my life is devoted to that."

"But you saw Emil and either wanted to kiss him or smack him," Paisley said with a smirk.

I lugged softly. "Yeah I did."

"I think it's wonderful." Kara said in a quiet voice. "He's been through so much: he deserves some happiness."

I looked at her, "he wants nothing to do with me, so we're never going to find out if anything will ever come of this."

It was Autumn that laughed this time, "he'll try to outrun it." She shrugged, "but I don't think they can."

"Some of them run straight for it..."

"Or rage." Crissy cut off Daxx.

"There's always raging." Paisley added.

Reagan turned and picked up her glass of water and raised it in the air, "I am very pleased Kinsley is to be the last mate for the last brother." She smiled at me, "she just fits."

"Absolutely," Kara smiled at me, "give him hell," she shrugged, "he pretty much has to forgive anything you do."

Daxx laughed, "she would know, she shot Raf in the ass with an arrow."

I turned back to Kara, "I'd heard rumors..."

She nodded, "they're true."

"We've got your back, sister," Autumn nodded.

"Welcome to the family." Alona said with a smile.

I felt a little overwhelmed. These were princesses and queens, and I was just a guard and yet, they were welcoming me without hesitation. For a brief second my mother entered my thoughts, oh *that* was going to be a discussion like no other. I cringed and looked around, "I apologize now if you ever meet my mother."

"Oh?" Alona leaned forward. "Why is that?"

I sighed loudly, "she believes a woman should never fight, and always being in frilly dresses," I motioned around the tub, "I don't think any of us would meet with her approval."

Daxx snorted, "anyone tries to stick me in a frilly dress..."

"It won't happen." Alona said quickly, "my fellow *queen*."

Daxx nodded, "Oh yeah." She smiled, "I call the shots," she sobered, "well, unless Mitz has her heart set on something."

The sound of music rang out. Paisley turned around and picked up her phone. "Hey, babe, what's up?" She frowned, then nodded. "Okay, we'll be there shortly." She hung up.

"What's going on?" Daxx was already standing up.

"Quick meeting to go over things found in some heads." Paisley stood up. "I'm going to grab a quick shower and meet everyone at the palace meeting room."

"I am hoping for a few hours of sleep before we go rushing anywhere." Alona said, as climbing out to of the tub.

"Yeah. Grabbing naps here and there is starting to wear on me." Kara picked up a robe.

I got up. I felt better after talking to them but was still a long way from comfortable. A battle would help me work through my emotions. I just wanted things to work out. I'd spent years getting to this point and wasn't ready to give it up, not one bit of all I'd accomplished.

Chapter Nineteen

Everyone filed in slowly for the meeting. I grabbed a coffee and went to sit in the chair that gave me the best view of both entrances into the room. Regardless of what my standing was, that was ingrained, I needed to be aware of my surroundings.

The first thing I noticed was the other guards weren't here. That had me second-guessing if I should be here. I started to get up when Daxx looked at me and shook her head. I sat back down.

The women's expressions were somber, making me think more was going on than I was aware of.

Arius came into the room his expression was scarier than I'd ever seen.

Bethany leaned over closer to me. "Troy saw who—" she frowned, "saw the face of the father of Rena's baby."

I put my hand over my mouth so no one could see what I said. "Does Emil know?"

Bethany nodded, "they all do."

I sat back in my chair. Knowing that fact explained the vibes in the room.

"Everyone," Troy walked over to his chair, "Rena will be here shortly." He cleared his throat, "I haven't told her yet."

"You're doing the right thing," Alona said quietly, "having us all here to support her when you do." She nodded her head in a regal way.

Troy gave her a long look, then nodded and sat down.

As if on cue, Rena came through the door, behind her was a young man carrying a box. She motioned to the table where the two kings were sitting. He walked over and set it down.

"Thank you, Kristopher." She motioned to the door. "If you want to start on the next pile, I shouldn't be too long."

He gave her a smile and then left the room.

"You have an assistant now?" Emil looked to the door he'd gone out, then got up and shut it behind him.

Rena stood there and looked around. "He was working in the kitchen, but he's absolutely brilliant with scheduling and organizing, so I borrowed him."

"It was cleared with Mitz?" Chase asked.

Rena nodded, "yes, she said it was a much better fit." Rena motioned to the box, "I have ten more upstairs. *Ten.* This place is killing forests in *all* the realms with all the unnecessary paperwork." She pointed to the box. "In this one is items I have no idea what to do with."

Chase leaned forward and picked up a page from the box, he looked at it then dropped it like it was soiled. "Agriculture report." He looked at his twin.

Troy cringed then cleared his throat, "so what are you proposing?" He gave the box a long look before looking back to Rena.

Rena huffed out a breath and sat down. "I'm proposing you let me determine what positions and /or reports are obsolete." She motioned to the box once more, "agriculture reports were probably important when your grandfather ruled, but we don't rely on them now with modern methods of tracking." She looked around the table. "I was given a list of obsolete positions in the kingdom, I'd like to designate each department to have a functional committee and then we," she motioned to the kings, "you, get the final reports from each instead of fifty a day from twenty something different departments."

Chase looked at Troy, then smiled at Rena, "you can reassign anyone you wish to make that happen."

Rena smiled, "I'd like one more person, in addition to Kristopher, so we can go over those reports and compile them, so you get the summaries all in one report."

"Oh, I like that idea." Troy said with a big smile. He nodded. "Let Mitz know what or who you need, and she'll make it happen."

"Thank you." Rena smiled. "Honestly, I don't know how you've survived this paper avalanche this long."

Chase laughed, "I'm sure somewhere in Alterealm there's a whole city of buildings filled with reports we had no idea what to do with."

"I will be thankful for less paper on my desk." Troy admitted.

"Oh," Rena put her hands on the table and clasped them together. "There will be no paper. It's all going to be electronic." She looked at the box of papers. "the only paper you'll see is if something needs signing in an official capacity."

Emil looked down the table to Victor, "She's going to have to interview many people, is there somewhere other than the palace she can hold them?

Victor glanced to Rafael, the Michael, "we will find a suitable place that is secure."

Emil gave him an abrupt nod and leaned back again.

"I want a job." Crissy sat forward. She pointed to Bethany, then Paisley, "we all do."

Victor looked at her for a moment, then turned to Troy. "Cristy and I have discussed she would like a position in the archival area."

Troy nodded slowly, "as she's one of the princesses, it would have to be a supervisory position."

"I want one in the legal department." Daxx said abruptly, "something close to bounty hunting."

"Oh, I'd like to be on a committee that deals with events

and things." Paisley gave Arius a hopeful look.

"Definitely the entertainment area for me." Bethany said.

"I could help in medical," Reagan looked at Quinton, "leaving my gloves on."

Autumn turned to Michael, he held up his hand, then looked over at Rena. "Perhaps you could let us know which areas you're going to need people to oversee and we'll find a fit for the ladies."

Rena nodded, "I have ideas already." She turned to her father, "I have one for you too, Dad."

He gave her a surprised look. "You do?"

She nodded, "Yes, I think you should help those that are born with Alterealm DNA—help them understand what they are and get them through it." A look of pride was on her face, "no one could do it better than you."

Emil smiled at her. "I do have the experience."

She nodded, "you do."

"That's a marvelous idea." Alona said. "We have so many in safe houses that are too unsure to leave them again."

Emil looked at her for a moment. "I will do whatever I can to help them."

Rena looked thrilled. "I've heard talk you can find Arwan now."

Chase nodded, "we're working on it."

"There's teams checking locations now." Quinton said, then looked over to Michael, "before we go rushing in."

"I can't wait." Daxx said.

"There's a lot of healing to do." Rena said, "after all that's happened." She nodded slowly, "I look forward to helping in any way I can once this is over."

Troy rubbed a hand down the side of his face, giving Emil a quick look. "I believe we've found the man." His tone was expressionless.

I watched Rena and knew the moment she grasped what he was saying.

"So-so you do have him?" She nodded slowly, "that's a good thing. The doctor can do his tests and he won't," she looked down at her hands, "can't hurt anyone else."

The room was silent.

She glanced back over to her uncle. "You're not asking me to go confirm it's him, are you?" She looked at her father, then back to him, "surely you can look in his mind and," she shook her head, "and…" Covering her mouth for a moment, she closed her eyes. "I don't think I can."

I stood up. "I'll go. Tell me which one he was." I looked at Victor, "I spent a lot of time watching while I was on that island."

"I was mad at you for a while." Rena said in a thoughtful tone, "but then realized if you hadn't been there, they never could have gotten on the island to get us." She held my look, "you were in as much danger as the rest of us."

I shrugged it off, "I'm trained to defend myself; you weren't." I nodded, "tell me which one he was."

She took a deep breath and exhaled it. "His jaw, the one with the lopsided jaw."

I closed my eyes and then opened them and nodded. "I know that one. Looks like his had his face rearranged by someone too many times."

Rena nodded then took a deep breath and stood up. "Thank you, Kinsley." She gave me a quick unfelt smile. "I'm going to get back to work now."

The room was silent as she walked out.

Troy looked at his phone. "I have to go speak with Elder Arian, then we'll meet at the cells?"

Arius nodded. "I'm just going to suck back this cup of coffee then go back."

Autumn got up; gave me a look I didn't understand then turn toward the door. "I'll be at the cells."

Michael jumped up. "He has to be alive for the doctor to do his tests."

She stopped and looked at him. "I know." She started for the door, "how much blood do you figure the doctor needs?"

Michael glanced at Emil, then went out the door after her.

I sat back down and picked up my cup. All of this needed

to end. There had been nothing but chaos for months now.

"What do you mean you are trained to defend yourself?"

I looked up to see Emil standing in front of me. He looked huge with me sitting so I got up. "I'm a guard, it's part of my training?"

"And you required it on the island?" His expression could have been chiseled in stone at that point.

I shrugged, "it was more of creating distractions then defending myself." I blew out a quick breath, "I had to stay off the radar."

"But men tried to force themselves on you?" He stood there with his hands on his hips glaring down at me now.

Why was it everything he said or did when he was near me felt offensive? I hadn't asked for any of this. He couldn't have it both ways. Either I was friend or foe. "Look, Emil..." I changed my mind with what I thought I wanted to say. "I got off there unscathed." I lifted my hands then dropped them back to the table. "We got all the women off there. That's all that matters."

He just stood there, his blue eyes searing holes into my own. I could see the tension in his jaw and for a few seconds I thought I'd be pissed too if Rena was my daughter.

"Look," he leaned down closer to my face, "I have buried five wives," his voice was barely above a whisper, "each held my heart during our time together." His cold stare locked on mine. "I do not want this, am not looking for a *sixth* time." His tone was defensive now.

I leaned in closer, no way was I backing down from this discussion. "Does it seem like I'm pushing you either way?"

He just stood there, breathing on me. "I just want it to be clear that I am not doing that again."

I nodded slowly. "You know what your problem is, *prince*?" I didn't wait for him to answer. "You keep thinking like you're human." I leaned back and looked him up and down, "I don't know if you've noticed but you've outlived the humans."

He clenched his jaw a few times, his eyes shooting darts at

me. With a jerk of his head, he turned on his heel and stomped out the door.

I watched the door slam, then something inside me broke. Before I knew it, the cup on the table was flying through the air and shattered against the door. I hadn't even lifted my hand. I watched the coffee drip down the door. Reality crashed back down when I saw the faces of the remaining royal family, looking at me. "I am *so* sorry." I whispered. "I'll get something to clean that up."

"Don't worry about that."

I glanced to see Mitz standing to the side of the door.

"I envy that skill. I'd love to toss things at people without touching them." She gave me a big smile.

I took a deep breath and then exhaled slowly. No one else said a word. "I'll go to the cells now." I said to no one in particular then made fast work of exiting the room.

Chapter Twenty

I opened the door to see Autumn standing on the other side of it.

She grinned at me. "I didn't know if you knew the meal schedule, so I thought I'd come get you." She tucked her hands into the pocket of her hoodie. "That was pretty decent, what you did for Rena."

I stepped out and closed the door. "I think she's a lot stronger than I am." I hadn't planned on eating with the royal family after earlier. "Is the man still breathing?"

Autumn made a noise of disgust. "Unfortunately." She motioned down the hall. "Arius has banned all of us from seeing him, even himself."

"That might a good thing." I shrugged, "so the doctor can do tests…"

Autumn shrugged, "yeah. The baby being healthy is the most important thing."

"So how do you feel about being called Mom?" I smiled at her.

"You know, I wanted this and still do," she made a face, "but I still can't *feel* it in my gut, you know?"

I nodded, "I'm sure a lot of parents feel that way until they hold the baby."

"You think so?" She put her hand on my arm and stopped me.

I nodded. "I think so."

"Okay," she nodded and released me, "okay then." She shrugged, "let's go eat. We're taking the whole night off to sleep." She laughed, "I don't even know the last time I slept more than a few hours."

We walked in silence for a few moments. "I'm sorry about earlier." I said quietly. "About that scene."

She made a short noise. "Don't sweat it." She grinned at me, then shook her head, "I get it. When you aren't drooling over their bod, you want to kick their teeth in." She chuckled, "It's messy."

I couldn't help but to smile. "Yes, it is."

I'd walked through the dining room in the palace, when I was learning the layout of the building, but I never thought I'd be sitting at the table. I watched Emil come in, he stopped and looked at me, then sat in the furthest possible seat. Leone and Bethany came in behind him, paused and looked where he sat, then sat beside him. I didn't know if he'd just rearranged their usual seating because of me, but I couldn't dwell on it. I was tired, hungry and just wanted to go lay down and sleep—if I could shut off my brain long enough.

The rest of the family came in and took their seats, more than one gave Emil an odd look, no one spoke out loud.

A few women came in carrying trays and placed them in the center of the table. Mitz came in after they left with a smile on her face, as always. She was carrying a basket and I couldn't help noticing that the men watched that basket, hopeful looks on their faces.

She stopped beside Leone and held out the basket. "Phone."

Leone jolted like she'd hit him. "But..."

With a shake of her head, she held the basket closer. "No phones tonight. You're all going to have one quiet and complete meal, start to finish." She nodded and held the basket closer.

Leone pulled out his phone and put it in the basket. "We'll have to sort through them later." He mumbled.

Bethany dropped hers in, then Emil did as well.

Mitz paused and took out of one of the phones, she pressed the button then snickered. "Oh, I think the screen backgrounds will tell us fast enough whose phone it is," she looked back to Leone, "superman."

There were several chuckles around the table.

"I didn't…" he looked at Bethany, then sat back and crossed his arms over his chest.

When Mitz walked out with a full basket, the room was oddly quiet.

"I feel like I've been grounded." Chase said.

Rafael nodded, "I don't think she's ever done that before."

Quinton shrugged, "I'm not going to complain about an uninterrupted meal." He reached over and picked up the closest platter.

Arius looked back toward the door Mitz had gone out. "She'll check them if they ring, right?"

Victor passed a dish to Crissy, "I'm sure she will monitor them for anything important."

"I'm okay without a phone." Crissy smiled and looked in the dish he'd handed her, then shook her head and passed it to Daxx.

Autumn put some food on her plate. "I'm looking forward to downtime tonight."

Bethany nodded, "me too. I'm going to start it with a hot bubble bath."

Leone smirked, but made no comment.

"I think I'll read." Kara said.

"Oh?" Chase glanced down the table at her, "have a new dictionary, cupid?"

Kara rolled her eyes, "no, a thesaurus."

Rafael laughed and nudged her with his shoulder.

"I'm looking forward to waking up feeling pumped for the

day." Autumn waved her fork around, "anyone want to go for a run with me in the morning?"

"A run?" Bethany grimaced, "like on purpose?"

Autumn laughed, "yeah."

"I'll go." I wasn't sure if I was invited, but I'd missed my morning jogs since starting at the palace.

She gave me a thumbs up and put the food into her mouth.

"Stick to the patrolled area we discussed." Michael said softly.

Autumn nodded, "you know it."

The mood continued to be light as everyone ate. It felt good, to just relax for a moment. No pressure about what I should or shouldn't do.

Alona pushed her plate away. "Is anyone else excited for life after Arwan?" She smirked, "I don't know what we're going to do with our time, but not having to guess his next step will be wonderful."

"I, for one, will have a years' worth of prisoners to go through." Arius said with a smirk.

"It's not done after we get Arwan." Crissy said, then looked back down at her plate.

Daxx paused mid-bite. "What do you mean?"

Crissy gave her a blank look, "oh, I see other things that aren't us, but are." She nodded and picked up her glass.

"Meaning?" Quinton leaned forward and looked down at her.

Crissy frowned for a moment, then the look cleared, "well, I see Prince Bastian and the woman and bus." She nodded, "and the prophecy says it's not done." She slumped her shoulders, "I mean it could be talking about other things, but I think we're still involved even after we get that mage." She looked at Victor, sighed and then took another drink.

"The nine brothers' prophecy?" Leone looked at Michael, who shrugged.

"Mmhmm," Crissy put her glass down. She looked like

she wanted to get on her knees on the chair but continued to squirm around in her seat. "Yes. The end of it."

"Criss, what does the end of it say?" Daxx glanced around the table, "I don't think any of us have it memorized."

"I know I haven't." Alona stated.

"Oh," Crissy smiled and closed her eyes, "Together the brothers nine, with mates of strength," she opened her eyes and looked at Daxx, "that's us."

Daxx only nodded her head quickly so Crissy would continue.

"Will rule and protect all of Alterealm and the other realms within their reach." Crissy finished and nodded once more.

"Well damn." Michael mumbled.

"So, we're on cleanup after this?" Leone turned to Rafael.

Rafael shrugged, "I don't see how we can help deal with rogue residents from Solrelm or worse FaTerra." He turned to Troy, "they'll just fairy magic our asses and it's game over."

Troy gave him an odd look for a moment. "A collaboration to end this on all fronts may be necessary. The women's realm is ours to police, so if there are things transpiring there, we'll have to."

Paisley sighed and set her fork down. "Can we just focus on finding Arwan and ending our part of it?"

Bethany nodded, "yeah, please let us have a small victory before we're bouncing from realm to realm," she lifted her hand, "or whatever."

"I agree with the ladies." Victor set his cup down. "We need to bring justice to Arwan and then we can proceed with the other aspects."

I just sat there. I couldn't speak on any of this. I knew what Crissy saw came true, and that the prophecy had been right so far—other realms and the war continuing? I didn't know if I was built for that. I glanced down the table to see Emil watching me, his face wasn't showing enough of an emotion to gauge what his thoughts could be.

"Do we have locations from the glass thingy yet?" Daxx

asked.

"Any with snow?" Crissy gave Troy a look with her eyes huge.

Troy paused and looked at her for a moment. "We have a few, it's a long process comparing things that we're getting from the ones we sent back from the park, and pinpointing and matching them with what Romulus is unraveling."

"Good." Autumn nodded. "I can't wait to crash their parties."

"You're sure of this snowy place, Crissy?" Alona pushed her plate away.

Crissy bobbed her head a few times. "Yes. The feeling I get with it is," she glanced to Victor, "intense."

Victor gave her a look of adoration, before looking to the others. "It's overwhelming for her."

"Okay," Kara turned to Rafael, "we need to get winter gear ready."

Rafael gave her a quick smile. "Mitz is already on it." He motioned to Crissy with a jerk of his head, "as soon as she told us the first time, I discussed a list with Mitz."

"Something that won't restrict movement?" Leone asked him.

Rafael nodded, "we went over that. She's confident she'll be able to come up with something."

Quinton glanced to Michael then Victor, "I'd hoped we were done fighting in the snow."

Michael sighed, "if it's where Arwan is, I'll do it naked if need be."

Autumn laughed, then sobered when he looked at her. "Sorry," she shook her head, "I just pictured that."

Michael scowled at her for a moment, then turned to Troy. "We have a location," he patted his pocket, then remembered he didn't have his phone, "that I know has been confirmed."

"You've sent teams in to check?" Troy set his fork down and placed his elbows on either side of his plate, clasping his hands together. "Are they able to confirm numbers?"

Michael exhaled slowly, "not as of yet, just the location and movement." He glanced to Arius, "we haven't been able to see inside."

"What kind of place?" Chase leaned back and rested his arm on Alona's chair, running his thumb over her shoulder in an absent movement.

"A building," Michael huffed out a breath, "that we'd never think to look inside."

"I am so glad we got that piece of glass." Bethany looked down the table to me, "no more wandering into portals and finding spells."

I'd only been present for the cave of water, but I'd heard stories about the other things they'd gone through in the past months. "I'm all for confirmed locations and shutting them down."

"We're going in the morning?" Quinton asked between bites.

Michael nodded then looked at Rafael, "we have the guard ready to go at a moment's notice."

I silently blew out a breath. I didn't miss that feeling. Being put on standby was the longest, tensest thing ever. Knowing you're going to a fight, but not knowing when led to some long sleepless nights and pacing, a lot of pacing.

"Does Romulus know how many locations yet?" Daxx looked around, "is that something he can figure out from that glass?"

"I don't think it came with a table of contents." Chase said with a grin.

Daxx rolled her eyes at him, "I just meant, does he have a ballpark number?"

"I ordered him to rest." Victor stated quietly, "he was making less sense than usual and hadn't stopped since we brought it back."

"The tablet is under lock and key?" Michael queried.

"It is." Victor inclined his head.

"Okay," Reagan nodded her head slowly, "the next few days are going to be busy."

"And then some." Leone added.

"Think there's any dessert tonight?" Quinton picked up the tray in front of him and put more food on his plate.

"Are you eating for two, brother?" Chase smirked at him.

Quinton paused and gave his brother a bored look. "We never get to finish a meal." He jerked his chin toward his plate, "I'm finishing this one."

"Planning at breakfast?" Paisley stood up and picked up her plate.

Troy and Victor both nodded.

"We'll have more information by then." Michael said and sat back in his chair.

Autumn got up and took his plate, then stacked her own on top. "I'm taking these to the kitchen." She smiled, "and to thank Mitz for the quiet meal." She bobbed her head then turned toward the door.

Paisley nodded and followed her with more dishes.

"Great idea." Bethany did the same.

"It is." Chase leaned over and kissed Alona on the cheek. Standing up, he picked up their dishes, then watched Quinton shovel in another bite. With an amused look, he went down the table and reached over and took the plate Quinton was just aiming to take another forkful from. "Don't want you getting chubby, brother." He quickly walked out of the room.

Quinton sat there with his fork in the air and watched his brother leave.

Reagan covered her mouth as she tried not to laugh.

Dropping the fork on the table, Quinton stood up. "I'm going to ask for a plate to go."

Chapter Twenty-One

I couldn't sleep. Every time I closed my eyes my head filled with so many things, I should have had a complete breakdown from it all. Getting dressed, I wandered through the palace. It was hauntingly silent. I paused and looked down at the floor and smirked. No creaking floors here.

My mind took me through the last while: back to the island, to the beginning of my guard training, and even my mother popped into my head. If that didn't make for an uneasy night, nothing did. I loved my mother, despite how hard she made it, but I couldn't make her beliefs my own. I was proud of what I'd done with my life, my father was as well. I had days where I hoped, even prayed, for my mother to birth another daughter. To have a child that would fill all her ideals of what a daughter should have to be.

Then my stupid brain would toss Emil in the mix, just to cover all areas of my emotional bouncing ball. Emil was my mate, half the realm knew that now, including him. If I'd been in any other position, I would have shouted it from the rooftop. I glanced up the stairs and mentally nodded, even this rooftop. He was, aside from his hot-headed emotional outbursts, a noble man. He'd survived trials I couldn't even begin to fathom. He was loyal and committed to family, that was very clear. Even though he hadn't known about this realm and his birthright for the first three centuries of his life, he still stepped up and took on the war his brothers faced. I don't know if I'd do such a thing, but it spoke volumes about his character that he had. I turned and went to the stairs that led to the third floor.

I needed to fill my head with purposeful things, not this tidal wave of thoughts swirling around and trying to swamp me. I needed to see the realm I was protecting. A tangible reminder of towns, villages, and evidence of the lives I was fighting to maintain. What better place than the balcony of the palace?

I walked into the room at the end, noting there were pictures on the wall now. I smiled, Alona did love decorating. Silently, I opened the glass doors and stepped out into the refreshing night air. Moving past the furniture, I opted to stand at the railing and look down. There were scattered lights as far as I could see. From here I could make out the area surrounding the underground chambers, a good reminder of what I was working for. For too long the royals had been forced to live underground. I rubbed my hands along the solid railing, affirming that their living peacefully in this palace was something I would do anything to achieve.

I inhaled slowly and looked out over the land.

"It's serene, isn't it?"

I almost collapsed on the cold stone. Turning, I saw Emil leaning around a chair he sat in, looking at me.

He smirked for a moment. "I didn't mean to frighten you."

I swallowed and forced my breathing to settle. "I was," I motioned in the air, "having trouble sleeping."

"Mmm, seems to be going around." He looked in the other direction for a moment. "Autumn just jogged by here a few minutes ago."

"Oh." I blew out a steadier breath, "she's very energetic."

"Yes, very driven." He motioned the other chair. "Have a seat."

I wasn't sure if it was a request or order, but my knees were shaking, and sitting wasn't a bad idea. I moved over and sat down. He sat there, the light from the moon shining down on him. He was a very handsome man.

"Look," he leaned forward to rest his elbows on his knees, "I'm sorry about my behavior lately," he shook his head slightly, "I seem to have lost control of rational thinking and managing my own actions."

I wasn't sure what to say about to that, so I kept my mouth shut.

He huffed out a breath, and leaned back, "There are moments I feel like I'm in some sort of dream." He ran his hand through his dark hair, "one moment I'm at the bank assessing if a move to a quieter, cleaner city is attainable," he shrugged, "I mean, it's easier to hide in the constant motion and chaos of a large place, but my heart," he gave me a steady look, "my heart needed some peace and solace."

I just sat there, listening to the angst in his voice. This was a man that had suffered in his life.

"That's neither here nor there," he leaned forward again, only to sit back once more, "you see how ridiculous this is, don't you?" He snorted softly, "My children are over two hundred years *older* than you," he shrugged, "well, Abe is one hundred and eighty-seven, but close enough to two hundred."

I realized he'd given more than a fleeting thought to the fact that I was his mate. "I don't see it that way." I said quietly. I glanced over the view again, "I've been born into this." I turned back to look at him, "family trees vary here a lot, but," I shrugged, "it's normal."

"Mmm," he watched me for a moment, "I guess that's me thinking like a human again."

I suddenly regretted my words from earlier. "But you're not," I watched his reaction, "human or *just* human."

"No. I'm not." He tapped his hand on the arm of the chair, watching himself as he did it. "I didn't know that until just recently, though." He glanced at me from under his lashes, "it's not something one would ever imagine, is it?" he smirked, "oh I must be a different race and from another realm." He rolled his eyes at his words.

I smirked, "I suppose it isn't."

"You grew up knowing there were other realms and beings of all matter." He sat back and crossed his arms over his chest, "I grew up with a mother having a tattoo down her arm about two hundred and fifty years before that was acceptable." He nodded slowly, looking between the rails to the land below, "we moved constantly, she was always melancholy and looking over her shoulder," his eyes sought mine again, "and never explained why."

My heart ached for him. "Does knowing change any of it?" I asked in a hushed voice.

He was quiet for a moment. "No. No, it doesn't." He inhaled deeply and then exhaled slowly, "that's why I'm in this fight. That's why when we catch that bloody lunatic Arwan, and assist the other realms if need be, I'll be out there finding every lost soul that's running from their own shadows for reasons they couldn't fathom and helping them." He held my look. "Helping them have a better life without the constant fear of someone finding out they're different."

I quietly cleared the lump in my throat. "I think that's an amazing and admirable thing to do." I searched his eyes for a moment. "Most wouldn't you know; most would never look back." I'd seen a lot of people that were just dark and selfish at their core. "I've never been over there myself," I made a scoffing noise, "except to that island and the amusement park."

Emil smirked, "those aren't very good examples of what that other side holds." He rolled his eyes, "Well, to be honest there are a lot of things wrong over there, but nothing that's the fault of any other realm."

"Maybe I'll go over sometime." I shrugged, "I could help those in the safe houses or something." I hadn't thought it through beyond that, only knew that I couldn't stay in this post with the royal family and see him every day.

He looked at me for a moment, then turned to look out over the land once more.

I didn't know what else to say, making light conversation seemed shallow. I turned and looked out over the closest village to the mountain. I nodded to myself, that was enough for one night, I thought. Sighing out loud, I stood up. "I think I better go try and sleep."

Emil stood up and looked at me. "I didn't," he motioned to the chair I'd sat in, "I wasn't saying anything against you," he studied my face, "you know, that right?" He touched his chest. "This is all me and the life I've missed. It has nothing to do with you." Placing his hand on my arm, he gave me a brief encouraging look, "you're a spectacular person." He nodded, "sincere, truthful," he made a small grimace to that, "a hell of a warrior." He smiled this time, "even though you kind of scare me when you can move things without touch…"

I inhaled sharply. It felt like my heart was breaking, which was insane. I didn't know this man. I would never know this man. His words hit me as being a goodbye. I wasn't as ready as I thought to say goodbye to the idea of having a mate. "Thank you, prince." I inclined my head and stepped back to go.

"Kinsley." He reached out and touched my arm again.

My breath was stuck in my throat. I'd never had a simple touch feel like so much more in my life.

His eyes searched mine.

I stood there unable to speak a word.

Something went through his eyes and everything changed once more. He lifted his hand away in slow motion. "You're a beautiful woman." He whispered so quietly it took his words a second to register. With that, he spun on his heel and went through the doors so fast he was almost a blur.

I lifted my arm and looked at it. I felt that there should have been some sort of brand or mark that labeled me as his. Inhaling slowly, I rubbed my hand across the spot his hand rested, hoping to remove the feeling.

With my hands on my hips, I turned and looked out over the country. My resolve, no, choice I had been fooling myself with was gone—if it ever was there to begin with. Biting my lip, I shrugged and then shook my head. I still had a job to do. I inhaled deeply. I wasn't going to walk away from an assignment. I may not be Rena's guard, but I had a job to do. A task I'd been asked to be part of.

I backed up still watching lights flicker across the land, I was doing my job, then—well, I had no idea, I'd figure that part out later. Turning, I went back into the room and closed the doors softly.

As I went down the stairs, I saw Autumn opening a door.

"See you for our run at seven, before breakfast?" She grinned, "work up an appetite."

I still couldn't find my voice, so I gave her a quick salute and descended the stairs as quickly as I could without landing on my face at the bottom.

Chapter Twenty-Two

I liked running with Autumn, she kept pace and there wasn't any of that chatter people thought was required. All that could be heard was the in-synch fall of our shoes on the ground and gentle breathing. It was nice, having another female to run with. I always felt like I had to run harder and take longer strides with the men.

Four guards rode past us on their horses, I gave them a simple acknowledgement with a bob of my head, I didn't want to throw off my rhythm.

I wasn't feeling much better than I had last night, but this was helping. Jogging a hundred miles wasn't going to erase Emil's touch from my mind, or his words from my memory, but my head was clearer. If I could keep it up, my resolve might not be so cracked either.

We followed the path and turned to run across the field surrounding the guards' yard. I smiled briefly as we hadn't needed any signals to let the other know where we were going or if we were continuing. As we passed a few trees in the middle of this space, two guards were standing under them, talking. For a second, I figured they were just taking shelter under the tree for a break. Six paces later, I glanced back over my shoulder.

"What's up?" Autumn asked, not even sounding out of breath.

"Did you notice something missing?" I glanced at her. We both slowed slightly but kept moving.

"They had no horses." She said.

I hadn't thought of that, although being on foot was also a norm. "Patches." I said. I put my arm out to slow her until we were both walking.

She stopped and stretched to the side, then squatted down to work out her legs. "Patches?" She glanced back in the direction the men had been.

"They were in uniform, but they didn't have the silver patch on their shoulders." I bent forward, then straightened and rolled my shoulders.

"Good eye." She said quietly. "I think we should go ask about that." She started to walk.

"Hang on." I touched my pocket, then realized I didn't have a phone. "You have your phone?"

Nodding, she handed it to me. I took it and opened the contacts and found the captain in her list. I dialed it and hoped he wasn't busy.

"Autumn?" Rafael answered.

"No, it's Kinsley, we're out for a jog, I forgot my phone."

"Okay, what's going on?" His light tone was gone.

"Saw two guards by the trees in the south field near the yard." I turned and looked to see if I could see if they were still there. "They had no patches, sir."

"I see. Did you recognize either one of them?"

I could hear voices in the background now. "No, but with all the guards called back from other posts it's possible I just don't know them."

"All my guards know to have the patch visible. It's mandatory."

Autumn gave me a questioning look, then shook her head an held her hand out for the phone. She took it from my hand, "Raf, yeah, we're going to go ask them." She shrugged. "I'll put it in my pocket." She nodded and then tapped the screen and tucked the phone back in her pocket. Turning, she adjusted her hood, so it was hard to see who she was and started back toward the trees.

I followed alongside her.

"You'll know right?" She glanced at me.

I nodded, knowing she was asking if I'd know if they were actual guards.

"Good. I wouldn't want to lay a beat-down on any of Raf's people." She smiled at me, then walked faster.

"They should know you." I said simply.

She glanced at me.

I shrugged, "your kind of famous with the guards, after Eunice."

She snorted.

They were still standing under the tree when we got there. "Hey guys." I said, not sure how else to start this.

Autumn stopped right beside them. "Taking a break?"

The one to the left glanced at his buddy for a second. "Yeah."

Autumn stretched her one arm, like she was doing a cool down from the run. "Those new uniforms?" She looked them up and down.

The man gave her a confused look. "Uh, yeah." He pushed his sleeve back and held his hand over a porter. It wasn't a guard's porter.

Autumn bobbed her head. "Cool." In a move so fast no one could anticipate; she swept her leg out and knocked him off his feet.

I lunged for the second guy as he shoved his sleeve up. "Not so fast." I said, then everything blanked for a second.

When the fog cleared, I realized he'd ported us somewhere. I snapped out of it faster than he did and lunged at him, jabbing my elbow in his face. He reacted slowly I added a fist to the nose for good measure. The sound it made, combined with the pain in my hand told me I'd broken his nose. I glanced around, to make sure we were alone. We were in trees—somewhere. He was bent over holding his face. I looked down at what I was wearing and realized I had nothing that I could use to confine him. Bending down, I lifted his fake guard's coat and saw a belt. "Take off the belt." I commanded him.

He squinted at me above his hand.

I spotted the porter on his arm and quickly took it off. He still hadn't moved to take off the belt. I sighed and lifted the jacket and undid his belt. "Don't make a move or I'll smash it some more." I warned him.

Once the belt was free, I shoved him back toward a tree until his back hit it. "Sit." He slid down the tree, blood was dripping between his fingers. I wrapped the belt around his waist and the tree, jerking it tight. I did it up and hoped he didn't get stupid and try to leave. When I went back around the tree, he was holding his sleeve against his face. "Tip your head back." I looked around again. "Where are we?"

His look would have killed me on the spot if that were possible. He made a move that looked like a shrug.

I glared at him. "You used a porter and don't know where it comes out?" I continued to look until I decided he wasn't going to speak. "Great." I turned and investigated the trees, there was nothing that way. If I left to go see what was in the other direction, he'd get free and leave. Or that's what I would do. I went back toward him. "Do you have a phone?"

He gave me a hard look, then reached his bloody hand into his pocket. With jerky movements he freed it from his pocket, not an easy task when you were tied to a tree.

I took it, then wiped it on my track pants. Pacing away a few feet, I squatted down and put my back to a tree. I looked at the phone. It dawned on me then, I was holding one of their phones in my hand. I opened the screen and brought up the message log. There was a long list. Hopefully my stupidity in landing here without a phone would be offset in my favor because I had his phone. Had they gotten phones before? I didn't know. I know they wouldn't port to the cells, nothing with a trace of metal could.

I brought up the dial screen and then stared at it. My

mother's words popped into my head. The *technology is bad for us*, and the part where *no one remembered a phone number anymore* especially. I blew out a breath, then started dialing, there was only one number that I knew by heart. I should, I'd called it thousands of times.

"Hello?"

I almost shouted into the phone. "Dad."

"Kins? What's going on?"

How did I even start to explain this? "I was out for a run with Princess Autumn and we found two guys lurking about."

"Are you all right?"

I waved my hand in the air. "I'm fine. I just don't know where I am, and I don't have my phone."

"How did you get there?"

"The jerk used a porter..." I held up my other arm and looked at mine. I looked over at the guy. I couldn't port him back to the palace or either of the other two locations on my porter. The tracker. "You need to call the Captain and tell him to use my tracker. I can't port this guy back. I won't take a chance that this is a set up."

"You have a tracker?"

Leave it up to him to zero in on that. "Yeah. That's a totally different conversation for another time. Call the Captain, please, or Ira and he'll get a hold of them."

"Okay, sit tight, I'll call the calvary." He said in a funny voice.

I grinned, even though this wasn't the time. "Okay. Give them this number too."

"Will do. Watch your back, kid." He hung up.

I closed the screen, checked the battery level. There was twenty percent, so hopefully they didn't take too long. I clutched it in my hand and then stared at the man tied across from me. The phone rang. I looked at, and for half a second wondered if the call was for me or the guy with the swollen face. I answered it. "Hello."

"Kinsley." It was Rafael.

"Sir—Rafael, I don't want to bring him back to any of my

porter options." I looked at him, "in case he has a transmitter or something on him."

"Good call." It sounded like he was walking somewhere fast. "Michael is checking now to see if we can use your tracker to find you." There were mumbled voices.

"Is Autumn okay?"

He laughed softly, "she is. The guy, not so much."

I nodded. "Good."

"Just stay on the—it's unlocked. The phone you're using."

"Yeah." I wasn't sure what that meant.

"We've never been able to get through the security on other ones. Don't turn it off." He said quickly. There was more talking I couldn't really make out. "Okay, we know where you are. It's about a five-minute jog to you from a location we know. Hang tight, we'll be there soon."

"Okay." I stood up, "I'm in trees, if that's helpful."

He snorted, "It is." More talking. "Do you need someone to stay on the phone with you until we get there?"

I made a face. "No. I don't want to drain the battery and have the phone turn off."

"Fair enough. See you in a few." The line went quiet.

I looked at the phone again, checking the battery, now that I knew it was an important find. I got up and walked a few feet in the other direction, trying to see something through the trees. I turned around and looked at the guy. "Why here?" I lifted my hands and motioned around him, "what's here?"

He held my look, and it didn't look like he was going to reply for a few seconds. "They don't work properly."

It was hard to understand him with the swelling. "The porters don't work?" He didn't make a move to tell me he was planning on replying. "So, they're not programmed properly?"

He winced when he lowered the material from his face. "They don't always work," he huffed out a breath, then made a moaning noise, "between realms." He finished.

I looked at him for a moment. He wasn't planning on saying more. I studied the porter; they really weren't anything like ours. Stepping back from him, I glanced around again. So which realm were we in? "Does it bring you out close to where it's supposed to?"

Something flashed through his eyes, but he wasn't planning on sharing his thoughts. He didn't make a move one way or the other.

I nodded, that was fine. We'd search near here.

Chapter Twenty-Three

Rafael was the first one through the trees. Prince Michael was right behind him.

"We got her." Rafael said while holding his hand over his ear.

I went over to him and handed him the phone and porter while watching *Michael* go over to the man, he pulled his hand away and looked at his face, then used the port box and sent him to the cells.

Arius came through the trees. "There's no one around." Arius reported.

Emil was next, he stopped and gave me a quick once over, when he frowned.

I looked down to see the blood on my pants. "It's not mine." I said quickly, then forced my head to turn and look at Rafael. "He said the porters don't work between realms, so where you come out isn't where it's programmed for.

"Really?" Michael took the porter band from Rafael. "Does it bring them out close to where they're meant to be?"

I shrugged, "I asked him that, he didn't answer but from his reaction, I think it does."

Arius turned in a slow circle, "we'll check the area, see what's close by."

Michael nodded, "I want to get this phone to Elder Arian and her team, I'll be back with help." He nodded to Rafael, then vanished.

I looked out in the direction they'd come in, "what's out that way?"

Emil finally looked away from me to glance over his shoulder, "a road, no buildings."

I watched the captain typing on his phone. "What realm are we in?" I shrugged, "if it doesn't work realm to realm, then I know it's not mine."

Arius shook his head. "No. It's the girls' realm." He looked at Emil, "I'm going to check out that way," he pointed, "come with."

Emil looked at me for a second, then turned to Rafael, "any way to tell if this area is on the glass tablet?"

Rafael looked up from his phone, "I'm asking now. Troy has brought Romulus to Michael's office to see it on the map." He motioned with his head toward the trees, "just scout our immediate area, backup is on the way." He smirked at me, "and Autumn is bringing your gear."

I blew out a breath of relief. "Good."

I felt much better with my blades and a proper jacket on. I glanced down at my track pants, I wouldn't win any fashion awards, but at least I could defend myself.

"There's a factory over here." Quinton's voice came through the earpiece.

"Working or abandoned?" Michael asked.

"Looks like it's still in use." Emil's voice made me pause in step.

I needed to focus and stop acting like some infatuated schoolgirl. Frowning, I glanced behind me to see Detrick and Gudrun right there. They were taking this whole guard the prince's mate thing very seriously.

"Rea, can you go over and see if there's any of your green haze around them?" Daxx asked.

"On my way. It's not *my* green haze, but I'll look." Reagan told her.

"Just hold there." Troy said in a soft voice over the mic, "we're not rushing into anything without information."

"It's really bugging me." Autumn's tone was louder than the rest, "what were they doing just standing outside the yard?"

I nodded but kept walking.

"You think this is a set-up?" Paisley sounded distracted.

"Alona, Crissy and I—with guards, are circling behind the factories to check out this side." Kara told everyone.

"Eyes-wide." Rafael said.

"I don't know if it's a set-up, but it's bugging me." Autumn continued.

I squatted down and looked out from the trees to see what was on the other side. I didn't hear movement, but knew my *guards* were still right on my heel. "Is the commander keeping a watch around the yard perimeter?"

"He is." Rafael answered.

"I have Elder Udela and Segos questioning them now." Troy said in a hushed tone.

"Izzy will find out something." Kara whispered. "There are people just standing behind the factory, behind a small shed."

"More like lurking, trying not to be seen." Alona added.

"Break time?" Bethany asked.

"I don't think so." Alona whispered. "A few of them are armed."

"Which end of the building?" Victor's question came across as more of an order.

"Furthest from where Kinsley landed." Kara answered.

"Just keep watch." Chase said in a hurry, "trying to get in and out in the middle of the day is going to be difficult."

I stood up and stepped out of the trees, Detrick was right beside me. "There's a field on this side, I can't see any buildings." I glanced to Gudrun as he stepped out, he nodded his agreement. "Do you want us to double back or go around the perimeter?"

"Stick to the trees." Leone replied.

I nodded and motioned for the men to go back, Detrick stepped aside and motioned for me to lead. I blew out a quick breath and started walking. Is this how people I watched over felt? Like you had someone standing on the back of your shoes? I made a mental note to give them a bit more space from now on. If I ever got another post, that was.

"Just roads over here." Leone said through the call. "We need to know what that factory is."

"Already on it." Arius informed him.

"Ira just messaged, Romulus confirms this area is one of the locations in the glass, or near here." Rafael told everyone.

"It has to be the factory," Daxx stated, "where that guy was trying to port to. Armed people don't just hang out at factories."

"Seems to be a normal factory on this side." Quinton said quietly. "Few trucks being loaded, deliveries coming in."

"Compost." Arius said abruptly.

"Is that a new way of saying oh shit?" Chase asked.

Arius made an amused sound. "Could be, but no. It's a compost plant."

"That explains the smell." Alona said. "Crissy is back here looking around for cattle."

"No cattle." Crissy stated, her voice sounding very nasal.

"They're working out of a compost plant?" Paisley sounded confused.

"Website seems legit." Paisley stated, "boasting the use of vermiculture."

"Vermi what?" Daxx asked.

"Oh." Paisley's tone changed, "It's a type of worm used to break it down, or something like that."

"Worms and rotting waste. Lovely." Alona didn't sound amused.

"At least they're being creative with their locations." Bethany stated.

"I could use less creativity and more kicking ass." Daxx replied.

We worked our way back through the trees until we met up with Leone, the kings, and Michael. Spreading out we moved through the trees in the direction Quinton and the others waited.

"I can knock them out with a few arrows." Kara said.

"Hold on that for now." Troy said as he walked past me, "we don't want to alert anyone that we're here."

"Are we just going to sit here?" Quinton didn't sound happy.

"We'll have to wait until shift change." Victor answered. "There are more than a dozen cars in the lot. We don't know how many civilians are inside."

"Not to mention the traffic to and from the factory." Leone added in.

"We'll leave two teams to watch," Troy stopped and pulled out his phone, "one at the front and one behind." He started typing something.

"I'll go meet them at the yard and bring them to the front." Rafael said.

"We have another fun place to go today." Chase smirked as we cleared the trees and came up behind them.

"Yeah?" Autumn gave me a nod when she saw me, I felt better that she was still in her jogging outfit. "That place checked out?"

Troy nodded, but still used verbal confirmation for those that weren't standing her with us. "It has."

"Can't wait." Daxx smiled at him as she cleared the trees.

Emil turned and looked at me, again giving me a once over. "I'll head around to the back, and keep watch until Rafael is back with the team." He glanced at Troy to see him nod in reply.

I turned to Detrick and Gudrun and motioned with a jerk of my chin to go with him. They both followed him without question. I turned back to see Troy give me an amused look, but he made no comment.

Daxx put her hand over her mouth, "we're going to need masks for this one."

I had to agree with her. The smell the slight breeze was bringing to us was potent. I tried hard to not inhale through my nose.

"Arius and I will stay here and wait for Raf, if you guys want to go back." Leone stated as he stepped out of the trees to stand with us.

Chase looked around and then pointed to Mac and Felix. "You two can stay with them."

The men both nodded and went over to stand where they could keep an eye on the road leading to the factory.

"We'll convene at the meeting room in the palace..."

"Can we just start calling it the war room or something?" Daxx interrupted Victor. "It's bad enough we have two dining rooms to keep straight."

"Summit room." Crissy said excitedly, "we should call it the summit room. I like the sound of it."

Chase grinned, "hence forth the old throne room shall be named the summit room."

Daxx smirked at him. "That works."

Someone cleared their throat through the mic. "We'll convene at the summit room once the watch is in place here." Victor stated, while looking around at the others.

The Rafael turned and nodded to me. I took that as being dismissed. I opened the porter and pushed the button that would take me to the palace. I at least wanted to get changed before this meeting took place.

Chapter Twenty-Four

I ran through the hall afraid I was already late for the meeting. I still didn't know why I had been bumped to the front of the line when I'd gone to feed, but I was glad for it.

"You didn't get enough running in this morning?"

I skidded to a stop, my heart in my stomach and spun around. Chase was leaning against the corner with a smirk on his face. "I didn't want to be late…"

He waved his hand in the air, "none of us are ever on time." He smiled and straightened from the wall, "I prefer to make a fashionably late entrance."

I nodded, then cleared my throat. "I had to go feed…"

"I heard." He started walking down the hall, "from now on you can call and someone will come to you," he glanced at me, an amused expression on his face, "until my brother man's up."

He'd heard? I felt my cheeks heat and didn't know why. "I'm okay with going there." I walked beside him, despite feeling like I should be behind him. Some protocols weren't easily overwritten.

He appraised me for a moment, "If you must, then, but we do have people approved to come here." He shrugged it off. "I wanted to speak with you before the meeting." His tone was more serious now.

"Of course." What could he possibly want to talk me about?

"I work closely with the designers that fill our armory." He kept walking, "I'd like you to help with some designs."

"Me?" What did I know about designing weapons?

Chase nodded slowly, "Dynamo helps often as well, but as we all know she doesn't really need a weapon in her hands."

Dynamo? I frowned.

He smirked, "Autumn." He stopped walking.

"Oh, right. No, she doesn't require a weapon." I couldn't help standing straight, keeping my hands behind my back. All the royal brothers made me feel like I was only three feet tall.

He motioned to the blade strapped to my back. "That lighter design was made hoping I could persuade some of the ladies to use it..." he lifted his hand, then dropped it, "but as you have probably noticed they all prefer different weapons."

I nodded, still not sure where this was going.

"I'm trying to incorporate a smaller concealed blade within the larger blade," he paused for a moment, an odd look on his face, "for those times when the larger one isn't feasible." He looked at me directly, "I'd like you to help with that." He started walking again. "I got the idea from Emil, and his butterfly blades that hide in his sleeves."

I kept walking, while trying to picture Emil's jacket. There were blades hidden in the sleeves? "I'll do what I can." I focused on the floor. "Maybe something small like a throwing knife could be hidden in the hilt somehow..."

He grinned at me, "like a false handle." He nodded slowly, "we tried something like that, but it came lose too easily and the sword would land on the ground when least convenient."

I stopped and pulled the blade out of its case and looked at it. Balancing it on one hand, I pointed to just below the handle where the blade and hilt met. "Placing it below where the main weapon is gripped would work." I frowned, "I'm not sure how to design it to work though, getting it out quickly."

Chase nodded slowly, "we'll let the designers come up with that idea."

I returned the blade to my back. "We will?"

He smiled at me, "yes, you will be the one that tests and evaluates them, being sure to tell them how badly they've failed if it doesn't work."

I straightened my shoulders back. "Yes, sir."

Chase chuckled. "I think we can probably dispense with the sir and majesty parts."

I almost said sir again to acknowledge what he said.

He leaned closer, "in case you've forgotten," he whispered, "your family now." With a grin he walked into the summit room.

I went in behind him, still not sure how I'd just been selected to help with weaponry. I wasn't going to complain, too often the female guards were passed over for the larger males standing beside them. I noted all but a few of the royal family were already here. I rushed over to the seat I preferred and was just about to sit when my phone rang. Pulling it out of my pocket, I glanced to see it was my dad. I answered it and headed to the corner by the thrones. "Dad?"

"Well you sound fine."

I cringed, realizing I should have let him know all was well. "Yes. Sorry I didn't call."

He chuckled. "I knew you would be okay, I just called…"

"Because you're in the shop hiding from mom?"

"That could be it." He sounded amused. "Listen, I was talking to some of the other retired guards and they were saying there's a possibility of being called back."

I turned and looked over at Captain—at Rafael, I thought quickly. "I could ask."

Rafael gave me a curious look and set his cup down and came over.

"Hang on." I lowered the phone as he reached me. "It's my dad, he's heard retired guards have the option to come back to help?" I covered the end of my phone with my other hand, "I think he's going stir crazy in his retirement."

Rafael smirked and held out his hand.

I gave him the phone.

"Mister Hinton." Rafael nodded, "we could use a hand at the new detention site." He nodded, "my nephew is getting it set up, but we've had to call back the guards that were helping there." He smiled, "I'm sure he could use a guard's expertise in setting things up." He shook his head, "no, you don't need to I'll send someone to bring you over." He smiled, "Thank you once again for your service." He held the phone out to me.

I put it to my ear. "Welcome back." I smirked.

"Your mother is going to hit the ceiling when I tell her." He cleared his throat. "Tell me are things really as bad as I've heard?"

I sobered. "Yeah it's bad, but we're on it now, so hopefully it will be over soon."

"I have faith in the royals." There was a pause, "how did you go from a personal guard to being in the mix with the royals?"

I blew out a breath, trying to figure out how to tell him. I'd planned on it, but not this soon. Emil walking into the room cued my mouth to speak again. "I found my mate." I whispered.

"What?" He was silent for a second. "That's wonderful."

I turned my back to everyone in the room. "Is it?" I hissed.

He chuckled, "I know I gripe from time to time, but yes it really is." He cleared his throat, "have you..."

"No." I answered before he could utter the words. I was forty, yes, but this was my father. "It's—it's complicated."

"Is it a guard?" His voice elevated, "is that why you've been moved?"

I blew out a breath, not knowing how to tell him without saying it and having the entire room hear me. "No, it's not a guard." I was almost hiding behind the thrones now. "It's one of the royals."

The silent was deafening.

"A prince? Prince Emil is the only one…" He gasped, "you're the mate of one of the royal brothers." He said softly.

"Yes."

He cleared his throat, "bring him when you come to get me." He paused, "I have to go your mother is calling me."

The line went quiet. I looked at the phone, then tucked it back into my pocket. I turned around to see Rafael was still standing close enough he probably heard every word.

He gave me a big smile and nodded his head once before walking back over to where he set his cup down. "Emil, after the meeting, I need you and a guard to go to Kinsley's family home and get her father."

Emil jolted like someone had smacked him. "For?" He gave Rafael a cautious look.

Rafael motioned to Arius with his cup. "I've reinstated him to help Ellis set up the security in the cells." Arius looked pleased with the idea.

"His knowledge will be quite valuable." Victor said as he sat down.

Rafael nodded, "You'll be leaving a guard there as well."

"Leaving a guard there?" I looked from Victor back to Rafael.

Michael took off his jacket and hung it on the back of a chair. "As a precaution?"

Rafael nodded, "we've done it with every other family relation." He turned to Michael, "one of the second years from the perimeter posts."

Michael sat down. "I'll go through the list."

"No female guards." I blurted out. Everyone paused and looked at me. I glanced to Rafael then back to Michael. "My mother has," I inhaled slowly, "issues with females being guards."

Michael raised one eyebrow at me, then inclined his head. "A male guard it is."

"Wait." Paisley perched on the edge of the table, "she has issues with female guards, but her *daughter* is one?"

I blew out a breath then nodded. "Yeah."

"Well then." Paisley shook her head slowly and got up. "I thought most women would be proud to have their daughter treated as an equal."

I slipped into the first chair near me and put my hands on the table. "My mother is, unique."

Rafael chuckled quietly. He'd met her, he knew. He turned back to Emil, "if you go to the guard house, Ira will give you a temporary porter set to the right location."

I gave him a quick look.

Rafael shrugged, "we have the coordinates to all of our guard's homes."

I glanced at Emil without turning my head. He did not look happy about being volunteered to do this. "I could…"

Rafael shook his head, "you go nowhere unaccompanied." He motioned to the door, "you'll have your own guard, Emil, and the guard staying there with you."

I turned to glance at Autumn, she shrugged. "Okay." I submitted, knowing that arguing wasn't going to get me anywhere. "Which one?"

Rafael gave me a curious look.

"I have two that are so close on my heels it's like we're sharing the same pair of boots."

Daxx laughed. "I thought my boots felt stretched."

Troy gave her a blank look for a second. "Take whoever you think would be best." He sat down.

Chase hugged Alona, then they sat down. "I've persuaded Kinsley to help with the weapons designs as well."

Autumn grinned, "that's perfect." She sat down beside Michael, "I can tell them how to use them, but have been having trouble showing them." She shrugged, "they're not warriors."

I nodded, "I'm happy to help." I glanced at Emil's arms resting on the table, wondering if he had the blades hidden there now.

"Okay." Daxx lightly smacked her hands on the table. "Let's talk about going to kick some ass."

Troy gave her an affectionate look. "We'll get there

shortly." He motioned around the table, "there are many things to cover."

Huffing out a breath, Daxx sat back. "Okay."

Michael grinned at her, then turned to look at Leone. "Romulus has discovered a few things about that tablet."

"Sleep helped, I'm sure." Leone said quietly.

"Most likely." Michael put his hands on the table. "Several of the locations Arwan was controlling with the tablet," he glanced to Troy, then Chase, "we have already shut down."

"Really?" Chase sat forward, "which ones?"

Michael glanced at his phone, "the warehouse, park, asylum, the wasteland," he looked up at him, "both of those, the wrecking yard..."

"How many are left *not* closed?" Quinton got up and went over to the coffee pot.

"Four." Michael answered.

"So, he'll have to be at one of those?" Bethany asked.

"Most likely." Michael nodded.

"Do we know the last few locations?" Reagan asked as she accepted a cup from Quinton.

"Two we do, well after Kinsley landed beside one today, we *now* know three." Michael told everyone.

"Then we have two locations to go hit today?" Daxx sounded excited.

Michael lifted his hand, "they're being watched right now."

Daxx leaned onto the front of her chair. "But we're going there today?"

Troy grinned and shook his head. "As soon as we get the word it's safe and there are no civilians, yes."

Daxx bobbed her head. "Okay. I can work with that." She grinned at Autumn who smiled back at her.

I looked at Rafael. "Was that phone or porter useful?"

He shrugged, "the phone had some contacts we're looking into," he leaned back in his chair, "their porters don't work once they've been taken off."

I frowned, "how does that work?"

He lifted his hand, "the science team believes its connected to their tattoos."

I nodded, even though I didn't know anything about that sort of thing.

"However, the fact that you got him to tell you that the porters don't work accurately between realms, was the most useful information we've gotten in a while."

I glanced around the table, "how's that?"

Emil gave me a quick glance, "it explains why we could never figure out why we found some where we did, here, over there..." he nodded, "now we know why."

"So," I looked back to Rafael, "now you're not wasting resources following nothing."

"Something like that."

"I've been thinking..." Kara played with the glass in front of her, "when I was hit by that portal..." Everyone looked at her, "the mage that did it was being controlled by Arwan."

Victor nodded, "that's correct."

"Okay," she sat up straighter, "so what *if* Arwan was trying to give the last mage in his circle," she waved a hand in the air, "or whatever, a quick out to escape?"

"Yeah?" Paisley nodded.

"We'd beaten him pretty bad that day," Kara continued, "Romulus crashing his ward at the tracks, us taking down his mages..."

"You think he was trying to take the mage to where he's hiding in the snowy place, but made a mistake because of what we were doing?" Crissy was up on the chair on her knees. She looked so excited, "Yes." She said loudly, then turned to her mate, "it makes sense, Vic." She nodded, "it's near there." She smiled, "the snowy place I'm seeing."

He looked at her for a moment, a soft expression in his eyes. Clearing his throat, he turned to glance at everyone else around the table. "It does stand to reason that even Arwan can make a mistake when under pressure."

"So, one of the locations is near where Kara landed?" Rafael looked over at Quinton, "can you set up a team to do some exploring there?"

Quinton nodded.

"I think we should put trackers in their porters for this." Michael added.

Troy turned to Chase for a moment, a silent exchange took place. "Yes." Troy nodded and looked back to Michael. "All of them are to have trackers and coms, linked into a call to be monitored here."

"Abe has been helping out in the communications room." Emil said.

Leone nodded, "he's fast on the keyboard. Knows all that techy stuff."

"Set him up to monitor the teams at these locations." Chase turned to Michael, "get them all trackers too, Abe can monitor those at the same time."

"I'll get him a few pairs of eyes to help out." Arius was typing on his phone as he spoke.

"Kara," Alona said softly, "I'm meeting Mitz shortly to go over the cold weather gear," she blew out a breath, "your approval would be helpful."

Kara nodded. "Not freezing again is my plan."

Quinton paused and looked up from his phone. "We should send the snow team over with snowmobiles…"

"Cloak them as hunters or something also." Bethany chimed in.

Quinton nodded and turned to Victor.

Victor inclined his head. "We can arrange that."

Daxx jumped up. "I'm stoked." She grinned. "We're ending this."

Troy chuckled, "you will get to kick ass today." He held up his phone. "The team at the factory and the church have just sent their reports." He glanced over to Emil, "Rena has things like that sent to all our mail."

A few of the brothers picked up their phones and checked them.

"That's awesome." Leone said as he tapped the screen. "Why didn't we think of this sooner?"

Paisley snorted. "Because you're men and old."

Arius gave her a hard look.

She shrugged, "it's true, you're stuck in the past with administration." She smiled at her mate, "except your maze of cells, they're top of the line."

"Church?" Alona leaned forward and held out her phone.

Michael nodded, "an abandoned church. It's been condemned for years."

"A church, winter wonderland, a fertilizer factory, what's the fourth location?" Bethany asked.

"We don't know yet." Leone told her.

"Okay, well let's hope it's not musty tunnels and flooding caverns." She shrugged, "right?"

"We can only hope." Michael stood up. "We should be able to go to the church in about an hour and a half."

"Fertilizer factory will be closed for the day after that." Quinton got up.

"Better pack snacks, boys." Daxx grabbed her jacket off the chair, "there will be no stopping in between." She nodded and headed for the door.

"She's not wrong." Troy got up. "figure that out." He looked at Leone.

Leone got up, "what? You want us to carry backpacks with our lunch bags in them?"

Troy smirked, "maybe something a little different than that." He walked out of the room.

Leone looked from him to Rafael, "how—we've never carried a lunch into battle before…"

Rafael shrugged, "guess you better call the caterers then."

Leone's jaw dropped, he glanced to Victor who shrugged. "Well…" He swore under his breath. "I'm going to find Mitz." He jogged out of the room.

"You're going to tell him, right?" Bethany turned and looked at Chase.

Chase grinned, "eventually." He stood up.

"You guys are evil." Alona smiled.

Chase laughed, "I didn't see you telling him we were

joking."

Alona lifted her hands up, then shrugged, "who am I to interfere with brothers?"

I got up slowly, trying to figure out how they all knew what was going on.

"Family hotline." Paisley tapped the side of her head.

Emil sat there shaking his head. "I honestly don't know if finding my family was a good thing or bad some days." He smiled and stood up.

"Have fun meeting your in-laws." Chase said with a smirk and held his hand out to Alona.

The amused look on Emil's face faded as he watched them walk from the room.

Rafael glanced to me, then blew out a breath. "Michael has already messaged Ira about the guard going to stay there."

I avoided looking at Emil completely. "I'll go get Gudrun to take with us."

Rafael nodded slowly but was looking at his brother.

I left the room as fast as my feet could carry me. This was going to be bad. My mother and my mate, I wasn't sure who would glare at me the most. My mother because I was taking Dad and leaving her a guard. Or my mate because he was my mate and was going to have to survive my mother's opinions.

I blew out a breath and headed for the courtyard where Detrick and Gudrun were waiting. Life would have been simpler if I'd chosen a different profession. Like—being a ballerina or something. Not that I could dance, but it had to be simpler than what I was going through, right?

Chapter Twenty-Five

I sighed in relief when we landed a few hundred feet from the house.

Gudrun looked around us. "This is a nice plot of land."

I sighed again, "it's peaceful and boring."

He chuckled, "peaceful is good when you're on a break."

"I'm okay with this location." The guard, Nyle, who was assigned here said quietly. "I was outside the mage's dome last week."

I cringed, "that's a rough post."

He gave me a wide-eyed look, "you have no idea."

Emil still hadn't said a word.

My father came out of the house, walking toward us. I could tell from his expression that my mother was at her finest right now. "I'm sorry guys." I whispered.

"For?" Emil turned and looked at me.

"See that crease in my dad's brow?"

They all turned to look at my father.

"Yeah." Nyle answered.

"There's only one thing in the universe that puts that there." I glanced at them, then back to my dad, "my mother, when she's off on one of her rants about the guard." I almost said and the royal family, too, but managed to bite my tongue.

My dad stopped in front of us. "How bad is it?"

He grinned, then rubbed his hand across his jaw. "She's going to need reassurances that I won't be going into battle." He looked at Gudrun, then smiled and put out his hand. "I heard you were back."

Gudrun shook his hand vigorously. "And just in the nick of time too."

My dad laughed. "I didn't hear all the details, but I was under the impression you were in a bad state."

The seasoned guard nodded. "It wasn't pretty, but my niece has the gift of healing, so here I am."

"Your niece is one of the princesses?" My dad asked him.

Gudrun nodded. "She is."

"I think you know more than we do half the time." I said hoping we could get this visit over with.

My dad shrugged, "old guards stay in touch." He stopped talking and looked at Emil, then bowed his head. "Prince, I'm sorry, I was just so surprised to see Gud again."

Emil shook it off, "not a problem..." He held his hand out to my dad.

"Rowan." My father shook his hand.

"Rowan." Emil motioned to the house, "shall we get this over with."

My dad laughed and looked back at the house.

"Where's Warin?" I glanced around.

My dad started walking toward the house, "you know your brother, he's off doing whatever it is he does."

I snorted, "yeah." I glanced at Emil, then back to the house, "did you tell Mom about..."

My dad looked at my mate before answering. "No. Thought if you wanted to share that, it was on you."

I jammed my hand in my pocket and grasped the bands with the trackers in them. "Know any other way to explain to her why a guard has to stay here, and she and Warin have to wear bands with trackers in them?"

My dad stopped walking and opened his mouth, then shut it and shook his head.

"Remind me to punch my brother in the face later." Emil said under his breath.

I nodded but had nothing to add.

We stepped into the small foyer and just stood there. It seemed very small after being in the palace. I looked around, as always it was spotless.

My mother came out of the library.

"Hi, mom."

She didn't smile or bother with a greeting. "Why is your father being called back?" She glared at the others. "He's retired."

I nodded.

"He's being reinstated as an advisor." Emil said calmly. "To oversee the new rehabilitation facility."

She stared at him for a moment, then bowed her head respectfully. "I'm sorry, Prince, I didn't notice it was you."

Emil offered her a polite smile. "That's fine." He motioned to Nyle. "Nyle will be staying here for the foreseeable future, as will another guard when his shift is over."

My mother frowned. "We need a guard?" She looked at my father.

I watched dad heave a sigh. "Yes, as a precaution."

"Where are you going to be working that we need a guard?" She looked from him to Gudrun.

Gudrun straightened, then bowed his head. "Gudrun Dalston, 'mam."

"Are you staying too?" She put her hands on her hips.

I wanted to back out the door and hide.

"No ma'am. I'm Kinsley's guard."

I was sure the whole realm went silent in that moment.

"Why does my daughter need a guard?" She gave me her accusatory look that she should trademark. "What have you done?"

I opened my mouth, but before I could say anything, Emil stepped forward.

"She hasn't done anything, Mrs. Hinton." He cleared his throat, "she's my mate." He took a deep breath, "and as part of the royal family, she must have a guard."

I dropped my head forward and squeezed my eyes shut tight for a second before straightening again. I looked at my mother. Standing in front of me was a creature I'd never seen. In my life. Just like that, the woman that had hounded me over every detail of my life was smiling and glowing like a flower opening in the bright sunlight.

"Well," she smiled at Emil, then grabbed and hugged me, "that's wonderful news." She turned to my father, "wouldn't you say, Rowan."

My father stepped forward and stood beside her. "I would indeed, dear."

I felt like my brain had forgotten how to speak. Who was this woman and what had she done with my mother?

Emil cleared his throat again, "we have bands that you and your son will be required to wear." He looked at me and held out his hand.

I prodded myself to make my arm move and pulled them out of my pocket.

Emil took them and held them out to her. "They have trackers in them." He offered her a charming smile, "we can't be too careful in watching over our extended family."

Once again, the woman occupying my mother's body nodded and smiled. "Of course." She made a cute little laughing sound, "and thank you for thinking of us." She took the bands and looked at them. "Does it matter which one I put on?"

Emil shook his head. "No. I will let them know that the first one activated is for you, as your son isn't here."

She made a tsking noise and looked at my father. "You should find a position for *him* while your advising the royal family."

My dad opened his mouth, then shut it again and smiled at her. "I will look into it."

"Would you like some tea?" My mother asked Emil.

"Sadly, we can't at this time." He said politely, "we have urgent business to attend, but I'm sure Kinsley will invite you to the palace for dinner, soon."

"The palace," my mother crooned, "of course. Absolutely." She smiled at me.

Smiled at me in a way I hadn't seen since she'd squished me into a ridiculous gown for my cousin's wedding, fifteen years ago.

"You must be so busy, Kins." Another smile.

I was starting to get creeped out by this new person.

"Go. Go," she waved to the door, "I don't want to interfere with royal business." She turned to my father, "you'll be back for dinner?"

My dad nodded. "Of course."

"He will have a porter to get to and from here, Mrs. Hinton." Emil said.

"Agnes." My mother laughed and grabbed Emil and gave him a quick hug, "we're family after all."

Emil stepped back, "Agnes." He bowed his head, then looked at me, "we should get going."

I nodded. "See you—" I reached behind me for the doorknob, "see you later, Mom."

Emil looked at Nyle. "Your porter will take you back to the yard when your replacement is here for shift change."

Nyle nodded but looked too shell-shocked to speak. I didn't know if it was because of the mate thing, or if the vibes coming off my mother in waves were crushing him too.

My father kissed my mom quickly, gave Nyle a pat, then nodded to Emil.

When we were out of earshot, I looked up at my dad. "Who the *hell* was that?"

He laughed, "I have no idea, but I haven't seen her that happy in eighty years."

"Well," Emil glanced over his shoulder, "that was better than the reaction I anticipated—I think." Stopping, he blew out a breath. "I'm still punching my brother in the head, though."

"Which brother?" My dad asked.

"The Captain." I told him, "he's the one that sent Emil with me, on purpose."

My dad chuckled. "He'll regret that when she gushes all over him when she sees him."

I dropped my head down and looked at the ground. "Can we just go and beat on the bad guys now?" I put my hand on Emil's arm and gave him a *now* glare.

My dad chuckled as he touched Emil's shoulder.

Chapter Twenty-Six

"How are you doing, Cutie?" Chase's voice came over the earpiece.

"Almost to the top." Crissy answered.

I leaned out and looked around the corner of the building. I tried to see where she was climbing the old building but couldn't see her. I checked behind me to see Gudrun and Detrick checking all around us.

"How did I get elected to sneak in from the basement?" Rafael asked. "These boards are almost impossible to remove silently."

Someone chuckled. "I suggested it." It was Emil.

"Really? Here I thought I outranked you." Rafael said in a hushed voice.

"Perhaps." Emil answered, "but I felt you were up for the task, *little* brother."

Someone laughed softly, "now you're feeling my pain, Emil." It was Quinton.

"Speaking of pain, how did the meet and greet go?" That was Chase.

I turned to see Gudrun and Detrick again, the looks on their faces told me this was not what they expected to hear when we were moments from breaching the building.

"My mother-in-law *adores* me." Emil said, enunciating each word. "Oh, and I invited her for dinner at the palace as soon as we resolve this Arwan thing."

His mother-in-law?

"Wonderful." Alona said. "Mitz and I were discussing the possibility of a formal dinner for extended family just this morning."

I cringed, "Formal?" I hadn't meant to say it out loud but now it was too late.

"I am not wearing anything poufy and no one is sticking a bow on my ass again." Daxx growled.

I nodded but was able to keep my mouth closed, this time.

"I was thinking more of dressing for dinner, not a ball." Alona said.

"I don't know what that means." Kara said.

Someone made a quiet noise. "Ditto." It was Reagan. "Is that like a dress and brushing your hair or a gown and tiara?"

"Oh, I want to wear a tiara." Crissy said. "I'm up."

"We'll have to open up the jewel vault." Chase said. "How does it look, Cutie?"

"We have a jewel vault?" Alona whispered.

"Can we discuss this later?" That was Quinton.

"There's five out behind the church, I can't tell if they have weapons." Crissy said.

"We see them." That was Arius.

"Okay. Just a second."

I looked around and nodded at the guards behind me. We'd be moving shortly.

"No one on the side by the graveyard." Crissy reported.

"I'm good with that. I wasn't going in there." Paisley said.

"Our three elder warriors have the graveyard covered, Paisley." Michael informed her.

"Good."

"Everyone be careful of the floors; we don't know what state they are in." Bethany warned softly.

"You stay away from all windows and stairs." Leone told her.

"No worries there." Bethany answered, "I plan on standing in the door and blasting anyone that moves from there."

"No one on the other side but Rafael and his team." Crissy said.

"We see the front." Michael told her.

"Stay up there, Cristy, inform us if anyone is coming toward the building." Victor told her.

"Will do, Vic." She said in a tone that didn't hint at a bit of anxiousness.

"Reagan and I are in place." Alona said, "our guards with us."

"The watch wasn't sure how many women were in there, but your only objective is to get them into the van." Troy said.

"Gloves on until they've been checked over by the doctor, Rea." Quinton said softly.

"I know the plan, Quint." She replied sounding amused. "As soon as it's clear, I check for portals."

"We can get in now." Rafael said. "Basement seems empty."

"Hopefully you can get upstairs from there." Kara said.

"I'll find a way. You in place?" He responded.

"Yeah, I found a nice tree across the street." She told him. "No one coming out the front will get far."

I leaned around the building and looked at the only tree in the vicinity. I couldn't see her but had to admit it was a perfect spot for her with her bow.

"Is Bart in the tree too?" Daxx asked.

Kara chuckled, "No, he's helping keep an eye on the van."

"Everyone ready? Here we go." Arius said softly.

"Fight well, brothers." Chase said.

"And if you can't, we sisters have you covered, *brothers*." Kara stated.

"Sing it, sister." Paisley said with a chuckle.

I motioned to Gudrun and we made our way across the street. As we reached the end of the fence near the church, I spotted Emil and Arius crouching at the bottom of the stairs. Behind them were Paisley and Bethany. We hadn't been able to find any recent schematics for the building, so we only had a rough plan once we were in the door. I glanced around, there was no one in sight, which was good because the witches of the temple were helping Romulus with the tablet, meaning none of us were cloaked.

Rafael's team was coming from the basement, which should bring him out at the back of the church. He was to force any found in the back to move to the front. Emil's team was taking the main floor. My guards and I, along with Daxx and Autumn, were to get to the second story and clear the upper loft area.

Emil glanced at me, giving me an 'are you ready' look. I nodded. No fancy words were necessary. I knew my training and after the day I'd had, was more than happy to be doing it right now. Fighting I knew, other aspects of my life, not so much.

"The ones out back have been dispatched." Victor announced.

"Found the way up." Rafael said in a hushed voice.

Arius nodded to Emil and they moved slowly up the stairs.

My guards and I moved to follow the princesses into the building. Normally I'd gripe at them going first, but after seeing what they could do, I was okay with being the last one in.

In the few seconds it took for me to cross the threshold, chaos was unleashed inside. People scattering in all directions. Our teams chasing them down.

"Stairs on either side of entrance." Paisley said in a hurry.

I didn't pause to watch what was happening. Turning left I ran toward the stairs.

"We've got the right." Daxx said abruptly. "Time of worship is over, boys."

I smirked, then sobered quickly as we went up the stairs.

"Steps missing on the left." I said to let anyone that may follow us know. It slowed me down more than I would have liked to get my short legs to reach over the gaps. With the landing in view, I grabbed the rail and leapt over the last step.

Autumn and Daxx weren't in sight yet, so they must still be taking out those on the stairs.

I looked around quickly. Aside from a few seats near the balcony, there was a door at the back—and about eight guys blocking the path that way. "There's a room up here."

"No women yet down here." Bethany said.

"Two more doors to check." Paisley said.

"Rea, need you to check the basement. There's a door here below the stairs." Rafael sounded like he was fighting as he spoke.

"Take Bart and Derian and go check it out." Alona said, "we have here covered."

"All clear up here." Crissy reported.

With Detrick on one side and Gudrun on the other, I advanced further into the loft area. I knew they had me covered, so I did a fast inventory to see what was lying around that I could use to our advantage. The men blocking the door had that all too familiar cocksure expression on their faces. "Time for distraction." I said quietly to let the men with me know what was going to happen.

"Be up there in a sec." Autumn said.

I glanced at a plaque coated in cobwebs hanging on the wall behind the men, as they were walking slowly toward us. It hit the floor and the men jolted, spinning to see the source of the noise. While they were looking, I looked over at the other wall. There was nothing but a bottle sitting on the floor. I focused and lifted it, hoping they were still staring on the plaque. A second later I flung it against the wall.

As they the men backed toward each other in the center of the room, warily looking all around them, Daxx and her team came up the stairs.

I nodded to myself. I liked these odds better.

"Let's clear a path so we can look in that room." I said

softly.

"No portal by this door." Reagan reported. "I'm moving to look upstairs."

"There has to be one somewhere for this to be on Arwan's tablet." Alona said quietly.

"Two approaching from the left." Crissy said.

"I see them." Kara answered.

"Can you hit them from there?" Rafael sounded winded.

"Yeah." Kara's tone indicated pure focus.

Gudrun and Detrick stepped in front of me to take on the men that had decided it was in their best interest to break from their little huddle. I stepped to the side and advanced on the next one heading this way. I chanced a glance at the princesses up here, I couldn't help it, that was ingrained in my training. Autumn and Daxx had Arwan's soldiers well in hand.

I ducked as the man coming at me took a swing with his sword. Judging by the way he swung, he was a novice at using a large bladed weapon. His stance didn't cover his swing radius. He had classic tells and made a snarling expression that warned me that he was going to take another swing. Thankful for the gloves I wore, I grabbed my own blade and blocked his weapon with my whole sword. The shock registered on his face. With a quick, you bore me expression, I lifted my own blade away from my hand and caught his in the motion. It hit the floor, much to his surprise.

I nodded my head once as if to say, that's right this little woman just out did you.

With a roar of a wounded animal he lunged for me, his big hands outstretched. I feinted to the right, then stepped left and swept his legs out from underneath him. He went down, bouncing off the railing on the way to the floor. I heard the wood crack and made a note to avoid going near it. Stepping over him, I put the tip of my blade against his throat. "Need a port box." I said.

"On it." Daxx appeared beside me and vanquished the man to the cells without ceremony. "We need to get to that door."

I turned to see Autumn, Woods and Tim working to draw four of the men away from it. Daxx sidestepped and dispatched the man Detrick and Gudrun were standing over.

"Go." Detrick said, "we've got your back."

Gudrun lifted his sword without comment and motioned with his head for Daxx and I to head toward the door.

One of the men broke off from the others and came charging toward us. He ducked around Detrick and flew past Daxx. Gudrun spun, trying to catch him as he went past, but the man avoided that too. I braced myself, ready to move in whatever direction he chose.

He didn't attempt to go around me or even avoid me, he barreled right into me and sent us both airborne into the fragile railing. I heard the cracking of wood and used my free hand to grab for whatever it could contact.

"Got her." I heard Paisley in the earpiece.

"Don't let go Kinsley." Bethany said.

I looked up to see I was holding the railing that wasn't attached to anything. Paisley must have stopped my fall.

"Bust that door." Daxx said.

I kept my breathing even, focused on my grip of the aged wood.

"I'm going to hold the rail there." Paisley said slowly, "on my say, let go of it."

"We're beneath you." Arius said. "We'll catch you."

"Okay." I dug deep for that trust they instilled into us during training. Truth be told, I was struggling to access it right now. I didn't dare look down, so I had no idea how far I was falling.

"Let go of your sword." Emil said in an even tone.

I hadn't even realized I was still holding it. I was just focused on not moving. I didn't know if Paisley was holding me or the rail and didn't want break whatever focus she had. "Releasing it now." I warned them. I didn't hear it hit the floor, so someone must have caught it. That was a small comfort, if they could catch that, then a body should be easy, right?

"Four women up here." Daxx said. "Autumn just dealt with the last jerk."

"Found the portal." Reagan reported.

Objective completed. I felt better for that.

"On three, Kinsley." Bethany said softly.

I nodded, not knowing if I'd find my voice if I tried to use it.

"One." Bethany said in a hushed tone.

I did notice there wasn't another sound coming through the earpiece.

"Two."

I closed my eyes and waited for the count.

"Three."

I opened my hand and crossed both arms over my chest. The weightlessness only lasted a breath of time before I landed in someone's arms. The air left my body in one soft *whoosh*. I heard the railing hit the floor with a loud, cracking sound. I opened my eyes to see Emil looking down at me as he held me against his chest.

"You really have to stop dangling from things." He said lightly. His expression did not match his tone at all.

I remembered the roller coaster. "I didn't expect to be tackled."

He leaned over and set me on the floor.

With my feet touched down, I finally took a deep breath. Glancing over I nodded my thanks to Paisley. She smiled in return. Arius stepped over and held out my sword. "Thanks." I lifted it from his hand and twisted to put it in the case. My arm griped with the movement. Of course, I cursed silently, it had to be the same arm that's barely recovered from the last injury.

Looking up from the floor, I watched Autumn and Daxx come down the stairs with four scared women sticking close together. Seeing them made the aches I was going to suffer worth it.

"Porting Romulus here to shut down this portal." Quinton

said abruptly.

"I'm getting down now." Kara stated.

"Cristy, port down now." Victor said.

We all exited the church behind the women.

Michael was looking at his phone. "There's only one car left at the factory. Small cube vans arrived after the last worked left." He glanced over to Troy.

Troy nodded, "we need to keep a team here to keep watch for any late arrivals for the next day or two."

Rafael watched Kara walk over then pulled out his phone. "I'll get Ira to bring a team." He turned and looked back in the building. "They can just camp out inside, now that the portal is closed."

Leone appeared beside me. He held up his hand and then tossed a paper bag at Rafael. "Here's your lunch." With a hard look, he turned to Bethany. "I'm porting over to the factory, you come over with Rafael." He ported out.

Rafael grinned at Michael.

"How'd we do with the layout of the factory?" Chase asked.

"It's rough." Michael told him. "We know the building layout, but not how the plant inside is set up."

Chase nodded and turned to his twin. "I'll get the rest of the guards for that."

Troy nodded, "Set them up around the outskirts to be a net when we breach."

Chase turned to watch Alona as the van pulled away. As if she knew, she glanced over her shoulder and nodded to him. "I'll come with you."

"See you there." Michael and Autumn ported.

I blew out a breath and nodded to Gudrun. He opened his porter when I touched his arm.

Chapter Twenty-Seven

We waited in the trees while the others got into place.

Detrick came over and leaned down beside me. He showed me the earpiece in his hand. I frowned and took out mine.

"How bad is it?"

I gave him a questioning look.

"Your arm." He said. "I saw how you were favoring it after the church."

I rolled my shoulder and tried not to wince. I failed. "It will be fine."

He looked like he wanted to say more, then glanced behind us to where several of the royal family were standing.

I grabbed his arm. "It *will* be fine."

He blew out a breath. "You're a guard, but you're not—" he glanced behind us again, "I should report your injury."

I shook my head. "They'll bench me." I whispered. "Look, this Arwan jerk tried to drown me —and the queens and *all* the princesses…"

"What are we whispering about?"

I almost jumped out of my skin when Leone spoke from beside me.

Detrick cleared his throat and straightened. He gave me a

panicked look, then turned his eyes to stare at the ground.

"Okay," Leone tilted his head, "what's going on?" He did something with the earpiece, I hoped it was to mute it.

I gave Detrick a hard look before turning to look at Leone. "I strained my arm dangling from the railing." I said quickly.

Leone stepped back and looked at me. "Same arm you just got off medical for?"

I nodded.

He winced, then put his hands on his hips and looked over at Rafael.

I closed the distance between us. "I'm good. I can do this." I nodded.

He didn't look convinced.

"They tried to drown me and your mate. All the mates." I waved my other hand around.

Autumn came over. "What's up?" She looked from Leone back to me.

Leone motioned to me, "she strained her arm in the fall."

Autumn nodded, "no doubt that was one hell of a hit you took." She nodded slowly, "is it the shoulder or whole arm?"

I shrugged my shoulder. "Bicep, forearm area."

She turned and glanced toward Michael, then touched the earpiece. "We have a few minutes?"

Michael turned and looked at her then nodded.

She grinned and touched the earbud once again. "Let's take a look." She turned back to me.

I was suddenly the center of attention. Daxx and Paisley both looked at me with curious expressions. I put the earbud in my pocket. Sighing, I pulled the strap over my head and held my weapon out to Detrick. He was smart enough to avoid making eye contact at that point. Shrugging out of my jacket, I tossed it in his general direction.

"Everything all right?" Reagan came over.

I blew out a breath, knowing that Quinton wasn't going to be far behind her.

Autumn lifted my arm and looked at it. "Is this what

you're recovering from?"

I looked down at the scar that ran from my lower bicep to just past my elbow. "Yeah. The doc cleared me."

Rafael was now standing beside Autumn.

"You could sit this one out," he motioned to the left of us, "or do clean up outside…"

I shook my head, "I'm good."

Reagan turned to Quinton.

He shook his head, "you need your strength." He turned and glanced over at Emil, who stood back with Arius.

"You a righty?" Autumn asked.

I nodded.

"Okay, so this isn't your sword arm," she nodded. "Lift your arm over your head."

I sucked in a breath and lifted my arm above my head. It took all I had to not wince with all the eyes on me.

Autumn held her hand out to Detrick. "Hand me her weapon."

Detrick complied.

She held it out to me. "Again, holding this."

I took the sword in my good hand and looked at it. I glanced around to see everyone was in the loop now. Arius put his hand on Emil's shoulder and said something to him. Whatever it was caused Chase to turn and smirk at his brothers. Emil gave Arius a hard look and then started stomping toward where we stood. I don't know what he said, but Emil was not happy with it.

"Ah, a mate to the rescue." Chase said with a note of amusement. He stepped back so Emil could stand in front of me.

He took the sword from my hand and I thought, this is it, I'm being benched. Handing it to Detrick, he grabbed my hand and started walking with long strides into the trees, dragging me along.

I was almost running to keep up. He suddenly stopped and I almost ran right into him.

"Shut up." He said, then pulled the earpiece out and

stuffed it in his pocket. He looked at my arm. "If you were injured you should have said something."

I tried to shrug it off, "it always aches to a certain extent."

He frowned and then took my hand and grasped my hand. "Then why aren't you still off on medical?"

"I was reinstated to guard your daughter in a warded palace." I said quietly.

He took a deep breath and released my hand. "You still should have said something."

I wasn't sure why he sounded so upset. Yes, not being at the top of my game may hurt the team, but I had Detrick and Gudrun as my shadows, literally.

With jerky movements, he unbuttoned his jacket. His sword case was next, without thought he tossed it on the ground and took off his jacket.

I continued to just stand there. I was stuck between feeling cornered into special behavior and wanting him to continue taking off layers. I felt my cheeks heat at his t-shirt hit the ground.

He leaned down and pulled a butterfly knife out of the cuff of his jacket. With a blurred movement the blade was exposed. He stood there for a moment and looked at me. "I've never done this." He shook his head, "my brothers and I tested, and I do have the healing blood, but," he shrugged, then stopped speaking.

"Look, you don't have..." He dragged the blade over his pec and grasped the back of my head in one fast movement. I didn't even know when I'd put my mouth on his chest, but here I was pressed up against his flesh, my lips sucking his royal blood from the wound. Licking over it, I lifted my face away from his warm skin. Red eyes were looking down at me. I'd seen the change of Alterealm eyes my entire life, never, not *ever* had the sight of them sent heat through me.

"Do you need to feed?" He tilted his head to the side as he grabbed the back of my head. "Feed." He commanded softly.

I bit him without a second's thought. I couldn't think

clearly enough to know if I needed it, but I had bitten him. I don't know who was in control of my body right now, but it wasn't me. I sealed my bite and lifted my head.

His chest was rising and falling as rapidly as I was breathing. With slow movements, he released me and stepped back.

I just stood there as if I were made of stone.

"Is it better?" His voice was hoarse.

A few seconds passed before his words registered. I lifted my arm up and down a few times. "It's like new." I whispered.

He made a deep rumbling noise, that I took as an acknowledgement.

I wasn't sure if I should thank him. "Thanks." I said so softly I wasn't sure he heard. I should probably go get my gear, I thought as I watched him put on his shirt, but I continued to stand there.

Picking up his jacket and swords he grasped them all in one large hand. Finally, he looked at me. I was almost disappointed his eyes weren't red. He stepped closer and I gave him a wide-eyed look. His hard expression softened. He touched the side of my face with his palm. "Next time say something." He whispered, then stepped back and put his earbud in.

I jolted and took mine out. I'd forgotten why we were here. Spinning on my heel, I headed back to the others as I jammed the earbud in.

"Guards are in place." Crissy reported.

Derrick held out my jacket as soon as I was close. He still wouldn't make eye contact with me. I slipped it on, noting that my arm hadn't felt this good since before my injury. Magic royal blood. That's what my brother and I used to call it. Turns out we were right. As I was putting my weapon back on, Gudrun came over and stood on the opposite side. I huffed out a breath, after we were done here, I needed to explain what personal space was. This was getting annoying.

Emil turned and looked right at me with a concerned look.

Damn blood bond. That's just what I needed a prince picking up on my emotions. I shrugged it off, giving him a quick nod. That's when I noticed everyone was watching me.

"We're good?" Autumn asked me.

I nodded, unable to find words that would convey how annoyed I was for the special treatment.

She pushed her hood off and shoved her sleeves up.

"Let's do this." Daxx said.

Gudrun held out a bandana. "For the smell inside."

I tried it loosely around my neck as we walked. We followed the team heading to the rear of the building.

"They're closing up the cube truck—van." Crissy said. "At the loading dock. The driver is talking with three other guys." She whispered.

I had no idea where she was, and there was no time to look around to figure it out. I paused and watched Michael point to Emil, then glanced at me with a jerk of his chin. Nodding, my two shadows and I followed Emil as he ran along the inside of the fence toward the loading dock.

He stopped and squatted down beside a transport trailer at the side.

There was no clear path to the truck without being seen.

I gnawed on my lip for a second. "Shit." I whispered. Shrugging out of the strap holding my sword, I held it out beside me. I didn't even need to look and see if Detrick was there. The weapon was taken out of my hand.

"Hold moving on the men out back." Emil whispered. "It's visible from loading dock."

"We're watching. As soon as you engage, we will." Arius replied.

"One distraction coming up." I said and stood up. I caught the expression on Emil's face as I went. He was not happy. I blew out a breath, I wasn't even sure what my own plan was. I almost groaned. Helpless woman always worked. I hated using it, had never used it, but there wasn't any time to come up with something else.

Pulling my phone out of my pocket, I held it in the air.

"Excuse me." I called out. The men turned and looked at me. "Hi." I offered a brief smile. "Can you help me?" I glanced behind me, "my car died." I looked at my phone again, "and I have no signal." I waved it around in the air. I lifted my chin so they would think I was looking at it, while I was checking for anything I could toss to distract them.

"Get them to turn their backs to the fence." Emil said softly.

I lowered the phone and pointed to the front of the building, "I don't even know what this road is called."

The driver closed the door and headed towards me. He pulled out his phone and looked at it. Probably checking for a signal

"Oh." I looked at my phone and stepped sideways, "one bar—come on," I moved toward the front of the vehicle. "Two. Great…" I pretended to type on it. "What's the road? I'm telling my friends," the other men their back to the fence, "to get here *now*." I said loudly.

I saw the guys clear the fence and knew I had about a second until he noticed. Jamming the phone in my pocket, I snapped my head back to see he had a gun in his hand. A gun. Coward. Without thought I used my skill to pull it from his hand and toss it in the other direction.

Now I had his full attention. He walked toward me, shoving his sleeves up as he did. The only weapon I had was a knife tucked into the back of my jeans. Why hadn't I come in full garb with all my weapons? I heard the motion around me but wasn't taking my eyes off him.

A large ball of energy smacked up against him, sending him into the hood of the van. He crumpled to the ground.

I turned to see Bethany there. She pulled the strap over her head that held my sword and shrugged. "Last second change of plans." She motioned with her head. "Let's go."

I put the sword case on and pulled the blade free. I followed her and Paisley, noting that my shadows were ass-deep in a battle with several of the men.

As we rounded the corner, I saw Autumn and Daxx

crouched down below a window.

"We're going in the front." Daxx said as she glanced in my direction.

"Hold. We're not in the back yet." Troy said.

Autumn and Daxx exchanged a look.

Daxx turned to look at Paisley, who shrugged. "Too late." She said as she shoved the window up.

Autumn hopped up and went inside.

I went over and knelt so the queen and princesses could use my knee to get up in the window.

"We're in the office." Autumn said.

Daxx and Autumn leaned out the window and pulled me high enough up that I could get my leg over the ledge.

Climbing in, I looked around. I motioned to the door on the other side of the room. Autumn moved and opened the door slowly.

Bethany moved to stand in the open door, energy arcing between her hands. She looked one way and then the other. "Office area clear." She said softly.

"Loading dock cleared." Arius said abruptly.

We moved down the short hall quietly.

"Van is filled with boxes." Emil said. "Checking them now."

"Knowing what we're looking for would be good." Alona said.

"There has to be a portal here." Reagan said. "Watch team reported only a few arriving."

"There are more than a few here." Michael said in an exasperated tone.

Bethany reached the end of the hall and stopped; I didn't pause to see if they had their own protocols as I moved to stand beside her. She glanced at me and nodded her head once before stepping out into the open.

I checked the other way, then followed as we moved along a row of stacked bags. My next move was to pull the bandana up over my nose and mouth. If they hid anything in these bags, I was not helping to check them.

The other women quickly put their bandanas on as well. Daxx advanced to stand beside Bethany as we walked out of the rows of fertilizer.

"Boxes have items in them that didn't come from here." Emil said quickly. "Leaving a guard here."

"So they're using a portal to bring supplies?" Alona asked.

"What kind of things?" Rafael grunted. The sound of metal on metal echoed through the earbud.

"Parts." A voice I didn't recognize answered. "Components." He told us.

"I don't like the sound of that." Kara said.

"Which means we haven't stopped their production of illegal devices." Chase said in a low tone, "Two more guards with Reagan now, we need to find the portal." His tone was not jovial for once.

"I have three, keep the guards." Reagan told him.

Someone made a noise of disapproval; I could only guess it was Quinton.

"Some of these parts are too big for porters or small bands." Rafael said.

"Find the portal." Kara said.

We found the packing area next and no bandana ever made could have hidden the smell in here.

Daxx froze and pointed to the far end.

There were four men standing beside a door. I glanced at Autumn, she nodded and started for them before I could take a step. Later when I wasn't in the mix, I was going to have to stop and think about how the family ruling our realm were not short on courage. However misplaced that may be in the middle of this war.

I caught up to her before they noticed either of us. I motioned to the left, she nodded and went left. I didn't pause to see if Daxx followed, just hoped she did. I went to the right and saw Paisley walking right for them. Bethany was right beside me now. "Four in the packaging area." I said barely above a whisper.

"They're guarding a door." Bethany added.

"Packaging area…" Reagan said softly, "we'll find it." She added quickly.

"Do not…"

I was pretty sure the captain was going to say engage, but the men noticed us and that spurred Autumn and Daxx into a charge, instead of silence.

"Too late." Paisley lifted her hands and the man swinging at Daxx stopped with sword in the air.

"Got him." Daxx said quickly and used her port box.

Autumn was taking on two by herself.

Bethany hit the man coming toward us with her energy, sending him skidding backward. I was there when he finally caught his balance and met his angry swing with my sword. Blocking it and then using my time-honed move, I unarmed him. Bethany hit him again, knocking him back from his weapon where it lay on the cement floor.

I advanced and swept his legs out from under him. He hit the floor. I moved over and placed the tip of my blade against his throat. "Stay down." I warned him.

"On my way." Daxx sang out.

She slid up beside me and used the port box to dispatch him to the cells.

Turning I saw Autumn had the last well in hand, with a nod Daxx took off back over toward her.

I looked at the door they'd been guarding. Bethany turned and gave me a curious look. I nodded. "Checking what's behind the door."

"Have care." Emil said, sounding out of breath.

"This is clearly," Chase grunted, "a favorite gathering spot for Arwan scum." He finished.

We could hear sounds of battle coming through the earbuds. I just wanted to check what they were guarding and get to the back to help the rest of the teams.

Bethany stopped and nodded when we reached the door. She raised her hands as I opened it slowly.

Both of us turned to the other when it was an empty storage room. Raising the sword, I motioned for us to go in and check the areas we couldn't see. She bobbed her head quickly as we moved with cautious steps into the room.

Chapter Twenty- Eight

A shiver moved over me, like the one that I got when I ported and then we weren't in the storage room.

Bethany hissed out a breath and pulled out her phone. I stood looking around as she dialed back in. We were in an abandoned kitchen, or cafeteria.

She tucked her phone back in her pocket.

I pulled mine out and connected.

"...what?" Leone barked into the earpiece.

"We're okay." Bethany whispered.

I moved over and looked out the window. "I think we found the fourth location." I said as quietly as I could.

"Shit." That was Emil.

"Come back through." Leone said.

Bethany and I turned and looked at each other. She shrugged.

"Negative." I answered. "We need to know where this is so we can shut it down."

"Kins..."

"Have care." Victor interrupted Emil.

I shrugged, happy he had. I wasn't sure what I would do if he'd given me a harsh order—or shown something softer.

Bethany rubbed her hands together, then held them in

front of her as we went out the open door. I didn't see any
arcs between her hands but hoped she could materialize them
faster with her hands ready.

We heard voices and crouched close to listen. There
wasn't anything important being said, it was just people
chatting with one another. I gnawed on my lip and looked
around. I jerked my chin to tell her to move along the wall to
the other door at the far end of counter.

She nodded and started in that direction.

We kept low to the floor and moved silently. Piled along
the counter were smaller boxes. They were new, not old or
dust covered. I hesitated for a second, debating on if we
should look in them. Bethany nudged me with her shoulder.
I leaned forward and pulled one of the boxes down.

We both investigated it to see several small components. I
looked at her, she shook her head, then reached in and
grabbed them and jammed them into her jacket pocket.

I looked back at the door. She crept slowly to it then
leaned down, almost on the floor, to peek out. Straightening
up, she gave me a wide-eyed look.

How many? I mouthed.

Her silent answer was *A lot!*

I bit my lip and looked around. I motioned at the door
we'd landed by. It was time to get out of here.

She glanced at her porter, then gave me a questioning
look. I shook my head. A princess wore her porter and
tracker at all times.

Sliding my sword back in its case, I reached under my
sleeve to undo mine. Pulling it free, I glanced around, then
sent it sliding to rest under the counter edge. With a nod, I set
the box back where I'd taken it from as she moved toward
the door.

"Hey."

I spun around to see a man carrying a small box was now
standing there. He tossed the box on the counter and came
toward us as he pulled a large knife from behind his back.
Blowing out a breath, I stood straighter and pulled out my

own. I hoped Bethany was heading through the portal while I distracted him.

He made a wide swing with his knife, jabbing at the end. That move showed he was skilled.

I stepped back to avoid contact with the blade and tucked mine into a defensive position, with my blade against the leather covering my wrist. I couldn't use my ability to distract him without alerting the others with noises in the kitchen. When he swung again, I blocked his forearm with my own. He moved too fast for me to score a hit on him.

Lunging at me; my hip hit the edge of the stainless-steel table and stopped my retreat. I felt the sting of it near my shoulder and knocked him back with a kick fueled by adrenalin.

Someone hit me from the side, and I found myself laying in the courtyard at the palace. Bethany was sprawled over me.

Pushing herself up to sit, she pulled out her phone and tapped the screen. "We're at the courtyard." She said, then frowned at me, "Kinsley got cut."

My brain cleared as I sat up, jerking my jacket off. I growled in annoyance. Blood ran down my arm. "Dammit." I hissed out a breath and pulled the bandana off my neck and held it over the gash. "They're going to start charging me for my jackets soon, the speed I'm going through them." I said, then looked at her.

"Reagan is on her way." She tucked the phone into her pocket.

I nodded, lifting the cloth to see if it was slowing. It wasn't. "Tell them about my tracker."

She made a soft gasp. "I forgot." Tapping the phone again, she set it on the ground. "Kinsley left her porter there. Can we use her tracker to find that location?"

"I'll port to over to Abe to see if he's getting a signal." Michael said.

"How is everyone?" Feeling like I'd failed again by getting injured. *Twice* in one day.

"Just cleaning up here." Paisley said. "Everyone is fine.

The usual bumps and bruises."

Someone snorted, "speak for yourself," that was Leone, "it feels like I have a second kneecap growing on my leg."

Bethany straightened up and stared at the floor. "What happened?"

"Some guy tried to take off his leg with the fork of a tow motor." Daxx reported.

"He's fine." That was Chase.

"It's nothing a feeding and meal won't repair." Quinton sounded bored.

Bethany crawled over and put her hands over the blood-soaked bandage on my shoulder.

"Keep crying, brother," Rafael said, "I may have to use bleach to remove this smell."

I started to feel lightheaded and pressed harder on my arm.

"You are not bathing in our room." Kara said.

"Shouldn't have rolled around in the bin." Troy said.

"Like I had a choice." Rafael said. "It was either that or get run over."

"Sorry," Paisley said, "I couldn't stop both of them."

"I'm glad you stopped mine." Leone said.

"I'll shower in my old room in the chambers." Rafael said.

"You can't walk on the carpets there." Alona said, "it will linger for months."

"What do you suggest then?" Rafael didn't sound happy.

"The bleeding isn't slowing." Bethany said as she checked under the cloth again.

"On my way." Reagan said quickly.

She appeared beside us. "Sorry." She dropped down onto the grass, "Quinton got nicked and I had to fight to get him to let me help."

I nodded. I couldn't gripe about one of the princes coming before me.

"We'll see everyone shortly." Daxx said.

Bethany moved out of the way and disconnected her call. "How bad is Leone's leg?"

Reagan dropped the cloth and put her hands over my slick red skin. "Troy is making him go get an x-ray before it's healed, to make sure it's okay to heal it."

Bethany nodded and stood up. "I better go to the hospital and make sure he does."

Reagan made a quiet noise. "This isn't healing."

I jolted and looked down at my arm. I looked at Reagan, her hair was almost grey.

Emil appeared beside us, then Quinton.

"It's not healing." Bethany said.

"Stop trying." Quinton said. "I'll go get the doc." He disappeared.

I had no idea what any of this meant.

"I'm taking her to my room." Emil bent down and scooped me up in his arms.

"We'll be there in a minute." Bethany was dialing her phone as she ran into the solarium.

I held my hand over my arm and then next moment I was in room I'd never been in before. Without a word, Emil went over to the bathroom and went in. He set me on the counter and grabbed a towel.

"Bastards are probably poisoning their blades now." He said as he pressed the towel against my wound. "I can't heal it until they clear out the poison." He met my look, worry in his expression. "They used this on Autumn before."

"Get her to the bed." Autumn came running into the bathroom. She grabbed the garbage can. "And we'll need this for the purge."

Purge was all I had time to think before I found myself lying on the bed. "The blankets…" I tried to sit up.

"Fuck the blankets." Emil said in a venomous tone.

Autumn stopped and gave Emil a look. "Call Ira, we need her blood type."

My eyes widened at that. "For what?"

"We just do." She turned when Alona and the doctor came through the door.

"I brought the antidote." The doctor said and came over.

"Leone will be here in a moment." Alona said. She answered my confused look next. "He's the same blood type and feeder."

I nodded and struggled to keep my vision clear. "A little weak." I felt like I should apologize.

Leone and Bethany appeared, he limped toward the bed.

I tried to sit up. "You should look after your leg first."

He dropped down onto the bed and held out his arm to the doctor. "No time." He gritted his teeth as the doctor put the needle in. Sliding up on the bed, he held his arm over his head.

I felt the needle go in but didn't really feel it. Small blessing there, I hated needles.

"Won't his blood heal the cut before the poison is out?" Bethany gave the doctor a worried look.

"Not intravenously." The doctor said in a distracted way.

I frowned, trying to figure out how ingesting it healed but through a needle it didn't. I started to feel dizzy and couldn't focus on my own thoughts.

"Prince Emil, if you could support her through this." The doctor said.

I felt the bed move and then knew it was Emil beside me, rolling me onto my side.

"You need to drink this princess." The doctor said.

I didn't know he was talking to me until someone pressed something against my mouth. I swallowed the bitter liquid. The taste alone almost made me gag. I put my head back against his warm body while trying to puzzle out if I should feel something in my arm after drinking that awful cure. As soon as I could focus enough to speak, I'd have to correct the doctor, I was not a princess.

I started to drift off and decided to go with it and get some rest while this stuff fixed whatever that blade had done. A few moments later my body had other ideas. The cramping started low in my gut and then felt like it hit every muscle in my body at the same time. My stomach clenched and I choked on the vomit trying to escape my body.

"Here we go." Someone in the room said.

Emil held me while my body rid itself of—everything.

I felt a cool cloth on my forehead and wanted to say thank you, but the next wave hit.

"When can I heal it?"

I heard Emil ask, but was too busy trying to breathe through the violent heaves to hear the answer.

I don't know how long this went on, I was incapable of speech or thought. The only thing that registered was my own heavy breathing and that the warm body holding me was still there.

"Help Leone to medical now." Someone said.

I was hot but cold at the same time. The bed was shaking, and it took all of my focus to see it was me shivering that was causing it. I felt a blanket cover me.

"Seal it." Someone said.

I thought it felt like someone was licking my arm but couldn't be sure. It was probably a wet cloth wiping the blood off.

"Go feed, I'll stay with her." Alona said. "Then you can give her blood."

I felt Emil move and wanted to ask him to stay but couldn't find the strength to form the words to speak. Blowing out a breath, my whole body was limp. I decided a short nap would probably be best at this point.

Chapter Twenty- Nine

"Kinsley."

My name was spoken so softly, I had trouble distinguishing if I'd heard or dreamt it.

"I need you to wake up for a few minutes."

I opened my eyes to see Emil leaning over me. I licked dry lips and the taste on my tongue brought it all back. I was awake now. "Did it work?" My throat was so dry I could barely get the words out.

He nodded. "Yes, the poison is gone." He sat down beside me.

I processed that. "Good." Inhaling, I checked that my stomach was going to behave now. "I'm going to have to find that guy."

Emil smirked, "retribution later." He said quietly, "right now we need to heal that." His eyes flicked to my arm.

I lifted it. The pain brought it all back again. "It's not bleeding."

He shook his head, "no, I sealed the outside, but the inside needs healing."

I nodded, not able to understand what he was saying. "Tell me it doesn't require any more elixirs."

His soft chuckle broke the silence of the room. "No. Just

some blood." He winked at me.

"Right." I tried to sit up, my head thrummed with pain. Wincing, I put my head back down. "I think I'm a little dehydrated."

Reaching beside me, he lifted a cup. "Here, take a few sips." He lifted my heavy head with one hand and held the cup near my lips.

I took a small sip and realized it was some sort of tea. I wasn't fond of mint, but right now if it got rid of the nasty taste in my mouth, I would drink the whole thing.

Lowering my head back down, he stood up and pulled his shirt over his head.

I glanced everywhere but his body, to try to hide my awkward feelings. There was no one else in the room. "Is everyone all right? Leone's leg?" I tried to remember more. "Was the cut on Quinton poisoned too?"

He picked up one of his switch blades off the table. "Everyone else is fine." He stood there, towering over me giving me a look I couldn't solve. "Quinton's cut healed immediately."

I swallowed nervously, "good." I blew out a breath, silently cursing myself for acting like a schoolgirl that had never been around a man without a shirt before.

Emil smirked and lay down beside me.

That didn't help me feel any more comfortable.

"It's all strange." He said softly, forcing me to angle my head and look right at him.

His face was scant inches from my face. I nodded in a jerky motion. "Yeah."

"I'm sure you'll feel better after this." He lifted the blade, "shall we?"

I appreciated he was trying to keep this clinical, however my heart dancing inside my chest wasn't allowing me to be that cool. In a smooth move, he dragged the blade over his skin and pulled me closer. I didn't pause to regret that he'd marred such a nice chest, I eagerly closed my mouth over the gash and took his blood into my body. As it sealed, I went to lift my head.

"Once more." He said in a gravelly voice.

I had no objections at all. Just the small amount I'd taken had eased the pounding in my head. I licked over the second cut to make sure it left no scar. "Thank you." I said softly, again not sure of what one should do in a situation like this. I looked back up at him. Red eyes met mine. I licked over the fangs in my mouth.

"Feed." He said as his eyes locked on my own.

I didn't hesitate. After blood loss it was hard to control the urge to feed and being up against his naked chest seemed to make it worse. Later when I could control my own body, I'd have to figure out why I'd never had these other urges while feeding, like I did now. It had to be the mate thing. If that was the case, how did mates ever leave one another's side?

Pulling my head back, Emil crushed my mouth with his own. He seemed to be starving in the same ways I was. I used my grip on his hair to pull my body up and closer to his, not wanting him to find a reason to stop.

Struggling to breathe, I looked at him when he ripped his mouth from mine.

"I have to taste you." He growled as his hot breath hit my throat.

I couldn't have uttered a word to save my life, I tipped my head back giving him access. When his fangs pierced the skin, I moaned in a way I'd only ever done when the situation was sexual.

His hot tongue moved over the wound, then he crushed me against his chest and held me there.

I don't know how long we lay there like this. I was in no hurry to move and he seemed to be on the same page as I was.

A knock on the door startled us both to move apart.

"Yes?" Emil's voice was almost deafening after the long silence.

"A heads up, Mr. Hinton is on his way up." Leone called

through the door.

I almost flipped off the other side of the bed, I moved so fast.

Emil got up and held his hand out to tell me to stay put. "Thanks." He said loud enough Leone would hear.

I watched him pull his shirt back on and move to turn the light on. I looked down and checked that I was decent. I had no idea whose shirt I was wearing. "I'm suddenly twelve again and getting caught kissing a boy in the barn." I whispered.

He glanced at me over his shoulder as he went to the door, one eyebrow raised, "we'll discuss this boy in the barn later." He opened the door and left it open.

Leone glanced in a nodded. "Guess we're blood now, huh?"

I remembered he'd had to give me blood. "Thanks for that."

He shrugged, "anytime." He looked toward the stairs. "At least there's no bond that way."

I looked to Emil, and then gave Leone a quick smile. "Yeah."

"Enforcer."

I blew out a quick breath when I heard my fathers' voice.

"I'm sorry for breaking protocol and asking to come..."

"It's understandable." Leone replied and motioned to come in the room

I sat straighter as soon as he walked in. "Dad?"

He assessed me as he walked toward me. "I was with Ellis when he got the call from his brother." He looked at Leone. "I just needed to see, with my own eyes, that she is fine."

I slid to the end of the bed and got up. Touching my shoulder, I looked down to see there was only a slight red mark now.

"May I suggest chain mail be placed in her sleeves?" My dad said to Emil with a smirk.

Emil glanced at me, amusement in his eyes. "It might be a wise idea."

Leone snorted, "you're going to be exhausted if you have

to heal her twice a day." He chuckled, "I know how tiring it is."

I gave him a look that said stop talking, then watched my father raise both eyebrows and look at me. "I'm fine." I said quickly. I turned to Leone, "did my tracker work?"

Leone nodded. "Yeah, we know where it is." He pulled something out of his pocket and held it up, "and this, they're making it there, is the main component for the illegal porters and stabilizers."

A breath of relief whooshed out of my mouth. "Great." I glanced from one man to the other. "When do we go shut it down."

Emil cleared his throat. "Tomorrow." He left no room for comment with that.

Leone nodded, "we have a team watching it now." He motioned to my arm, "they're prepared for us, so we need to come up with a good plan to get in and out without injuries."

"Can't we just take a pill or something that will prevent that poison from working?" I wanted to get back there as soon as possible and find that idiot that had been the cause of my having to drink that stuff.

Emil and Leone exchanged a look.

"That's a good question." Leone pulled out his phone. "Everyone is down in the solarium," he glanced to my father, "go down and grab something to eat." Turning he walked out the door with his phone against his ear.

I felt even more awkward.

"You should eat." Emil said.

"I'll head back to the farm." My father smirked at me, "I think it's best we leave out the details of your day for you mother."

I cringed, "yes. Good idea."

With an abrupt nod to me, he turned and bowed his head to Emil. "I will see myself back to the foyer. Ellis is waiting for me there."

I nodded. "I'll call you later."

"Thank you." He inclined his head to Emil again.

Emil said nothing, just gave him a quick nod as reply.

I didn't move or speak until I could hear his boots on the stairs. "Well." I looked at Emil. "I'm going to…"

Emil moved over to stand in front of me. "If I asked you to sit out when we breach of that building, would you?"

I had to give him points for asking and not trying to make it an order. "No."

His blue eyes searched my face for a moment. "Fair enough, but please stay with your guards."

I gave him a bored look. "I am a guard."

He shook his head as he walked over and picked up his jacket. "Not anymore."

Chapter Thirty

I hadn't realized how hungry I was until I was on my second plate. I blamed that awful antidote. My whole body was running on empty. Between bites, my eyes would meet with Emil's across the room. Each time our gaze connected a heated feeling moved over me as I remembered those moments in his bedroom. His look changed each time, he knew exactly what I was feeling.

I waited until Michael got up to get a drink and leaned closer to Autumn. "Is there a way to control the blood bond?" I whispered.

She snorted, then rolled her eyes. "I can barely do it *now*." She watched her mate stop and talk to Troy. "I think their age makes it easier for them."

I blew out a breath and sat back. "Great." I mumbled.

"I figured you would be able to," she shrugged, "being from here."

I shook my head slowly. "It's not really something we practice."

She nodded and went back to eating.

My brother and I, when we were younger had tried to see what the bond was all about. We'd used blood from each other's hands, and it hadn't been easy to sense anything. I'd talked to my father about it years later. and he said it wasn't something you could just choose to do. It didn't always work between two people. As I got older, I had to wonder if he avoided such a thing with my mother and her raging moods. They were true mates though, so I'm sure he could sense it without any other connection. I blew out a breath and pushed the plate away. I picked up my cup and stared into it. I had to get this under control. I couldn't allow lustful thoughts to fill my head in the middle of a fight.

"Everything all right?"

I looked up to see Michael sit back down. I offered a brief fake smile. "All good." I needed something else to think of. "How is the team doing finding the last location?"

Setting his glass down, he sat back and crossed his arms over his chest. "Nothing yet." He picked up his phone and checked it. "We switch the teams out every four hours so they can rest and warm up again." He lifted his chin to me, "you finding the other location cut hours of search time."

I shrugged, "I'll try to fall through portals more often."

Michael grinned, "hopefully after we find this winter location, there won't *be* any more portals."

Autumn tapped her hand on the table once. "I'm so pumped to end this once and for all."

"We all are." He gave her an affectionate look. Clearing his throat, he glanced over to Emil, then looked back at me. "Things are good?"

I suppose that was his way of asking me how the mating process was going. I gave him a blank look. "I guess." I said slowly.

His eyes lit with amusement. "It's a trying thing."

Autumn laughed out loud. "That's the understatement of the year."

Michael smiled at her, then offered a quick shrug. "It works out in the end."

Rafael stood up, tapping his phone. "They're having trouble getting numbers." He went over and filled his cup with coffee. "We may have to take Reagan over to see if there's other magic or portals in the works."

Quinton heaved a sigh and sat back. "I saw that. Large numbers going in, but no one coming back out."

"So there has to be a portal." Reagan said while watching Quinton's unhappy look change to a scowl.

"Maybe it's a portal to the winter location?" Bethany offered.

Troy turned to look at Victor, "we need confirmation from Romulus, that there's only two locations left."

I glanced at Emil, who was looking at me.

"Is it possible it's a portal that's not on that glass tablet?" Paisley looked from Troy to Victor. "Where no big magic is in play, just a way to transport quickly."

Troy sat back and rubbed his hand down the back of his neck. "It's possible."

Victor stood up. "I will go have Romulus check again." He touched Crissy's shoulder lovingly, then nodded before porting out.

Daxx shoved her plate back. "There goes my appetite." She gave Troy a stern look, "you said two more locations."

Troy exchanged a look with Chase before answering her, "that was our hope."

"Any more possibilities that you pulled out of heads?" Arius put his arm around Paisley as he leaned back in his chair.

Again, I caught myself looking over to Emil. He was paying attention to his brothers, but still turned to look at me at the same moment. We held the look a moment this time.

"Elder Udela and I have another meeting planned to go over things seen and heard." He glanced at his phone, then smirked at Chase.

Chase nodded, "*loving* the brief reports I can check everywhere." He looked over at Emil, "your daughter is brilliant."

A proud expression filled Emil's face. "She's kept the four of us on track for a few hundred years." He nodded slowly, "without technology."

Alona held her phone in both hands. "I'm tickled Daxx and I get the same reports."

Daxx nodded, then gave her mate a sideways glance, "it's nice being in the loop with *everything*."

Troy and Chase exchanged a look. Troy stood up. "I'm going to go meet the elder now at the meeting room." He gave Daxx and amused look, before turning to Chase, "care to join?"

Chase gave him a quick nod. "No. I'm going to have a nap." He yawned, "one of us should be rested. Tomorrow could bring some vigorous action."

Rafael set his cup down. "I'm going to go set up a team to go over with Reagan."

I stood up, "sir…"

He gave me an amused look. "Rafael." He glanced to Emil.

I bobbed my head once. "Right, Rafael, I'd like to go over with the team."

He raised an eyebrow. "Hoping to spot the one responsible for your injury?"

I opened my mouth, then shook my head. "Actually no. I just want to see it from the outside and come up with some breach possibilities."

His expression changed. "Meet me at the yard in five."

I nodded quickly, almost relieved to have something to do.

"Emil." Arius stood up, "I could use a hand in the cells."

Emil dragged his gaze from me to look at his brother. "You want to tag-team inmates again with our likeness?"

Arius grinned, "exactly that."

Leone stood up. "I'm coming to watch. The expression on their faces when the two of you walk in is priceless. They don't know what to do or where to look."

"It's quite funny." Kara got up. "Hearing their thoughts then." She turned to Emil, "they think you can fiddle inside their heads too."

Emil laughed and got up. "As long as it helps them talk, I don't care what they think of me." He started to follow Arius, then paused and looked at me. He didn't say anything, but the look he gave me, paired with the emotions that flooded in told me to be careful.

I nodded slightly, then looked at the floor, so we weren't standing there staring at each other.

"Well," Reagan stood up, "looks can say a lot." She smiled at me.

I shrugged it off.

"I'm surprised they didn't burst into flames a few times." Quinton got up and looked down at Reagan. "Just looking, no touching."

Reagan laughed quietly, "yes, dear. No healing."

Nodding, he leaned down and kissed her. "You will be the death of me."

She patted his chest, "not at all, I'll heal you before you expire."

Shaking his head, he motioned to the door with his chin. "Let's go check on the team coming back from snow country."

Michael nodded. "Then I want to see what Clairee has come up with."

Bethany watched Leone grab a handful of snacks off the table on his way out the door. "Clairee?"

Michael nodded, "Kinsley wondered if there was something we could take that would negate, or slow, the effects of the poison they're putting on their blades."

Everyone remaining turned and looked at me. I really had to stop calling attention to myself.

Autumn smacked me on the shoulder. "Good thought." She looked at Michael, "I am *never* doing that again."

I remembered she'd known about it as she'd prepared me. Not that anything said could prepare a body for *that*.

"I'll go see how she's doing." Bethany said.

Paisley pointed to me. "I'm going with you two." She nodded, "I need to scope out how I can help get us in."

Michael pulled out his phone as he headed to the door. "I'll tell Raf to just send your guards, ladies. We don't need it to look like a convention there."

Chapter Thirty-One

"There's no haze on this side." Reagan whispered.

We moved back toward the overgrown grass, keeping low to go look from another angle.

"I can't believe we don't have to be on coms to do this." Paisley said.

I glanced behind us to the guards. Detrick winked and pointed to his ear. "The guards are dialed in." I said softly.

Paisley and Reagan both turned to look at their guards.

"Captain's orders." Felix said with a serious look.

Paisley nodded and started moving again. "I suppose it makes sense." She paused and looked in the other direction. "In case we run into trouble."

"I'm hoping they think we got away and have no way of finding this spot again." I checked the direction we had already covered, looking for any signs of their people.

"Surveillance team hasn't reported any increase in guards." Reagan said softly.

Paisley nodded, then motioned to me, "we need to get Rena to put Kinsley on the report list."

Reagan nodded. "I already told Quinton to do that." She smiled at me. "She needs to be informed and owing to the fact that she was a guard, she has the experience the rest of us women don't."

I opened my mouth to correct them and say I was *still* a guard but decided in the middle of an open field when we were supposed to scoping out the place wasn't the right moment.

"Let's get behind that tree over there." Paisley pointed.

Gudrun moved alongside me, then passed me and headed to the tree.

I blew out a breath and looked down at the grass around my boots.

"You'll get used to it." Paisley said.

I glanced at her before following Gudrun.

"The constant guarding." Paisley added.

"It's not really necessary." I said and regretted that I sounded petulant.

"From the looks you and Emil were giving each other, I'd say it's very necessary." Reagan said, amused.

Paisley stopped and checked behind us again, "how's that going?" She looked at me, "with Emil?" She clarified.

"There's nothing to really…"

Gudrun crouched down.

I immediately followed, crouching.

He pointed toward the old school.

I raised up to look over the grass toward the building. There were four men standing near a door. Each had a weapon. I blew out a breath when one of them lit a cigarette then offered his pack to the next guy. Not sentries, just taking a break. I held my hand up with my fist clenched to tell the guards around us to hold where we were. I didn't need to look and see if they followed the silent command, we were all trained the same.

Reagan sat right down, crossed her legs and waited, facing the building. I didn't know much about her life before Alterealm, but clearly, she knew when to wait it out. I did know she was over one hundred and fifty years old though, so some quick math told me she'd seen a war or two in her time.

Paisley didn't look toward the building at all, she watched Gudrun to see what he was doing.

The men were still standing outside, chatting quietly. I didn't focus too much on what was being said, their demeanor told me they weren't even slightly worried about the prospect of being watched. I gnawed on my lip and thought about that. We'd checked two directions so far, neither had sentries or were watching for unwanted company. I looked at Reagan. "Can you see all magic?" I whispered under my breath.

She nodded, then tilted her head to ask me why.

No guards, I mouthed then jerked my head toward the building.

She frowned and then nodded, she understood what I was saying. Leaning closer until we were inches apart, she spoke into her shoulder. I was impressed she knew to do that so her voice wouldn't travel. "I'll have to get closer." She said.

I nodded and then turned to see Detrick and Felix were close enough to hear her as well. They both nodded. Looking, I watched two of the men go back inside. Another walked over to corner of the building and relieved himself. With a shrug to the man on the steps, the two of them went back inside.

"You think it's warded somehow?" Reagan asked.

I shrugged, "you'd think after the princess and I landing in there, they would at least have someone keeping watch."

Reagan looked at Derian, "ask Quinton his thoughts."

Derian smirked, probably because she knew who would be on the other end of the call. He backed up a few feet further from us and touched his earpiece.

I didn't pay attention to what he was saying, I was too busy looking around the building, trying to figure out how we could get closer without being seen. If it was warded, how would they be able to come and go from the building without being detected?

"He says we're not to get too close." Derian said.

I bit me lip. "Stay here, I'll be right back."

Gudrun stiffened.

"Relax, I just want to try something." I gave him a hard look and hoped I'd pulled off that commanding expression my superiors used on me.

He motioned to Detrick. "He follows at a distance."

I looked at Detrick, then turned to Paisley. "I want to see if it's an alarm or warning system."

She nodded and looked at Detrick. "Stay here."

With an uneasy expression on his face he nodded.

"Have them tell the watch team to move back further." I told Derian. "In case they check beyond the perimeter."

Derian started talking quietly again into the coms.

I didn't wait to hear what he said. I moved back in the direction we'd come from. At least it the building was only one level, so falling over railings wouldn't be an issue here. Unfortunately, it was a big structure with many doors and a lot of windows to cover at the same time. I was going to go all the way back to the first side we'd checked for portals. If it came down to it and I needed to hightail it out of there, I didn't want to endanger the princesses. I scowled at the ground. I was not a princess. I was not a guard. What the hell was I now?

I spotted the tree we'd stood by and headed for it. I kept watch for something to throw beyond the field to land closer to the building. I found something about thirty seconds later when I stumbled over a stone hidden in the long grass. It was about the size of a baseball and perfect for my test.

I got behind the tree and tried to judge the distance from here to there. I had no idea if I could throw it that far. I looked down at the rock in my hand as if to say, it's up to you. Nodding to myself I stepped out and whipped the stone with all the might I could find. That side of the building lit up as soon as the rock crossed some unseen barrier. I looked to see several large floodlights on the side of the wall.

When the door opened, I ducked back behind the tree. Two men came out it. Guns were in their hands. I snarled in their direction. Cowards used guns. They headed in different directions, looking around the area.

When one pulled out a flashlight and shone it into the field, I leaned behind the tree, watching the light reflect over the grass near me. The light disappeared. Ducking down I looked around the tree.

"Animal?" Another man stood in the doorway looking out at them.

"Probably." The one at the corner of the building said.

"Come on." The guy in the door said as he shrugged out of his jacket. "We only have a day left."

I frowned as they went back inside. A day left for what? Having seen enough, I double-timed it back to the others. My adrenaline was so high when I reached them, I was almost out of breath. I held up my hand as I pulled out my phone. I tapped my call list to call the Captain. Rafael, I thought as I raised it to my ear.

"Kinsley?"

I nodded, "the old school has motion-sensor lights."

"That's an obstacle." He said in a serious tone. "I wonder if it warns them inside too."

"I don't know." The others moved closer so they could hear what I was saying. "The guards have guns as well."

I watched Gudrun's expression darken.

"Shit." Rafael hissed out a breath, "hang on." I heard doors being opened and closed. "You're on speaker." He informed me. "It's Kinsley. The school has motion sensor lights, and the guards have guns."

I didn't wait for anyone else to speak. "One came out and took off his jacket," I cringed, knowing I'd just buried the main fact, "a heavy *winter* jacket." I added speaking each word slowly.

"Do you think there's another portal inside?" That was Michael.

"Not sure, we still have one side left to check." I glanced to Reagan, she nodded.

"Check it and get back here." That was Troy.

"Will do."

"Port to the palace, we'll be in the summit room." Quinton said.

"See you soon." I hung up the phone and tucked it in my pocket.

"Guns?" Paisley blew out a loud breath. "I hate guns."

"Yeah." I turned to Detrick, "we're to check the last side and get to the summit room."

"The man had a winter coat on?" Reagan looked toward the building.

I nodded, "Yeah somewhere in there is a portal to the winter hideout."

She glanced to Felix. "Let's go check that last side." She started moving. "Are they going to figure out what to do with the lights?"

I gave her a quick look. "I hope so."

"That's a good thing—in a way." Paisley said. "They must be running out of mages, it would be warded instead."

I hadn't thought of that. "There's only one mage I want to see."

She snorted softly, "get in line. I've lost count how many times he's tried to kill all of us."

Chapter Thirty-Two

I walked into the summit room, my shadows about a foot behind me. The others were already here. I wasn't taking any chances on needing a delay because I needed to feed, so I popped in for a quick top-up before running to the meeting. As soon as I stepped through the door, Emil zeroed in on me. His look was disturbing. I tried to sense if I could feel his emotions, but not a chance. He was completely closed off. So much for working this bond thing. I quickly glanced around the room when he stopped right in front of me. Something was going on, and no one else paid attention to who was coming and going.

"If you need to feed." He said in no more than a whisper, "come to me." He then spun on his heel and walked away.

My mouth dropped open. He'd known I was feeding? Of course, he'd known. He and I really needed to talk about the mates but not mates thing.

"Where is everyone else?" Paisley asked Arius.

I checked to see the Justice and kings, along with Rafael, were missing.

"Conference call." Arius said and leaned back against the table as he appraised, she was all right.

"With?" Reagan gave Quinton a soft look, then sat down.

"The other realms." Daxx said looking enthused.

"Oh?" Paisley went over and opened the fridge and pulled out a bottle of water.

"We may have help when we find the winter spot." Kara said.

Paisley nodded slowly, "stands to reason that if that is the main hub, there will be people from other realms there."

"Does that mean the other realm," she frowned and looked at Quinton.

"Veiltide." He supplied for her.

"Yes, Veiltide, does that mean they have found people involved from their realm too?" She sat down beside him.

"I don't know if they have, but Willis had them in mind at one point." Daxx crossed her arms and stood there looking at the floor. I wondered if she was tapping into her connection with the king to see if she could get a sense of what was happening.

"I heard it too." Kara said quietly. "When they were asking him about others." She nodded, "he thought about all the realms."

"I can't wait to meet them." Crissy looked excited, "I've read about each one."

"Oh yeah?" Autumn went over and sat on the table edge by where she sat. "What are they like?"

"We'll have to wait for that." Troy came in.

"Or we could just send all the ladies to sit in on a fifth-grade worlds studies class." Chase smirked as he came in the door.

Alona glared at him.

"Or not." Rafael grinned.

"So, are they sending people to help when we find the snow place?" Daxx straightened.

Troy nodded and went right for the coffee pot. "They are."

"We will have an informal meeting with all parties in the morning." Victor went over to Crissy, glanced at what she was doing in her notebook, then stroked her head gently.

"That's cool." Bethany looked at Paisley, "that we get to meet others from so many different realms."

Paisley nodded her agreement.

"They all look normal, right?" Reagan asked.

Chase smirked at her, "you look fairly normal to me, Rapunzel."

Reagan sat there, a look of astonishment on her face.

Everyone did.

Chase frowned, "she had healing hair…"

"To save my sibling from being beaten, I think we should discuss what was discovered about the school." Troy said as he sat down.

Alona looked like she'd rather be sleeping but looked to me and smiled. "I heard your call, guns?"

I nodded. "Yeah. Handguns."

"Great." Daxx looked to Paisley, "can you stop bullets?"

With eyes-wide Paisley looked at her. "I've never tried."

"And aren't going to." Arius said, in a tone that let everyone know *that* conversation was finished.

"I can probably knock a gun from their hand if I'm close enough." Bethany said.

"No dice." Leone shook his head, "bullets move faster than you can see."

"I can knock them out from a distance." Kara said.

"Which only works if all of them aren't carrying guns." Rafael looked at her.

"Are any of your archery students proficient yet?" Victor asked.

Kara thought for a second. "There's two that could probably hit a person." She looked at her mate, "they're pretty big targets."

He gave her a blank look for a second, then held out his phone. "Type their names, I'll have Ira send them to practice."

Nodding, she took the phone and started typing on it.

"Hitting the guards won't get us past the motion sensors." Reagan mentioned, hesitantly.

"Would they sense Rea if she was invisible?" Leone looked to Quinton.

"Even if she could get by, the rest of us can't, so then what genius?" he scoffed.

Leone frowned, "We're just tossing ideas around."

"If the other two archers could deal with those with guns, I could probably hit the lights." Kara said.

"Them shattering may draw attention." Michael said.

Victor studied Kara for a moment, then turned to Michael, "contact Elder Arian and see if her department can make an arrowhead with a charge."

"Like a power surge to blow the lights?" Michael asked him.

Victor nodded, "give her details and let her surmise how best it should be handled."

Michael nodded and got up. He went over by the thrones, his phone against his ear.

Troy looked to Reagan. "Did you detect any portals or magic?"

She nodded, "there's magic near the one door, probably a portal or how else did that man get there wearing a winter jacket?"

"We closed the one from the factory to there." Bethany said.

"So there is another." Daxx said.

"There has to be." Bethany turned to her mate. "If we get inside, we could get to the winter hideout from there."

Leone rubbed his hand over the side of his jaw, "that could drop us into something we're not prepared for." He glanced around at his brothers.

"Has the search team found anything?" I asked.

"Not yet." Emil looked at me. "It's hard for them to clear search grids in the snow."

I nodded. I'd been stationed in the Northern area; snow I knew better than I wanted to.

Rafael stood up and went over to a whiteboard that I hadn't noticed on the wall before. "Okay," he turned and looked at me, "give us an outline."

I'm sure the surprise was on my face for all to see as I looked at the marker in Rafael's hand. I stood slowly, noting that no one was objecting. Okay, I could do this. I went over and took the marker and put it on the board. Pausing, I recalled the shape of the building and made a rough outline of it.

I nodded more to myself than those watching me. "There are trees or something to hide behind in the fields on these two sides." I marked those on the board. "A river over here," I glanced across the room to Tim, "we could use the riverbed to stay out of sight."

Tim nodded.

"While the lights are taken care of." Kara's voice was close behind me.

I turned and saw most of them were standing behind me now. I nodded and turned back. "The lights are," I put an x in two spots, "here and," I marked the other ones I'd noted, "here."

"That's a lot of area to cover." Kara said.

Rafael was standing beside me now looking at the drawing. "We'll hold all action until they're dealt with." He said quietly. "Where are the doors?" He glanced to me.

I turned back and circled the spots on the lines where a door was.

"Lots of exits." Leone said.

"Or entrances" Autumn crossed her arms over her chest.

"Where was the heaviest concentration of haze, Rea?" Quinton moved so she could get closer to the board.

She tapped a spot that marked a door. "This one."

"Okay so it's guarded, no one enters through there." Michael said.

I remembered something and almost blurted it out. How could I forget to mention it? "I overheard the man wearing the winter jacket say they only have one day left."

All eyes were on me now.

"One day for what?" Alona asked quietly.

"I don't know. That's all he said." I gave Rafael an apologetic look, ashamed that I hadn't mentioned it sooner.

"Shit." Troy stood in front of the board. "That changes our timeline." He turned to Victor, "reach out to Elder Marinus and have him push the big meeting back a few hours." He looked back at the board. "The sooner we shut down this site, the better chance we have to interrupt another one of their plans."

Victor nodded and pulled out his phone.

"I think we need to move before daylight." Rafael looked from one king to the next. "It will be easier for Kara to stay out of sight and take out the lights in the dark."

Kara gaped at her mate. "You have more faith in my shooting in the dark then I do."

He gave her an affectionate look. "I *know* you can do it."

Biting her lip, she nodded. "Okay."

Rafael looked at his phone. "The team thinks they've found the last location."

All the men pulled out their phones and looked at it.

"Have them proceed with caution and get us some intel." Troy said.

"Tomorrow is going to be a busy day." Chase mused. He turned to his twin, "three hours enough time to get our ducks in a row?"

Troy looked from Michael to Rafael, "more than enough."

Michael pulled out his phone, "nap, eat, do whatever you need to do and meet at the armory in two hours, people." He walked out of the room.

"I'll be there, Iceman." Autumn called after him with a big smile on her face.

"With bells on." Daxx mumbled as she followed Troy out of the room.

I turned around and looked at the guards standing along the one wall. "Go, take the downtime then be back on time."

There were several nods, as well as smirks. Sith smiled at me and then made a dramatic display of bowing his head to me. I gave him a snarl just before he left the room.

Chapter Thirty-Three

I watched as a few chatted while most were wandering out of the room. What was I going to do with my time?

"I'll show you to your new room." Emil said.

"I have a new room?"

He nodded his head slowly, "yes, Mitz said the room with the daybed was too small."

I frowned, "too small for what? I only sleep in it." I grinned, "and sleeping doesn't seem to happen much around here." I followed him to the stairs.

"I think that's the first thing I'm doing when this is over."

My room was upstairs? "What's that?"

"Sleeping until I can't sleep no more." He said with a smirk.

"I'm used to little sleep." I told him, "guard posts don't allow for much sleep."

"I gathered as much." He looked straight ahead, "the lady's guards keep the same schedule we do." When we reached the top of the stairs, he glanced toward Rena's room, then turned and went down the other hallway. He motioned to the last door. "This is your room."

I opened the door and then paused. Best to go into battle with a clear head, I thought. "Can you come in for a sec, I'd like to talk to you."

Emil raised one eyebrow but followed me in the room.

He flicked on the light and I stopped, frozen on the spot. The room was huge. I looked at the bed. The bed was huge. "This is ah…" I glanced into the bathroom, "a bit much."

"It takes some getting used to." He admitted, "mine is just as big with the balcony as well."

I turned and looked around again, then spotted another door and went to open it, it was a closet. I was just about to say someone else's clothes were in here when I spotted my bags on the floor.

"Everything in there is yours." He stood beside me now.

I walked into the closet; a bit giddy that it was big enough to walk into.

"Ah, your new gear." He motioned to the end of the left side.

I looked over, there had to be ten different jackets and pants hanging there. "I feel guilty that I've gone through quite a few." I gave him a quick look, "there's no chain mail in the sleeves, right?"

He grinned. "Sadly no, Mitz laughed at me when I asked."

I wasn't sure if he was being serious. I cleared my throat, remembering why I'd invited him in. "Yeah, listen, this," I motioned between us, "mate stuff." He just stood there, "I know you don't want it, and I appreciate what you did for me—" I frowned, "twice." He still hadn't moved, was he even listening? "But I can't have distractions when I'm trying to focus…"

Emil finally moved and held up his hand. "I'm not intentionally distracting you."

I needed room to move. I shrugged and walked past him out of the closet. "I know, that's not what I meant." I stopped in the middle of the room, trying not to be distracted when I saw that the furniture in the room all matched. "I'm not saying it's your fault, or that you're purposely doing it…" I turned to find he was standing right behind me. I moved over to look in the bathroom and was momentarily speechless. The décor wasn't fancy, but the tub was the most inviting tub I'd ever seen. I just wanted to tell him to leave so I could fill it to the top and float peacefully. I shook my head. "I know you don't quite understand the way true mates work," I looked to make sure he was not behind me before I turned and stood in the doorway, "not being from here." I shrugged. "But we need to agree that this fight is more important than," I motioned to him then back to myself again, "this draw we're feeling."

He nodded his head slowly and I thought, great that was easy, then his expression changed. "Are you saying that it's easy for full Alterealm people to ignore this *mate* thing? It's something that you can chose to ignore?"

I opened my mouth than closed it for a second. "No. No, it's not really something most would want to do." I felt like my mouth was betraying everything I had just said.

"I see." Again, a slow nod, "I thought it was just me, being weak and not able to control it."

I scoffed at that, "ah, no." I lifted my hand, then lowered it, "I've heard stories of some pretty intense reactions."

"Then you're not asking me to deny that I feel a strong physical attraction to you?"

My heart picked up to that. I had to focus to not look happy at hearing those words. "I think what happened after I drank that awful gunk was a clear enough demonstration that we are physically drawn to one another." The whole time my mouth was moving, I was trying to figure out how I'd lost the point of this talk.

Emil crossed his arms over his chest and nodded once again. "I will admit when you are in the room, I find myself looking at you more than I would others."

What did that mean? Others? I shrugged because I honestly didn't know what to say.

"You seem to look at me as often."

I walked across the room to stand beside a small sofa. I touched it like that had been my purpose all along, to feel the furniture's texture. "Like I said a true mate is a generally hard to ignore."

He followed me and stood behind the sofa. "Right. It is indeed difficult." He cleared his throat, then put his hands into his jacket pockets. "I had been wondering how I was to broach the subject, but as you're clearly fine with talking out the logistics," He pulled out his hand, a silver chain and pendant dangling from it, "this is yours."

I looked at it. It was one of the royal amulets. I blinked and looked at it, then to him. Another blink and my eyes strayed back to the circle with the sun and moon engraved on it. The same sun and moon emblem the entire realm knew to be the royal emblem. I opened my mouth to tell him that was not mine.

"You have to wear it at all times." His eyes connected with mine. "Orders." He added in a softer tone.

"I don't see…"

"If we run across any in battle that know this side, they are to know your status." He walked around the sofa and went behind me. "The meeting tomorrow with the other realms, you need to wear it to be there."

I frowned at the carpet as he placed the cool metal against around my neck. I needed to be part of that meeting. His hand lingered against my neck for a moment longer.

Moving back to stand beside me, he tucked his hands in the pockets of his jeans. "I meant it earlier." He cleared his throat. "When you need to feed." He tilted his head ant looked at me, an uncomfortable expression on his face. "We may not want this, but it *is* there." Emil's iris's flared as he watched me. "I can't change something that has been ingrained since time began, so we are just going to have to find ways to work around it."

We stood there, inches between us, just looking at one another. I felt a calming effect being this close, but it was nowhere near calm inside my mind.

"I will be back in an hour to collect you and head to the armory." He inclined his head. "You'll need to feed before we clear out that school."

I watched him walk out of the room and just stood there. I shook my head slowly and looked down at the floor. That talk had veered so far from what I'd intended, I felt stunned. I stomped into the bathroom then just stopped to stare at my reflection in the mirror, my eyes locked on the pendant that rested against my collarbone. I was wearing a royal amulet. I blew out a breath. I really was mated to a prince.

Chapter Thirty-Four

I kept looking around the building, even though I knew we were well concealed. I glanced behind me to the witch who was keeping us cloaked. I didn't know who had come up with the idea but was glad they had. It allowed us to be much closer to the building.

"I'm staying with Kara. To carry her arrows. There's a lot of them." It was Crissy. "Oh, right, Bronx is staying too. Derian is going to help guard the door." She mumbled something. "The one with the portal."

"Have care, heart." Victor said

"You too, Vic."

"Ward is up." Leone announced. "I wouldn't want to cross it."

I frowned and looked behind us wondering what that meant.

"Do not go outside the perimeter we discussed." Victor told us plainly.

Daxx looked at me and raised her eyebrows but made no comment.

"Light two out of commission." Kara reported.

"Knew you could do it." Paisley said

"It's not easy." Kara sounded like she was running. "I have to hit the metal part with the suction tip and not the light part." She paused. "Then it sends a burst of power through it and fries the wiring."

"Did you bring spare arrows?" Rafael asked.

"Two extra." She said in a whisper.

"You've got this." Bethany said.

"Shh." was the reply.

The line went quiet.

"Third light down." Crissy announced in an excited tone.

"Where do you want me when I'm finished?" Kara asked

"Corner by the first light, there's two exits visible." Rafael answered her.

"Sounds good." She replied.

"Watch out passing by any windows." Alona said. "Every movement is visible out here. They can see you once you're not cloaked."

"Oh yeah?" Quinton asked, "can you see how many are inside?"

"With the binoculars Chase got me I can see the rocks on the moon." Alona told him. "I've seen at least twenty inside. There are others at tables doing something, but I can't make out what."

Someone chuckled. "I wanted you to be able to give the Elders a heads up if anyone got away."

"If the ward works as planned," I recognized Elder Drusla's voice, "it won't be much sport for us while they're laid out on the ground."

"You never know." Troy commented, "there may be some that aren't affected."

"I do not care if they're on the ground or flying, we are ending this." I recognized Elder Sego's voice.

I glanced at Detrick, who shrugged, he had no idea either what the warnings were about.

"Last light down." Emil reported. "Kara and Crissy are at the corner with us."

I frowned and focused on the ground. Just hearing his voice, even as we were walking into battle caused my stomach to tighten. I had to get a handle on this. There was no room to think of anything other than the fight right now.

"Shall we get this going?" Chase asked.

"Time to party." Daxx nodded and started moving toward the building.

"Call out when you're in place." Rafael ordered.

"Fight well brothers," Emil said, "and sisters."

"Always do," Daxx answered for the women.

I turned to see the witch was moving with us as we went.

"I could get used to going in unseen." Reagan said.

"You should stay outside with the witches, Rea, in case we need a medical assist." Quinton said.

"I'm sorry, who are you and what have you done with my mate?" Reagan said sounding amused.

"Just—go with it." Quinton didn't sound amused.

"Oh, I will." She agreed.

"I think he's fond of your hair streaks." Alona said softly.

"I'm fond of her intact and whole. These assholes have guns, so we may need her help." Quinton said gruffly.

"In place." I announced

"Same here." Leone confirmed.

"Ready on this side." Emil said softly.

"We've got the portal side covered." Michael said, almost inaudible. "Five right by the window near the portal."

"We're in place. Babe, you and Beth cover the portal." Arius whispered, "stop anyone from coming or going through it."

"Will do." Paisley answered

"Try not to fall into it." Leone said

"Shush." Bethany whispered.

"On three people." Chase whispered. "One."

I pulled my blade free and moved closer to the door.

"Two."

"Three." Daxx said quickly and burst through the door when Tim pulled it open.

I was right on her heels.

We didn't have to go seeking, there were four men right inside the door. Daxx tackled one, knocking him away from the others. I engaged the next closest and was relieved he was using a blade and not a gun.

"Jackpot." Chase's voice came through the call. "So many naughty slags."

Someone chuckled. "So, you're the one that borrowed my dictionary." Kara said, like we were sitting around a table and not in a fight.

I spun to deflect a swing from the man in front of me and spotted another out of the corner of my eye. Kicking the first one back I saw he was frozen in mid-swing.

"Port him, Daxx." Paisley said.

"One," Daxx growled, "sec."

Bethany knocked back my second opponent with one of her energy balls.

"I've got him." Detrick stepped in front of me. "Get the princesses to that portal."

"It's like they're lining up for recess," Chase said, "so easy to take out."

"Speak for yourself, brother." Rafael grunted.

"Letting one with a pistol go out the door." Victor said calmly.

"We'll get him." Kara said.

"I'll port any that they take down." Michael said hurriedly.

"Another with a gun near the portal." Arius said quickly.

"We'll take him out." I told him. I grabbed a serving tray on my way out of the kitchen. I had no idea what it was made of, or if it would stop a bullet.

We rounded the corner and ran down the empty hall to the door at the side. As we darted through the entrance, I skidded to a stop and sent the tray flying at the only man standing there. It hit him in the head, and he crumpled to the floor. A gun fell from his hand.

"I thought you were going to try to deflect bullets with that." Bethany said with a smirk.

I shrugged, "I'm improvising. We need a port here." I pointed my sword at the man on the floor and watched him.

"On my way." Leone said.

"Portal is guarded." Paisley said.

"Three headed out the front." Troy said in a clipped tone.

"You could let one try the barrier, Kara, I'm curious." Alona said.

"You may get your wish; he ducked my shot." Kara sounded annoyed. "Garrett, he's headed your way."

"I see him." A male voice said.

Leone skidded around the corner and dispatched the unconscious guy to the cells. He straightened and looked at the tray on the floor, then smirked at me. "Ladies." He gave Bethany and Paisley a quick salute and headed down the hall again.

I looked to Paisley, silently asking if they were good. She nodded and went off following Leone.

"He's down." Garrett informed us.

"I feel like I'm doing laps out here." Michael said.

"Good cardio." Autumn retorted without hesitation.

The main area was mayhem. There were a lot more people here than we had anticipated. I quickly noted several were in winter garb. Rafael was trying to beat back two at once, I didn't pause but rushed over to lend him a hand. I blocked the one's swing and dropped down and kicked the side of his knee out. He stumbled back. I used his recovery against him and advanced until he had nowhere to go.

In a move I didn't anticipate, he busted the window with the handle of his blade and rolled through to outside.

"Four got out at the back." Daxx said, annoyed.

"Three at the side." Quinton growled.

I didn't stop to announce another had gotten out, just dove out the window and rolled to my feet. I looked to see which direction he'd gone and followed him. "Chasing one toward barrier." I said quickly. How this man was running that fast after the kick to his knee, I had no idea. Desperation was great for an adrenalin boost.

I was closing the distance between us when he fell to his knees and started throwing up. I stopped abruptly. "I think he just went through the ward." I stared at the man, almost feeling bad for the way he was retching.

"I will come dispatch him." Elder Drusla said in a leisurely tone.

I looked at the man for a moment more. "Yeah, he's not going anywhere."

"Need a hand," that was Kara, "they're coming out like ants in a colony."

I jolted and started running back. I could see there were at least fifteen running in different directions. "Where did they all come from?" I ran faster.

"Basement." Leone huffed.

"There's a basement?" Alona asked.

"Yeah." Rafael growled, "Rea need you down here to look."

"On my way." She said quietly, "I'll be invisible."

I intercepted a man heading back to the building and tackled him to the ground. He landed on his face. I put my knee in the middle of his spine and looked around. "Need a port here when you can." I watched Michael run around the corner.

"Could use a hand here, brother." Michael sounded out of breath.

"Trying." Leone sung back.

"On my way." Victor said.

The guy under my knee tried to get up. I scowled at him and tapped the back of his head with the handle of my sword. "Stay down." I warned him.

"I'm out of knockout tips." Kara said.

"Use anything you have." Rafael said loudly.

"Fine." She answered, "but I'm only taking out legs, not killing."

"Arms, legs, an ass or two, it all works." Chase sounded amused.

Leone came running in my direction. When he was almost to me, I stood up and he dropped down and ported the man to a holding cell. Standing, he turned and surveyed how the others were doing.

"Building is empty." Troy announced.

"Stay at the portal, babe." Arius said quickly.

"We are." Paisley replied.

"There's no haze in the basement." Reagan informed us. "I think they were resting down here."

Leone jogged away in the direction of bodies scattered on the ground. I glanced to where Kara stood and decided they'd been her targets.

"There's sleeping bags stacked in the corner." Reagan said.

"Drop the ward." Victor announced.

I started walking toward the others as they came out of the building.

"Are we closing the portal?" Daxx asked.

"Can we lock it from this side so it can't be used?" Paisley asked.

"Elder Marinus, please bring Romulus to the building." Victor ordered.

"On our way." The elder replied.

"All guards port back and grab some rest. Report to the yard after breakfast." Rafael said.

I paused in step, not sure if I was included in that order or not.

"I'm going to see if Abe has heard from the team." Quinton said. "If they've confirmed the location, we'll need to start programming porters."

I stopped by Daxx. She looked quite pleased with the results. We both turned and watched the Elders, Alona and Romulus come toward the building.

"Everyone else go get some rest. The meeting is after breakfast." Michael said.

I looked at Emil as he came around the corner, assessing quickly that he was uninjured. When I reached his face, I concluded he was doing the same to me. "I'll see you at breakfast." I said and then used my porter to take me to the palace.

Chapter Thirty-Five

When you're running on no sleep for too long, even a three-hour nap could feel like eight I concluded as I went around another corner in the hallway of the underground chambers. I paused again and checked the map on my phone. Despite wanting to be assigned here for years, now after almost getting lost twice, I was very happy I hadn't been.

I peeked in a door to see it was the dining room. Several of the women were already seated at the large table.

"Ah, that feeling of victory when you navigate the hallways successfully." Alona quipped.

I went straight for the coffee urn. Normally I was all about green tea, but today felt like it was going to be a coffee kind of day. "I am thankful for the map." I told them as I poured a cup.

"It was interesting making it." Paisley said with a yawn.

I nodded and sat down a few chairs away from her.

"Seriously, none of the others?" Daxx asked with a confused look on her face.

I watched the women shake their heads, all looking amused.

"I'm sure I would have noticed something like claws." Alona said with a smirk.

"I call Arius beast, but not because of claws." Paisley shrugged.

Daxx sighed, "it only happened that first time, but still..."

Mitz stood in the doorway holding two plates. She stopped and stood there. "Who has claws?"

Everyone looked at Daxx.

"Troy." Daxx said in a quiet voice.

"Oh." Mitz set the plate in front of Crissy then went around the table and put the other in front of Autumn. "I only know of one other that had them." She grinned, "scared my sister so much that first time." She nodded. "Ancient ones say it's the sign of the creator of twins," she paused, "or something like that."

Everyone watched her walk out of the room, then jerked their heads to look at Daxx, openmouthed.

Daxx set her cup down. "That's dumb." She scowled, "what does one have to do with the other?" She stood up, "I'm dealing with this *right* now. Even if I have to have him declawed." She ported out.

"Well then." Alona cleared her throat. "That's..."

"Yeah." Bethany nodded.

I felt like that was a discussion I could have lived without hearing. "Where is everyone?"

"Having a pre-breakfast meeting before *the* meeting." Kara said with a yawn. She motioned around the table, "we were invited but it was too early for me to listen to all of them."

Reagan nodded. "Quinton said it would be the bunch of them all suggesting things that no one else would agree to, but he went anyway."

"Oh. I see." I took a sip of the coffee and regretted my choice immediately. I set the cup down and leaned on the table. "I'm looking forward to meeting people from the other realms."

"I can't wait." Crissy piped up. She nodded and took a bite of her toast.

"I just want to find Arwan and shut him down for good." Autumn looked around the table.

"Amen to that." Alona said softly.

I stood beside the thrones where the women were all standing.

"They're sending their strongest." Crissy said, the excitement on her face quite clear.

"I wonder what that looks like." Bethany mused.

"I'm just glad we don't have to be all dressed up." Daxx nodded, tucking her hands in her back pockets.

"Chase said this wasn't the time for formal showcasing." Alona sat on the platform the thrones were on.

"I just want to get there and get it done." Autumn glanced over at Michael.

"All of the guys have already been there." Paisley said, "so they could port everyone else over."

"I think they just wanted to see it to come up with some sort of plan." Reagan said.

"Leone said it was carved under the snow." Bethany whispered. "I don't know how I feel about being deep under the snow."

"Vic says the people from other realms will help our safety and success." Crissy got up off the floor. "Elders are here." She moved around me and went over toward her mate.

I turned to watch the elders file into the room. They were in their black robes, and all wore somber expressions. I blew out a breath and jerked my chin toward the table. "I'm going to sit. The vibes in here are intense." I hurried over and took the chair where I could see the door clearly.

Emil made fast work of coming over and sitting down beside me. He leaned on the table, so he was close to me. "You haven't fed." He said in a hushed tone.

I shook my head. "Not yet." I held his look, "I'm good so far."

He nodded his head slowly. "You will once this has concluded." He leaned to sit in his chair properly.

I turned my head and spoke into my shoulder, "you know this mate, no mate dance is getting annoying."

Emil turned his head and looked at me, amusement on his face. His eyes flicked to the amulet I was wearing. "I couldn't agree more."

Ira came into the room and nodded to Rafael.

"Everyone ready?" Rafael went over and sat beside Kara.

Troy stood beside where Daxx had sat down. "Elder Landry, if you would." He motioned to the door.

The elder with the gentlest expression of all the elders stood up. "I would be honored, your majesty." He quickly moved over to the door. Ira handed him a piece of paper. The elder looked at it for a moment and nodded.

Ira opened the door.

"Representing Queen Amadine and King Osbert of Solrelm," he inclined his head as two men stepped through the door. "Prince Bastian and Tor Westergaard."

Prince Bastian waved his hand around then they walked to the table and took a seat. Once again, his hair was a mess and he looked very entertained. Tor, his guard had long out-of-date shaggy dark hair and I swear his eyes were black.

"Representing Empress Anata of Aridon," Elder Landry bowed his head again, "Princess Oriana, Prince Elaric with Peyton Sallow and Manton Fernsby."

They looked nothing like I had pictured of people from the realm of heat and fire. Not that I had any reference to back it up, I'd only heard talk of it while growing up. The Princess was tall, that combined with her muscled build was quite intimidating. Her short blonde hair was slicked back, which only made her almost yellow eyes stand out more.

She inclined her head, "Your majesties." Then motioned to the woman beside her and went to her seat.

The woman, I assumed was her guard as she followed and didn't lead, was my height and stocky. Her eyes were turquoise and interesting, but her expression was pure don't mess with me.

Prince Elaric nodded to the kings and made short work of going to sit down. He was as tall as his sister, had the same eyes and blond hair. Only his hair hung down his back in a braid. The prince's guard seemed completely normal. Neat brown hair, brown eyes—that never stopped moving.

"Representing Queen Aurora of FaTerra," The elder bowed, "Princess Aireese, Lady Mystral accompanied by Firo Loughty and Aslac Hatlen."

I'd seen the princess before; she was probably the most gorgeous woman I'd ever seen. Her long, pale, strawberry blonde hair was braided into an intricate pattern on her head. The Lady Mystral was just as lovely, with her midnight dark hair. The guards with them were most definitely the prettiest men I'd ever seen. Firo was so blond his hair looked like it glowed. Aslac wasn't as 'bright' but I'd still say he was too pretty to be a man.

They made quick work of sitting down, then turned to look at the Elder Landry.

"Representing King Erian of Veiltide," He bowed, "Prince Artesiam and Sorcerer Elgar."

A sorcerer? Was that the same as a mage or more powerful? Either way, having him here made me feel a bit better about finding Arwan. The Prince gave the room a quick appraisal.

"Art." He said with a quick nod.

He was tall but not overly muscular. I wouldn't call him out of shape though. His eyes were the truest green I'd ever seen. His shoulder-length, brown wavy hair was mostly pulled into a small bun at the back of his head.

The sorcerer had no features I would call distinguishable. He had dirty blond hair, brown eyes, and carried no visible weapons. His eyes appeared too small for his face were squinting and judging everyone in the room as he took his seat.

Elder Landry went back to his seat.

"Thank you for coming." Troy sat down beside his twin.

"Thank *you* for including us in this." Prince Art said with a smile.

"You found your ancient mage?" Bastian leaned forward.

"We have." Troy glanced to Michael.

"His last hiding place is in the caverns built under the snow." Michael stood up and went over to a large map on the wall I hadn't noticed before. "Here."

"Snow." Bastian shrugged, "I didn't think to look in places like *that*."

"Do we have a layout of these caverns?" Prince Elaric asked.

Michael came over and sat. "We couldn't get inside undetected."

"So, we have no idea what we're walking in on." Princess Oriana stated quietly.

"That is correct." Victor rested his forearms on the table.

"There's not a lot of nature buried under the snow." Lady Mystral murmured.

"Nonsense." Princess Aireese looked at her, "cold air is still air and there will be plenty of it."

"Do we have a rough plan?" Bastian leaned back and crossed his arms. "to avoid tripping over one another in there."

"Yes, I don't think we've ever all worked together before." Michael looked around.

"Not since the games were canceled more than a thousand years ago." Bastian stated.

"Games?" Chase sat up.

Elder Varus nodded, "it was a yearly gathering in your grandfather's time." She smiled, "a fun competition between five of the realms—each team has someone from each realm..."

Elder Udela nodded, "it had to be canceled because Willis Hubert's ancestors presented a threat to royalty."

"I understand you finally have him in custody." Prince Alaric looked at Troy.

"We do." Troy looked to Arius.

"He'll never taste freedom again." Arius gave the other prince a hard look.

"So," Princess Aireese glanced up and down the table of the Alterealm royalty, "it is my understanding that once we get Arwan, this will end."

Victor cleared his throat quietly, "we believe there are factions in each of your realms that have been working with Arwan," he paused and let his words sit for a moment, "once we have Arwan in custody we will strive to assist if you should have need, to find any from your individual realms."

A few of the visitors looked surprised.

"It's true." Princess Aireese nodded, "we have discovered some from FaTerra taking part in this."

"Solrelm too." Bastian sighed, "and from what we've found out all the realms are involved."

"Even the human side?" Prince Artesiam sat forward.

"I don't think there have been any leaders participating," Troy glanced at Chase, "but they've involved so many innocents that it may take a decade to get it entirely resolved."

Lady Mystral clasped her hands in front of her. "My aunt, Queen Aurora told us," she motioned to Princess Aireese, "of your discoveries." Her soft ethereal look changed to a hard one, "we are quite willing to help bring any to justice that took part in these despicable acts."

"We are in agreement there." Princess Oriana inclined her head to the Lady.

"Tor and I can get in and out of that cavern undetected." Prince Bastian shrugged, "unless it's crawling with our own kind, then it will be a messy soul slaughter."

I looked beside me to see Bethany giving me a wide-eyed look. I should have paid more attention when I was in school.

"That will be helpful to know what we're walking into." Prince Elaric nodded.

"We will deal with any magic or castings taking place." Princess Aireese looked to her cousin who nodded. Their two guards also nodded.

"As shall I." Sorcerer Elgar said in a low tone.

"The snow and ice are just hardened water." Prince Art grinned then turned to Prince Elaric, "I'm sure we can use that to our advantage."

"Indeed, we will." Prince Elaric smiled at him.

Prince Bastian looked at me for a long moment, then around the table at the others from our realm. "The slicing and dicing dance we leave up to you." He grinned at Chase.

"Can't wait." Autumn said. "Arwan tried to drown us."

Daxx nodded, "he has some serious payback owed him."

Prince Elaric laughed softly, "this could be fun."

"I have heard whispers that your mates," Princess Oriana looked at Troy, "all possess abilities."

Princess Aireese chuckled softly, "there's so much magic and energy on that side of the table I'm almost inebriated just sitting across from them."

Princess Oriana looked at her for a moment, then smiled at Troy. "Congratulations."

Quinton stood up suddenly. "Are we done with all the talk?"

Daxx got up and nodded her head at him. "Let's say an hour?"

Troy got up and gave her a gentle look. "We have winter gear for everyone." He motioned to Ira, "if you will follow Commander Ira, he will take you to get it."

Chapter Thirty-Six

I'd gone up to my room to regroup as soon as everyone had left the meeting. I just needed to wrap my head around this before it happened. Six realms, combining forces to shut down the atrocity we'd been living for months without pause.

I turned and looked at the winter gear laying on my bed. I nodded, okay, we could do this. *I could* do this. I pulled out my phone and checked the time. I'd put off going to feed until the last possible moment, so the effects would last for however long it took. I was starting to envy the elders that could go a few days between feeds. Then again, I was still comparatively an infant at forty.

A knock on my door had me almost jump out of my skin. "Come in." I called out.

The door opened and Emil walked in. He was carrying a winter jacket similar to the one on my bed.

I motioned to it. "Have you tried it on? Are we going to be restricted?" I'd hated the winter uniform jackets I'd had to wear before.

He lifted his hand and looked at it. "No, it was good when I tried it out." He looked down at his feet. "The heavier boots are a bit awkward though."

I nodded. "But prevent slipping." I paced quickly to the other side of the room. "I have to be honest here, I'm freaking out at the idea of being *under* the snow."

"No, you're not."

I gaped at him with a 'have you seen me' expression.

"You just need to feed." He tossed his jacket on top of mine. "You should know the signs by now, Kinsley, hunger first affects your mind, and it's running in every direction." He tilted his head and smirked, "I spent a year thinking I'd completely snapped before I knew I had to bite people to sustain life."

I hugged my waist and looked at him. "I can't even picture what that must have been like." Of course, I needed to feed. How could I be so stupid?

"Don't," Emil came closer, "try to picture it." He stopped right in front of me, "it wasn't pretty." His eyes held mine prisoner. "Our blood bond has worn off." He said softly.

I bobbed my head, "yeah it's not a long-term thing." The soft tone he was using was soothing.

"I was," he looked at my mouth briefly, "surprised when feelings of melancholy arrived without your presence inside me."

I licked my lips when he glanced at my mouth again. "We can't keep doing this mate, no mate dance, Emil."

"Mmm, so you said earlier." He reached out and brushed my hair back from my face. "I didn't know we were dancing around it."

My brain said back up. My body just stood there. "You don't want a mate, but you restrict me as a mate would."

He looked surprised. "I restrict you?"

"Yes. Ordering me to feed after the meeting."

He smirked, "and yet you haven't."

"Touching me, looking at me in a way a mate does," I uncrossed my arms and grabbed his hand that lingered on my shoulder, "but you don't want a mate."

"I don't expect you to understand it but having lost five..."

I nodded, "I know five wives." Why did that bother me so much? I released his hand and crossed my arms over my chest. "Do you still love them all? Or the last?"

He frowned. "I will always have feelings of fondness toward them..."

"You're not still in love with any of them, drowning in longings for a ghost."

He raised one eyebrow at me, "no, I know the difference between reality and fantasy."

"Okay." I nodded vigorously and backed up a few feet before turning and walking to the other side of the room. "So here's some reality for you," I glanced at the lamp on the table and debated on levitating it into his head, "this," I made a jerky motion from him to myself, "isn't a meet, fall in love and then marry thing." I gave him a hard look, "a true mate is nothing like you've ever dealt with before—or ever will again." I had no idea why I was so angry with him right now. "Having a mate is a connection you will never be able to feel with any other." Or so I was told I added in my mind. "Did your wives know who you really were?" He opened his mouth and I waved a hand, "I don't mean your real name—" I put my hands on my hips, "I mean every nuance that makes you who you are." I glanced at the lamp, then spun away so I couldn't look at it. "That is what a true mate is." Why? Why, was I arguing for mates all of a sudden? Where was that woman who decided that this wasn't what she wanted?

"Kinsley," Emil touched my shoulder making me spin around and face him. His expression showed pain and worry, I didn't know why. "Come here." His voice was low and calming. Putting his hand against the back of my neck, he guided me toward him. I moved like I had no control over my own actions. "Feed." He whispered against my cheek. Leaning down, he tilted his head to the side.

I moved before I realized it. Grabbing a handful of his hair, I moved his head to the side and bit into his neck. His essence was like nothing I'd ever had before. It felt like lightening moving through my body.

Emil uttered a low growl, and I was boosted up against his body. Licking over my bite, I jerked his head so I could attack his mouth. I wanted to climb inside him, consume all that was him. My tongue scraped over his fangs and that ignited a strong need inside me.

I felt my back hit the wall and hadn't realized we were even moving. Emil tore his mouth from mine and grasped the hair on the back of my head. Moving my head to the side, he bit into my neck without warning. I gasped and wrapped my legs around his waist.

This was insane. Completely out of control. I didn't want to stop. I needed... I needed... I didn't know what, but the need was burning through me.

He lifted his head away and his sexy red eyes looked into mine. "This goes way beyond lust." He said in a rasping voice. "I feel like I need to consume you."

I tried to swallow and ended up panting harder. "It's the drive to mark me." I looked at his mouth. "It's got me too."

Lowering his mouth, he dragged his lips over mine. "Is this something we should explore?" He covered my mouth in a heated kiss before I could reply.

I clung to him trying to be closer.

He lifted his mouth away and looked at me again. "With or without marking each other we're finishing this later."

I nodded, not able to find any words.

"If we don't go now—we're going to be late." He kissed my mouth softly.

I blinked. The fight. I'd forgotten we were taking out Arwan today. I slid down his body, a shiver of awareness filling me when I felt how much he wanted me.

"Get your amulet on." He said and released me. He moved and stood on the other side of the room staring at the wall. I watched his shoulders rise and fall as he tried to rein in his breathing. I was lost, there was no way I was walking away from this man, ever. Grabbing the pendant off the dresser, I put it on with shaking hands and turned to get my jacket off the bed. Emil stood there watching me. His expression told he was thinking as I was.

"Let's go get this lunatic." He said softly and put out his hand.

I grabbed my jacket and sword case and took his hand.

Chapter Thirty-Seven

I watched my breath in front of my face. I had hoped it wasn't going to be this cold, but of course it had to be, or Arwan's ice complex wouldn't last. Was the cold natural or had Arwan enhanced it? I turned to see snow, only snow as far as I could see. Natural, I concluded. I looked around to see others were prancing on the spot with their hands jammed into their pockets too.

"Can we hurry up the porting?" Leone's voice came through the earpiece. "I'm shivering so bad now there's two of everyone."

"That can't be all bad." Chase said sounded pleased with it.

"I have enough brothers, I don't need eight more." Leone said bluntly.

"We were waiting on Elgar." Troy said. "He required something."

"An electric heater?" Autumn asked.

I looked over to see she was jumping up and down trying to stay warm.

"I can't believe there's no ward or warning system in place." Clairee said then blew into her hands.

"He probably thought no sane person would think to look here." Reagan said while she bounced on the spot.

246

"Our witches will be staying outside after they get us closer." Bethany nodding to the woman standing beside her.

"Build a fire for warmth." Paisley joked, then nodded.

I turned to look at the four witches around us. They had a bubble or something around us so we could see each other but no one could see us. I didn't understand it, but I was willing to go with anything that got us in there to end this.

Romulus and the sorcerer from Veiltide appeared. Elgar held a long staff in his hand with a white stone on the top.

"Isn't that the staff of light or whatever it was called?" Daxx asked.

Elgar held it up. "It is." He inclined his head to Troy, "thank you for letting me borrow this." He smiled. "I think it screams sweet justice when I use his own weapon against him."

"That staff made my best friend turn evil." Bethany said.

"I assure you, princess, it *cannot* affect me." He smiled again.

A shiver went down my spine and I wasn't sure if it was the temperature or the icy expression in the sorcerer's eyes.

Paisley glanced at me, her expression said she was right there with me.

"Is this thing on?" Bastian's whispered.

"Yes." Victor replied.

"Okay, Tor and I have taken a quick walk about in here." He was talking so quietly I had to focus to hear him over the heavy breathing of people trying to stay warm.

"There's only one way in or out that we can find." Another male said. It had to be Tor.

"When you come in the main area, it branches off in four directions." Bastian reported.

The group started moving down the snow packed incline.

"What are the numbers like in there?" Rafael asked.

"Too many." Tor stated.

I glanced to see Arius and Troy exchange a look. The whole vibe of the group changed in that moment. No one remembered how cold they were, just what they had to do.

For months all of us had been trying to put a stop to the atrocities the mage was responsible for. This was our last chance to stop him. If we didn't get him this time, we were out of options.

"There are many flavors of souls in here." Bastian whispered.

"Some of ours are there?" Princess Aireese asked.

"Yes, some for all." Bastian said.

Princess Arieese and Prince Artesiam glanced at each other. I didn't know much about their realms, but the look did not bode well for their traitors.

"They shall be handled." Prince Elaric said quietly.

"Are you secure until we're inside?" Michael asked.

"For now." He answered. "Okay, quick rundown." He was louder now. "Once you enter there's a huge open area with about…"

"Thirty men hanging around." Tor added.

"Then there's a path to the right, minimal bodies there, nothing of interest in that direction." He supplied.

Rafael pointed to three guards and Leone.

Leone nodded and hugged Beth into his side.

"The path leading straight on seems to be quarters, again not too populated."

I watched as Troy motioned to Emil, Michael and Arius.

"The two paths to the left are a little more complicated." Bastian said in a hushed voice again.

"Complicated how?" Quinton asked.

"It's like there's some sort of sliding ice…" He stopped talking.

We kept moving, no one made a sound.

"Ice wall that I can't see how it works." Bastian finally finished. "We only got in to look because we followed someone else."

"I will look into this ice wall." The sorcerer said quietly.

"What is in the last direction?" Victor asked.

"A big door." Tor supplied.

"Yes, with fifteen men guarding it." Bastian added.

"Arwan has to be there." Troy looked around and then motioned down the middle of us. "This side can deal with the main area." He turned to look at his mate, "the rest of us will handle what's behind the wall and big door."

"Are you ready to enter?" Bastian asked.

I glanced to see the entrance was well hidden between snow-covered trees.

"In less than a minute." Chase informed him.

"On my word." Bastian said. "We'll create a distraction so all of you can get in."

I pulled the blade from my back and looked at my gloves. They stayed until I was ready to step through the door. I twisted my gloved hands over the handle, hoping to warm it before I had to put skin on it.

"Take no chances, ladies." Emil said while looking directly at me.

"Female warriors should be revered." Prince Elaric said softly.

Princess Oriana grinned, "that's not what you say when I best you, brother."

"Everyone be careful." Alona said.

"We're coming in, Bastian." Quinton said.

"Thirty seconds." Bastian whispered. "Tor is going to push over their supply cache."

Cursing under my breath, I pulled off my gloves and stuffed them into my pocket. I rolled my shoulders and unzipped my jacket. Now was not the time to discover a wardrobe restriction.

We filed into the cavern within a few seconds, then spread out so all of us had room to move freely. The men were scrambling to pick up crates and boxes that were spread out all over the floor. I paused for a second to look around. If I wasn't here to fight, I'd be in awe. It was like a giant ice sculpture inside. Glossy ice walls. I slid my boot and looked at the floor, it appeared to be ice, but wasn't slippery at all. There were tables and normal fixtures throughout. It had to have taken Arwan decades to make this. My appreciation of the frosty work of art ended when the men that had been trying to figure out how their supplies fell over noticed us.

Leone and the guards broke off and ran down a tunnel to the right.

Several moved forward to take on the men. I followed them. I wasn't going to leave them if they needed the help.

I engaged the first man I came to and leveled him before he could get in the first swing. Victor was right beside me before he could recover and dispatched him to our cells. With an abrupt nod to me he motioned for me to follow the others that were heading left.

I glanced to see Princess Oriana standing there with a smile on her face. She pulled a long narrow katana from the case at her side, it looked like it was glowing. Her brothers looked to be the same, only larger.

"Shall we?" She grinned at him.

"Let's." He advanced on the men scattering out to cover the hollowed-out area. Their guards were right there with them.

Autumn nudged me when I came up beside her. I was surprised she wasn't in the fray. "They've got this."

I nodded and walked beside her as we went.

"Can you remove it?" Prince Art asked his sorcerer.

Elgar nodded slowly, "I can take down the magic making it work, but I can't remove the ice."

The Prince backed up and motioned to the tall sheet of ice. His sorcerer closed his eyes for a moment. When he opened them, he began moving the staff in a slow wide circle. The stone on the top started glowing, emitting the brightest light I'd ever seen.

Turning my head to the side, I squinted to block out the brightness, but still wanted to watch what he was doing.

"We'll be there in a moment to clear the ice." Princess Oriana said.

"Barracks are cleared." Michael informed everyone.

"Come to us." Troy said in a tone that was a direct order.

Bastian and his guard appeared out of nowhere in front of us. He put his hands on his hips and watched the sorcerer.

The princess of Aridon came running down the tunnel, her female guard right behind her. She stopped and looked at the large wall. Stepping over, she held her hand against it. It began to melt under her touch. "We can take it down." She looked at Peyton, who nodded.

"I have no doubt you can, but we'll drown." Bastian said.

"I can move the water." Prince Art looked to Elgar who nodded.

"We'll take it after that." Princess Aireese said.

"Yes." Mystral agreed.

Troy stepped back. "Just get us in there."

"Just don't melt *all* the ice in here." Chase said.

"Don't worry, King Chase." Firo said, "water is air, air is water."

I chanced a look at Bethany, she was nodding, when I looked at Daxx she made a strange face. I'd have to think more about that later.

"Be at the ready, this is going to go fast." Princess Oriana said as her brother and his guard came toward us.

If I hadn't been standing and watching with my own eyes, I would have thought this was some fantastic dream. The Aridon's used their touch to make the ice wall into streaming trails of water. Before it could pool on the ground, the Veiltide males had it swirling up into the air. After that I don't know what our FaTerra guests did but it was water one second and not there the next. The only thing that did register was the temperature became more tolerable. I flipped the strap over my head and shrugged out of my jacket. By the time I had my weapons case back in place several of the Alterealm family had done the same.

As soon as there was enough of the wall gone, the Alterealm guards were through into the outer hall that held a large room and a big door. Men started pouring out of the room into the small space.

It was hard to fight and be sure you weren't going to hit someone on your own team. A sword swung past my head, I ducked down to make sure it didn't come back on the same path and decapitate me.

Princess Oriana caught the blade on its next path. With her hand. The metal changed to the fiery orange of molten metal. The holder of said weapon yelped and released it. With a satisfied look, the princess used the butt of her own weapon against the man's head and he crumpled to the ground.

Autumn went past me in a hurry, I didn't hesitate to follow her.

The men guarding the door were engaged by Daxx and the kings. I ran faster and placed myself in front of a swing that would have caught Daxx in the hip. She growled in annoyance then ported a man in front of her, then spun on the attacker. He took a wide swing and she dropped down and held the box out. He disappeared.

Princess Aireese touched my arm. "Go, find that mage, we have it under control out here."

I nodded and looked to Daxx. Her look screamed retribution as she turned and headed for the large wooden door at the end of the hallway. I turned to see the men from our realm were engaging a steady stream of combatants and realized it was up to the women to get us in the room and find Arwan.

Bethany stepped forward and put her hand on the door. She closed her eyes and inhaled slowly. Nodding she opened her eyes. "Stand back." She said quietly as she raised her outstretched arms gradually.

"Princess," Aireese's whisper came through the earbud, "use your fear, your anger. Hold everything he's done to wrong you in your mind…"

Bethany nodded her head slowly but made no reply. The arc between her hands grew and multiplied until it was too bright to look at. When she flung her hands toward the door, the sound of wood shattering echoed through our mics.

"Fabulous." Princess Aireese exclaimed. "We'll cover out here. Go."

At her urgent order we rushed through the door. The room was about the size of the royal's personal gym and objects were moving through the air in all directions. It was a gauntlet.

The door repaired itself and slammed back in place with a loud crash.

"Arwan, looking a bit tired there." Reagan said quietly.

I spun around to see a man standing on the other side of the room, with his hands in the air.

"Can't get a clear shot at him with all this stuff flying around." Paisley said.

"Beloved," Chase's tone was pleading, "protect our child." He said urgently.

Everyone looked at Alona, she had her hand over her stomach.

I turned and stared at a long table against the wall. With a flick of my hand I sent the chairs around it scattering in all directions. Squinting I focused on the table and lifted it in the air. I brought it over and set it in front of Alona, tipped on its side. "Work on getting that door open." I said. Crissy nodded and got behind the table with Alona.

"She's safe." I said into the mic.

Kara stepped to stand beside the table, her bow at the ready and pointing at the old man on the other side of the room.

The man took a few steps forward, his arms still raised in the air. "Ah, it's the lost woman." He was looking at Reagan. "You had me fooled, princess, I had no idea who you were." He inclined his head to her. When he lifted it, the objects in the air began swirling faster.

I watched the objects, none of them were harmless if they were to hit or drop on us. I bit my lip and looked around the room. I couldn't hold anything long enough to cover all of us.

"Distract his gaze, stop him looking at me." Reagan whispered into the mic.

"Take this." Daxx said quietly.

I turned to see Alona and Crissy prying the door with knives, trying to free it. We just needed to stall long enough to get one of those strong magic folks in here.

"Try to get the door open from out there." Alona said.

"We are trying." Chase sounded anxious.

I watched the items swirling in front of me and stepped forward when it was safe to do so. A book stopped a breath away from my face, then orange light deflected it in the other direction. Paisley and Bethany had my back. "Arwan it's over." I said loud enough I was sure he'd hear. "Your icy masterpiece is currently being thawed by the Aridons." I took another step, ducking when a bottle got too close. "The strongest fae from FaTerra are out there unraveling any magic you've used."

The man looked at me, his hands pausing for a moment.

The objects slowed when he did.

"They're here? The realms are all together?" He sounded doubtful.

"Keep distracting him." Reagan said in a low whisper.

"They are." I took a few more steps while the motion was slowed around me. "All six realms are here today. It's over."

He laughed. "You will never find all I have done."

"All of your generals are locked up." I moved forward.

He shook his head. "All they had to do was take out one of the mates..." he scowled and whipped his hands in a circle. The speed of the objects returned. "Just one and they failed."

"They tried hard, jerk, that's got to count for something." Daxx was beside me.

A blast of orange light exploded in my face and several of the objects hit the floor, clearing the path.

"You can't keep up your magic much longer, Arwan," that was Bethany, "you have no sources to draw from now."

"Do not use your port box, Huntress, only mine is set for him." Victor's steady words filled our ears.

"Almost." I thought I heard Reagan say.

I sheathed my weapon and decided I needed my hands free for this. I didn't know where Reagan was and didn't want to chance hitting her, but I couldn't just stand here and try to talk this evil being down. I focused on the first thing my eyes connected with and stopped it, then flung it to the floor.

Another blast of light energy cleared a few more feet.

A knife stopped an inch from my face, I froze on the spot. Then I reached out and grabbed it. I'd have to fall at Paisley's feet later and thank her.

"You can't stop me." Arwan snarled.

Reagan appeared out of nowhere behind him. She held the curved blade the Huntress used against his throat. "Wanna bet?" Reagan's expression was cold. "Hands by your side asshole or I'll skin you like a rabbit."

"Don't do anything you'll regret." Quinton said in an urgent tone.

"No regrets." Reagan growled out.

"W-what are you?" Arwan stammered. He moved his hands down and the echo of things hitting the floor echoed around us.

"Move back from the door. We're going to scorch the wood." Prince Elaric said.

"I can use heat to cauterize the bleeding."

Princess Oriana's words made all of us pause for a moment. Then the line went silent. They'd just muted what was happening outside this room.

Bethany went closer to Arwan, energy arcing between her hands. "Don't even breathe." She hissed.

I pulled my blade free and went to stand in front of him.

"Bind his hands, he's working on a spell." Kara shouted into the mic.

Nodding, I pulled the strap for my weapon over my head and held it out to Daxx as she came over. She took it and went over to him. Grabbing his arm, she jerked it behind him and the other arm followed. I don't know how she managed to tie the leather, but Arwan now stood there with his arms behind his back.

"Let's see you fling stuff at us now." Daxx muttered.

The sound of crackling filled our earbuds, I turned to see the wooden door was engulfed in flames. Steam began rising from it and then the door slid across the floor. Elgar stepped into the room and assessed the situation.

Right behind him Chase and Troy came in.

The scariest sight I'd ever seen was when Victor stepped through the doorway. His long strides brought him toward us. The expression on his face screamed vengeance.

"We need him alive, brother." Chase said as he enclosed Alona in his arms.

"He will live." Victor said as he stopped in front of Arwan, "for now." He did something with his port box, then held it in front of him.

The mage that had wreaked havoc on our lives and hundreds of others, disappeared.

I lowered my blade and breathed out a loud sigh of relief.

"Vic. Somethings wrong with my head." Crissy sounded upset. "They're gone." She said quietly.

Victor spun around and moved in her direction.

"Rea," Quinton's voice sounded strained, "we need you out here."

Reagan didn't pause, she just ran past the others and out the door.

I looked at Bethany, she frowned.

"Leone, what's happening?"

There was no reply. She darted for the door. I looked around and noticed only a few of the brothers were here. I ran for the door, followed closely by Paisley.

A few feet down the narrow hall lie Leone. Quinton and Reagan were beside him. The prince from Aridon and Lady from FaTerra all leaning over him. I looked around. Where were the others?

Paisley grabbed my arm and squeezed it. She didn't need to say anything for me to run after her into the first area we'd come into.

Arius, Rafael and Princess Oriana were leaning over someone. I rushed over and saw Emil's blade on the floor.

"We can't port him in this state." Arius said while looking at me. "Michael went for the doc."

I dropped the blade and slid across the cool surface. The Princess moved out of the way so I could get close to him.

Rafael was kneeling there, talking close to his ear. "You need to feed, brother. Fight through the fog and feed." The urgency in his tone scared me, I'd never heard the captain speak like that before.

I lay down beside him, trying to see where he was injured. His whole chest was soaked in blood. "Emil," I said softly with my cheek resting against his, "listen to my voice." I swallowed the lump in my throat. "You have to feed." Lifting my head, I stared at his eyes hoping to see some sort of response. His breathing was so shallow. His eyelids fluttered and barely opened, but when they did; he looked right at me. He was still in there I almost cried. I nodded and lifted my upper body up. "You have to feed." I said again. I felt a hand on my shoulder helping to hold my weight off him. I moved my hair away from my neck and leaned over his mouth. "Listen you obstinate man, feed. Now." I tried to keep my voice steady but failed.

I could feel his breath on my skin, it was so faint I looked at Arius, my eyes watering.

"Come on brother." Arius growled.

His mouth brushed against my neck; I held my breath. When he bit into me it wasn't very forceful, so I leaned into his mouth. I could feel his mouth moving in a feather-light movements and knew he was trying. I clenched my teeth against the pain, he wasn't coherent enough to use eufori to dull it. "He's trying." I whispered.

"That's it, brother." Rafael said in a calmer voice.

I could feel the draw and didn't say anything when I knew it was past the point I should let someone feed from me. Emil reached up and held my head in place.

"That should be enough to help." Arius said.

"Emil, you have to stop now." Rafael was right next to my face.

"Let him." I said in a voice that didn't sound like my own. I rested my hand against his head and closed my eyes.

"Emil, brother, you *have* to stop." That was Troy. I didn't know when he got here, but he was now.

"Get her." I heard Michael say. I felt hands on my shoulders and didn't have the strength to resist. Someone was moving me away from him. I should fight, I thought but couldn't hold the focus long enough to do it.

"Kinsley." It was Emil. He was all right.

I blew out a breath and closed my eyes, relief filling me.

Chapter Thirty-Eight

I opened my eyes and looked around. I had no idea where I was. Blowing out a breath I tried again and realized it was my new room in the palace. In no hurry to move I closed them again then tried to process the last thing I remembered. My eyes popped open. Arwan and the ice cavern. Emil.

I lifted my head.

Bethany was standing beside the bed.

"Hey, take it slow." Paisley sat on the edge of the bed.

"I'll go get Emil." Bethany disappeared from my sight.

"How's Emil? Leone?" My voice throat was so dry I could barely form the words.

"They're okay." Paisley said.

I dropped my head back to the pillow then went to brush the hair back from my face when I noticed I had a needle sticking out of my arm. I frowned. "Was I hurt?"

"No, not that way."

I looked at her again.

"We couldn't get Emil to release you." She said quietly.

"He needed it." I said trying to clear my throat so I could talk.

"You did it purposely?"

I looked to see Emil standing in the doorway. His expression was not at all happy, but he was alive and standing there, so I felt better. "Your injury was serious enough that they couldn't port you." I said softly.

Paisley stood up as he came toward the bed. "I'll go get you something from the kitchen." She said and left the room in a hurry.

"I thought I'd almost killed you." Emil stood looking down at me. "Have been tormented by the horror of doing so."

"I'm fine…"

"It's been two days." He enunciated in a clipped way.

"We're trained to give our life for…"

"Don't." He barked. "You've been lying here, comatose, for *two days*. We couldn't even rouse you enough to give you blood." Red eyes glared at me.

"Emil. I'm fine." I blew out a breath, "a little light-headed and groggy, but I'm fine."

"Emil, perhaps…"

Emil spun to look at Chase. "Out." He said as he stomped over and grabbed the door.

Chase looked to me than bowed in a dramatic gesture, "as you wish." He moved out of the way just before Emil slammed the door in his face.

Emil stomped in my direction, pulling his shirt off as he went. "I'm giving you blood." He said as he reached down and pulled a blade out of his boot.

"I think…"

"Don't," he waved the hand holding the knife around, "think." He glared. "Because the only thought in your head seems to be I must sacrifice *myself* for the good of the royals," he knelt of the bed, his arm still going, "for the good of the realm—for the good of the people." He pointed the knife at me, "that nonsense stops now."

I looked at his serious expression and then to the knife tip. "Prince, lower your weapon before I stab you with it." I said in an even tone. I couldn't have if I wanted to, but he seemed almost incoherent in his agitation. He looked at the blade, then lowered it. "Emil…"

Reaching, he placed a finger over my mouth in a gentle touch. "Shh, just let me do this." He nodded slowly, "I think I need to almost as much as you need it." His look pleaded with me. "Your mother is downstairs. The women have been trying to distract her for two days, Kinsley, I can't even describe what that's been like."

I scrunched up my face and looked up at him. "She's here?"

He nodded as he moved to lay down beside me.

"Oh my god, I'm going to have to apologize to everyone." I put my hand over my eyes. "I'm not in a frilly dress am I?" I was afraid to open my eyes and look.

He chuckled, "No, we managed to keep her out of the way while Alona and Mitz changed you."

"Thank the gods for that." I whispered. I opened my eyes and looked at him.

"Your mother is," his eyes rolled as he searched for the word, "exasperating at times."

I snorted, "you have no idea." I whispered.

"Mitz has her helping in the kitchen right now." He said with a smirk.

"Poor Mitz."

He grinned, "don't worry about Mitz, she has her in hand." He cleared his throat, "now, let me give you some blood so your recovery moves along."

I nodded as best I could while laying down. "Yes. We need to get my mother out of here." I glanced at his chest as he held the blade near it. There was a faint red mark on the right side. The mark was too wide to have been made with a sword. I reached out and touched it. "What did it?" I whispered.

"Axe." He said looking down at my hand.

With my eyes wide I met his look. "An axe? You took an axe to the chest?"

He nodded slowly. "Yes. I can honestly say I will never forget looking down and seeing it sticking out of me."

I closed my eyes, my heart pounding too fast to speak.

"Hey," he touched my face, "It's fine now. The mark will always be there because the Aridon princess used heat to seal it to save me bleeding out, but I'm fine."

I nodded. "But it's really over, we got him."

Emil smiled, "we did." He tilted his head, "there's a lot to clean up and the other realms are going to need a hand tracking down any of theirs involved, but all the realms are currently safe from the plan Arwan set in motion."

I blew out a long breath. "Okay, let's do this, we have work to do."

He chuckled but said nothing more.

I watched as he cut into his own chest and then assisted me in lifting my head to take his blood into my mouth. Before I licked to clean up any trace of blood on his chest, I could feel the difference. Magic blood indeed, I thought.

"Now feed." He said softly.

I almost attacked his neck. I hadn't fed in two days, how was I even still here? I thought as I took his essence into my body. Licking over it I rested my head against his shoulder.

"Now we can remove that needle." He lifted his head and reached over and pulled it from my arm. Lifting it to his mouth, he licked over the puncture from the needles. He stroked his hand down my arm then took my hand in his. "I don't know how my brothers withstood this." He leaned back, a pained look on his face, "watching their mates in battle and being put in so many life-threatening situations. I've been a raving lunatic for the past two days." He kissed my hand, "I was banished to my room." He frowned, "Banished." Taking a deep breath, he blew it out, "my room is in a great state of disrepair at the moment as a result of my banishment."

I grinned. It wasn't funny what he'd gone through, but his reaction was.

He gave me a playful hard look, then smirked. "Now," he sobered, "just one more thing and my heart may finally beat normally again." He squeezed my hand in his and looked at me.

I was about to ask what when he lowered his mouth to mine and kissed me with feather-light touches. He kissed along my lips, then trailed down my jaw. When he nuzzled my neck, I didn't even have to think to give him access.

When he bit into me, I hissed out a breath. Feeding has always been so detached for me, but with him it became something erotic, something I craved. He lifted his mouth away and hovered over my neck for a moment, his breath teasing against my skin. When he suckled the wound gently, a shiver went through my whole body.

Licking it, he lifted his head and attacked my mouth. With the arm that wasn't crushed between us, I grabbed the back of his head and held it so he couldn't pull away again. I craved his kisses more than anything I'd ever thought possible. He broke the kiss for a second and I tugged his hair so I could reach his mouth.

Emil had no problem complying with my silent demand and covered my mouth with his again. If my whole body felt like it was on fire just from kissing, I couldn't even grasp what more was going to feel like.

I turned into him and tried to get closer, he wrapped his arm around me tightly, letting me know he wasn't going to let me go. When he tore his mouth from mine, he continued to kiss my face, my neck and any other part of me he could reach in this position.

Lifting his head, his red lust filled eyes looked down at me. "I had no idea what I was doing." He said breathlessly.

I grinned and licked over my lip, I tasted blood from a nick one of our fangs had made. "I wouldn't say that."

He looked at me still, then squeezed the hand that was trapped between us. He looked tentative and wary.

I felt my fangs recede and pulled my arm out of his grasp. I'm sure my eyes have never been as wide as they were now, looking at the intricate design that weaved over the whole length of my arm. "Did you just..." I looked at it again.

"I did." He said in a confident tone. "And I'd do it again and tomorrow if that were a possibility."

I held my arm in the air, stupefied to see the mate's tattoo on it. "I..." Having no idea what to say. I shifted and looked at him. His blue eyes were watching me, a guarded look on his face. "I thought you wanted no part of this."

He nodded his head slowly, "As did I." He cleared his throat and propped himself up on his elbow, then took my hand in his. Our tattoos looked like an extended tattoo when our arms were this close. "Then I got to think about that for two days." His eyes flicked to my face, "I don't believe I've even slept." He tilted his head, then sighed, "the thought of being mated, I believed I'd already had my fill of in this life," he nodded, "but the thought of losing you made me feel things I've never felt—even in the grief when I lost my wives." His brow creased as he paused, "I thought a mate was no different than a spouse, but I have never been so wrong about anything in my life." Emil looked at our arms then continued speaking, "mourning a lost wife was, I thought, the hardest thing I would have to endure," his eyes flicked to my face, "thinking I'd lost you was worse. It was as if everything inside me stopped, the only emotion I could feel was rage," he leaned down and kissed me softly, "a mate is nothing like a spouse, a mate is a part of you that lies dormant," a pained look filled his face, "until I met you I thought I'd lived a full life." He shook his head slowly, "it seems I was just going through the motions until now."

Squeezing his hand, I lifted both of our arms and looked at them. "I didn't know we could," I felt my cheeks heat, "that one could be marked without..."

He leaned over and kissed me hard on the mouth. "Oh, there will be *that*, but I couldn't take a chance you'd say no." He rested his lips on mine as he spoke.

I grinned against his mouth. "I wouldn't have said no. I just didn't want it at first."

Moving his face away from mine, he gave me a curious look, "but then you changed your mind?"

"More like I knew I couldn't outrun it even if I tried."

He pouted, "that's not an encouraging answer." He scowled at me, "I've been losing my mind for two days and you just don't want to *outrun* it?"

I laughed.

A loud knock on the door had us both sit up and stare at the door.

"What?" Emil barked.

The door open and Chase leaned around it and looked at us. "Ah, good. All is well." He winked at me, "had us worried." He gave me a hard look. "Don't do that again." Chase looked back as his brother. "Dinner will be served in ten minutes."

Emil sighed, "I'll grab a plate..."

"No. No plate. You're both coming down for dinner." He nodded. "That's an order." He looked right at me, "your mother will be there."

I wiped my hand down my face. "My mother." I kicked the covers off my legs and paused to make sure I had something on. Relief went through me to see I had pajamas on, "we have to get rid of my mother, Emil."

"Now you have it." Chase grinned, "see you down there, princess." He closed the door.

I stood up and then looked at Emil. "I'm a princess." I felt like someone had just hit me with something.

"Yes, you are." He grinned, then motioned to the closet. "Get dressed." He pulled out his phone and looked at it. "I say we eat, talk a bit and still be back up here in thirty minutes, forty tops." With a smile, he came toward me and grabbed me around the waist and kissed me. "Then I'm declaring to all we are not to be disturbed, for the honeymoon period."

I felt my face get hot. "The honeymoon period?"

"Yes." He kissed me again, then stepped back. "I'll be back in five. Be ready." He ported out.

I stood there staring where he had been. Lifting my arm, I looked at it, a feeling of warmth and contentment moved through me. I was a princess. I laughed for a second, a princess of Alterealm. I shrugged; I could do that. My stomach rumbled, hunger hitting me. "Dinner, here I come." I remembered my mother and jolted for the closet. We had to get her out of here.

Chapter Thirty-Nine

I took another bite and looked down the table at my parents. Dad seemed to be taking it all in, then again, he wasn't a verbal thinker. I glanced at my mother; she was in her glory. I looked at my plate, there had to be a way to limit her visits, right?

Emil reached under the table and squeezed my knee.

I looked at him, and he gave me an understanding look. He could feel everything I did, and knew how much I needed to get my mom out of here. Taking another bite, I looked around the table.

"...but they're back." Crissy nodded, "and all different." She said, nodding again.

"I still can't believe they stopped completely for almost a day." Daxx said waving her fork toward her.

Crissy nodded, "I slept so hard."

Victor grinned, "I found myself checking her pulse too often." He glanced at Daxx, "I have never witnessed her sleep that deeply."

"I feel like I could run to the moon now." Crissy sounded excited.

"Please don't." Paisley said, "we'd have to follow." She leaned into Arius' shoulder, "actually, sleep felt amazing."

"Didn't it." Alona leaned back I her chair, "I don't think I've slept like that in years."

"Could be the pregnancy making you tired." Autumn nodded and pointed her fork at her, "Rena had that at the start too."

"Yes," Alona smiled, a soft light in her eyes, "growing a baby is tiring I've discovered."

"Congratulations." I said, then shrugged, "I'm a bit late but was—busy." I smiled.

"Thank you." Alona touched her stomach. "This app I have says it's the size of an apple right now."

"I may never eat an apple again." Daxx mumbled. "You're sure there's only one?"

Troy smirked at Daxx, then turned to see Alona nod slowly.

"So, Emil said there's cleanup to do?" I glanced at my mother, then to Rafael, he shrugged.

"We still have to keep an eye out for stragglers over here." Leone said.

A woman came in and began removing some of the trays and plates.

"Oh, let me help." My mother stood up and picked up her plate.

"Mrs. Hinton, you don't need to." Troy said.

"Nonsense, I had a wonderful time with Mitzie earlier." She waved her hand in the air, "I'll leave you to discuss important royal business with my daughter, the princess." She turned and went out the door.

I dropped my head down until it almost rested on my chest. "I am *so* sorry." I looked up and down the table to my dad.

He was smiling. "She'll be happy at home for a year after this." He rolled his eyes. Standing up, he came around the table and leaned down and kissed the top of my head. "I'll go try to get her out of here—now that she's seen you are perfectly fine."

I patted his hand. "Thanks, Dad."

"Anytime, princess." He said with a chuckle.

I watched my dad walk out.

"You definitely take after your dad." Bethany said.

I nodded. "Yes."

"Thank the gods for that." Chase said.

Troy nodded too. "Your mother," he glanced to the door, "is exhausting." He whispered.

I know, I mouthed.

"So," Chase looked at every one sitting at the table, "the brothers nine are all finally mated." He looked quite pleased.

"Just tell me we get to have a long vacation now." Leone said as he pushed his plate away.

"We could…" Chase frowned and pulled out his phone, he glanced at the screen, then tapped it and set it on the table. "Bastian?"

"Yes. Where is the little seer? Is she there?"

Crissy leaned on the table. "I'm here." She said loudly.

"The woman—the one with the bus, what did she look like?" There was a lot of noise in the background.

"I," Crissy stared at the phone, "I didn't really see her."

"I think I've found her." He mumbled something, "Kings, I may need that favor soon." There was the sound of sirens in the background. "Someplace secure in your realm. It can't be here, and it will have to be guarded." Bastian sounded like he was running. "Damn, why didn't I see this?" There was a loud siren blaring, "…the easiest way to take down the leadership of my realm…" the noise was too loud to hear what he said, "…take out the soul I can't live without, the one that I live for." The background noise stopped suddenly. "I'll call you later." The line went quiet.

Chase turned and looked at Crissy.

Crissy shook her head. "I don't know." She glanced at Victor, "I didn't see any more than that."

He reached out and touched her hand, then looked at Michael. "We better prepare a secure location for him."

Michael nodded and pulled out his phone.

"That answers the time-off question." Leone sighed.

"Oh, this isn't over for us yet, brother." Quinton motioned toward him with his glass. "Not anywhere close to over."

Epilogue

Sometime in the future...

She stood beside the love of her life as they looked down over the balcony of the palace.

"I'm tired, Ira, bone weary tired."

"You have every right to be, Mitz, my love, living as two for so long."

Smiling up at him, she nodded. "I kept my bond with my sister as long as I could. It feels void without her now."

"Queen Viola would have been so proud of you." He hugged her closer to him. "I'm proud of you." He looked back down at the children he'd watched rule and their children that someday would.

"She better be pleased. I would never suggest binding two souls the way we did—but knowing she got to see her children achieve all they have and knowing their lives were complete and happy made it all worth it." She smiled as she watched Rafael chase some of the children, to their utter delight.

"Are you ever going to tell them that you've been both their mother and aunt for centuries?" He gave her that look he always used when he was trying to influence her decisions.

271

Turning she looked back down at the future rulers of Alterealm. "I don't think I ever will." She sighed, "I don't want to change the way they see me." She rested her head on his shoulder again, "it wasn't all her, you know, I know all those children and their wants and needs."

He was silent, in the way he knew to be at times like this. Turning he looked at the new building just beside the palace. It wasn't as big as the palace but had taken almost a decade to build properly. The family had outgrown the palace and the underground chambers, but no one wanted to be too far from the others. "Have you decided yet? Are we to live in the new keep, or the new building above the underground chambers?"

She looked over at the building. "I think I'm going to take Quinton up on his offer and take some time off."

"The estate in the north?" He hugged her and tilted her chin up to look at him. "Whatever will they do without you, Mitz?" He gave her a playful smile.

She chuckled softly, "oh I'll be back." She inhaled slowly, then breathed it out. "There's something on the horizon, Ira, and we'll be needed here again soon enough."

Nine Sons' Prophecy

For the King's sons numbering nine...

Lives will change when new blood merges with those that reign.

Without mates, shall all sons remain until the time of the Huntress Queen comes to be.

At a time when lawlessness and chaos to be bred the huntress shall be born to keep the balance.
Hidden in another realm she hunts those lawbreakers and brings them to justice. Her destiny is concealed until the time of her need is upon Alterealm.
Neither of this world or her own, but of both.

When the marking unveils between her shoulders, the sundial will validate she is true and waiting to be found. The sundial will protect her from all manner of trickery and evil force and shield her from powers of all.
Her beauty and skill of the hunt will win the hearts of the brothers nine.
The Huntress Queen Daxx will stand equal with the throne and none shall fail to notice her right to be there.

Nine brothers must lay in wait for her to choose her King.
True mate to either twin King if the bond be made, she must select one or the other that can hold her heart right.

The Huntress's reign alongside her King will change the realms forever controlling the evil of both sides and bring peace to sun and moon.

For our King not chosen, a mate lies in wait, born of human blood. She will rule over his compulsion as no other could and bring him lifetimes of eternal peace."

To build the strongest realm the reign through all ages of time the brothers that remain will have their happiness found with only the one destined for them and no other.

The justice of righteousness will find, when he's not looking, a woman that sees all good and all evil from within. She shall hold a place in his heart as no other could. With his seer of truth at his side, the justice will prevail throughout the years of time.

For our loyal brother filled with the deepest sadness, he will find the touch of his woman will renew his heart and she is the only one that will be able to heal him inside.

A lost brother will claim his place beside the thrones with one that is equal to him in a way no other woman could be as she has the one thing he has sought through the years.

The keeper of peace will find his mate in a woman that is a champion for the meek. A woman without fear will bring justice to any whose morals faulter

Long prevailed the brother that controls thought will stand stronger when his mate that holds time is found.

The warrior brother that holds all law in his hand will be tempted no more when his female can give to him that which he desires the most.

The last brother of nine will stand stronger with his arcus mate at his side. Only she will be able to bring him the peace he's long sought.

Together the brothers nine, with mates of strength, will rule and protect all of Alterealm and the other realities within their reach.

KEEP READING FOR AN EXCERPT OF

Heart

Animal Senses Series

Book 1

By Jacqueline Paige

Chapter One

Blinking, Rayne glanced around. She was in the underground parking space in her apartment building and didn't even remember the drive. Her chest hurt, hands were vibrating and reality felt far away. Three times, she tried to extract the keys from the ignition, finally after fumbling she managed. *Come on, Rayne, get it together. Think!*

Her mind didn't want to accept the words that had come from Aiden's mouth, her fiancé. In all the years she'd known him, never had he used that tone. Scared her enough to send chills through her spine. She believed he meant every word. *I am not an idiot, I've always known he was a hard man, but the words turned my blood to ice and a part of me knows I'll never feel the same for him again.*

Taking a shaky breath, she groped around for her purse, feeling like she was moving through mud. Somehow, she managed to move and get out of the car. Her legs still felt like rubber, but she couldn't stay in the parking garage all day. Turning, she forced herself to move to the door.

What am I going to do? I can't marry a man like that. I'm not even sure if I can look at him now.

Stopping, she looked at the elevator door. Just the thought of stepping inside left her feeling suffocated and trapped. Hugging the purse again, she turned toward the stairwell. *Keep moving*—she had to.

Trapped, I am, aren't I? Trapped in a relationship. Just that one word showed her the next move. She had to get out of this relationship. Aiden was not her dream man, if such a thing existed, but he had been comfortable. Admitting that, she now accepted that the relationship was too comfortable to be real.

When she reached her third-floor apartment, she wasn't out of breath. But, as numb as she felt, she wasn't sure if she *was* breathing. Maybe this was just a dream and she'd wake up any second now. Giving herself a small reprieve, she let that thought marinate for a few seconds before reality came crashing back.

It took her two tries to get the key into the lock. *What had his associate said just before my world darkened? "We haven't found a body or any sign of him, Aiden."* Him, who? A body? *A body!*

As Rayne stepped inside her apartment the dreamlike veil lifted away, revealing reality. *A reality I'm not sure how I can live with.* She quickly locked the door, all three locks. Not it would protect her, Aiden had keys. Leaning back against the door she tried to calm down and think.

Aiden was some sort of mob, mafia...*whatever?* Standing there she waited to feel her doubts were unsubstantiated, but it didn't happen. Her fear *was* the truth. This explained the dangerous looking misfits he had in his employ. They had never quite *fit* she thought. Aiden wasn't a boy scout—she knew that. He was a powerful man, as his father had been, but what kind of power was now very clear to her. Closing her eyes, Rayne held a trembling hand over her heart, it was still beating too heavily. *I can't look at him again. Ever.* This only meant one thing...

She looked around the pretty apartment for a moment, taking two steps towards the kitchen before stopping. She had to leave, now. Everything was *his*. *He* paid for everything in this apartment, she worked in *his* gallery. Her whole world was controlled by *him*...

Moving in a slow circle, Rayne studied everything in sight.

Every. Single. Thing.

Bought by him, in one way or another. Taking a deep breath, she tried to exhale slowly. Failing, her breath huffed out in one loud whoosh. There was no alternative, she had to get out of here.

Today.

Right now.

Kicking off her shoes, she bent down, scooped them up, and headed towards the bedroom.

Faster than she ever changed before, the skirt was stripped off and tossed on the bed. Barely having both legs in her jeans, Rayne began pulling open drawers and cabinets, dumping the contests all over the bed. All she really owned were clothes, her beloved camera, laptop and a few mementos to remind her of her parents. All of it was going in her car. A thought made her freeze as she held the empty drawer over the bed— her car was in *his* name. Dropping the drawer on the pile, Rayne sat on the bed, defeated. In the mirror, a frightened woman stared back. Seeing herself was enough to jolt her back into action. Giving the frail looking reflection a determined nod, she made a solid decision. To hell with him. She was taking the car. He hated it, called it girlie, and complained it wasn't comfortable. *The car is now mine.*

Forty-five minutes later Rayne surveyed the bedroom. There was nothing left that she wanted. Leaning down and picking up the last bag, she went to set it with the rest. "This is pathetic, Rayne Andrews. Your entire life fits in six cases and a couple of purses."

She walked through the apartment for the last time, working out how to get all of the cases downstairs to the car without causing suspicion, when the ring of her cell phone pierced the silence. She looked over at her purse, the ringtone was Aiden's. A few seconds after it stopped, the phone on the table began to ring. *Can I do this?* Taking a deep breath, "Buy some time," she whispered aloud just before answering it.

"Hello?"

"There you are. You didn't answer your cell."

He may be using that soft tone, but she now *knew* what he was. "Oh, I was taking the garbage to the garbage room." Her hand shook as she held the phone and prayed that her voice didn't give anything away.

"Where the hell is that girl I pay to do that?"

Just the way he said it made her tremble. "I-it's Wednesday, Aiden. She doesn't come in today."

"Right. Listen baby, I may be here awhile. Could be most of the night..."

"That's—fine. I was heading to the spa shortly." Closing her eyes, she waited to see if he questioned that.

"Do you want me to come by in the morning to pick you up?"

For what? "Pick me up?"

He chuckled. "We have a brunch with Donny and his wife."

Letting out the silent breath she'd been holding. "Oh, yes please." *Please let me sound normal.*

"Okay baby. You go get all beautiful for me and I'll see you in the morning. Ten o'clock."

"Okay, Aiden."

"Love ya, baby."

"Me too." She hung up quickly. Suddenly gasping for air, Rayne tried to settle her nerves again. *Ten o'clock.* Looking over at the clock and doing the math, she had seventeen hours to disappear.

It took almost as long to get all the bags down as it had for her to pack them. Of course, if you're planning to pack your whole life up and vanishing, it would probably be easier if you didn't drive a *Cabriolet*. Fitting everything into the micro-sized car had taken more than one attempt. In the time it took to finish, she was much calmer about her decision to leave. Not that she had a choice, but she could always have a mini breakdown and cry her heart out, later. Right now, she needed a plan to figure out the next step.

The first stop was the gas station. Getting out of the car, she looked around, checking for Aiden or one of his men. *Great, paranoia already.* After she assured herself that he couldn't possibly know yet, Rayne walked over to the pump. As she lifted the card up to the slot, she realized that he could track her cards. As if the machine was going to grab it, she jerked her hand back and turned to get her purse. She'd need all the cash she had available. Looking over her shoulder again, she walked to the cash machine. This location was close enough to the apartment to not point in any direction— when she finally decided on which direction. Her hands weren't the steadiest as she punched in the numbers and requested the limit the machine would allow, the shaking increased when she grabbed the cash and stuffed it in her wallet.

Glancing around, she walked back to the pump, inserting a card to pay for the gas. It only took her a few minutes to decide she would hit a few more cash machines in the area to bypass withdrawal limits. Aiden might not drive by, but now she suspected he had people everywhere that would recognize her.

After the gas was pumped, she thought that a map would be a good thing, unless she planned to drive around Chicago endlessly—because that's the only place she'd ever driven. Reaching down, Rayne pulled out the nearest one, only to put it right back, it was a map of the one place she knew. Bending down, she studied the title of each map before spotting an oversized atlas with Canada in it. She grabbed that one. Before she could second guess the decision, she set it on the counter and waited for the clerk to ring it in.

With the receipt and atlas clutched in her vibrating hand, she went back to the car, hoping she could get through the next few moments without questioning what she was going to do next.

An hour later, she sat in an empty parking lot, trying to force a bagel down her throat. The atlas she'd purchased was propped against the steering wheel, endless lines of varying colors stared back at her. So many places and no idea where to go. She looked over at the glove box where she'd put her money—in a make-up bag no less. It had taken five different bank machines to empty her accounts of every cent she had. Her cards were now at their limits, accounts were empty and on a whim, Rayne had taken out a cash advance on the card Aiden had given her for emergencies. If this wasn't considered an emergency, she didn't know what was.

Focus, Rayne. Looking back at the map, she tried to wash down a bite with the lukewarm coffee. She knew making maps took a lot of work and was complicated in a way she didn't really care to understand, but they really weren't telling her anything. She needed her laptop and the internet to make a decision that the squiggly color co-ordinated lines weren't telling her. Sighing, she glanced around the parking lot. A hotel was at the far end. She reached down to pull the laptop case off the floor. Setting it on the passenger's seat, she opened it and hit the power button, praying for it to pick up a signal as she flipped through another few pages. There was a signal, not a strong one, but it would do. Bringing up a mapping site, she entered Chicago as the starting point. *Now what?* A starting point generally meant you needed a destination and that she didn't have. Flipping a few more pages, Rayne picked the first name that jumped off the page. Destination? Timmins, Ontario, Canada. Her heart was pounding as she hit enter.

Strangely, she felt relieved knowing she had decided on a location. Her resolve only faltered for a few seconds when she discovered there was a fourteen-hour drive to get there. Biting her lip, she looked out the windshield, not really focusing on anything. Was she ready for a fourteen-hour drive that would take her far away from Aiden? If she had translated the map correctly, where she was heading was right in the middle of nowhere. That meant there was less chance of her being found. Yes, she was ready. Picking up the notebook that was waiting for the details of *the* game plan, she started to jot down the directions, deciding after a few lines that she'd only write down the first five hours and then reassess her route from that point. She had no idea what it was going to be like driving this far.

Closing the laptop, she put it back on the floor and just sat there. Was she crazy for doing this? Yes, but she couldn't stay here and that left few options. She was alone, just like when her parents died. This time all the decisions to be made were going to be her own.

~

Her eyes felt completely dried out. Was such a thing even possible? She didn't know, but at the first drug store, she was getting some eye drops. Glancing at the time—again, Rayne squinted back at the road. *How long have I been driving now?* Four hours? No, closer to five, she needed to stop soon. A few hours ago, she had foolishly thought she would be across the border before planning a stop, but that wasn't going to happen. Driving at this speed meant she still had at least an hour and a half to go before reaching Mackinaw City and then another hour to the border. Considering the longest she'd ever driven passed an hour back, Rayne knew she wasn't going to make it. She had a newfound respect for people that drove for a living. The quick bathroom stop a few hours before hadn't been long enough. If she didn't stop soon, she was going to make mistakes and end up lost, or worse. Stopping would be for the best.

Blinking quickly, she tried to make her eyes not feel as dry and then focused on the sign she was coming to. A motel was thirty miles from here. Looking at the speedometer, Rayne attempted to do the math and calculate how long that would take, less than a minute later she gave up and decided it wasn't important. As long as she arrived at the motel before falling asleep. A few hours of rest, something to eat and a shower became the new goal.

After what felt like ten hours she could see the hotel's sign not too far ahead. Elation and a bit of pride filled her as she realized she'd made it to here without help. She was slowing down when she noticed two police cars sitting at the motel. All the hair on the back of her neck stood up. Aiden couldn't know she was gone already, could he? Would he involve police? Biting down on her lip, she thought he probably wouldn't, but she wasn't going to take any chances. Gripping the steering wheel tighter, her heart was crashing against her ribs at the thought that Aiden might find her. There would be more motels further away, and another chance to take a break.

It took several seconds for the sign she'd just passed to register. *I've done it!* She was almost to Mackinaw, at least that's what the sign had said. Taking a deep breath and fighting the grogginess that had been closing in for hours, she forced herself to keep going. Maybe a little air would help, not that it had a half hour ago, but it couldn't hurt. She rolled the window down, hoping it would help. Seven hours of driving, minus two very brief bathroom breaks and a stop for gas, and she'd managed to keep going. If she wasn't ready to pass out, she would be pretty impressed with what she'd managed.

After a few minutes of taking deep breaths she groaned, the open window wasn't working. Reaching for the radio, she fumbled with the buttons and flicked through the few stations that were clear, anything to sing to or even pretending to sing might work. She scowled at the radio. Turning it off, she stared at the road once again. "Okay," she tried to ignore how slurred her voice sounded. "Use your brain, get the blood pumping and drive." Wiggling a bit, she tried to sit straighter. "Great, my brain is already sleeping," she yawned while trying to see the sign that was getting closer. "Oh. Interstate one twenty-seven. I've been looking at that for what seems like forever," she mumbled to the eyes in the mirror. "And before that it was I31." She bobbed her head and tried to recall the roads before that. "One ninety...something, not that it matters really—It's not like I'm going to be going on the return trip," Rayne snorted and then laughed, not sure if it was delirium or exhaustion that had her talking to herself. "And what are you going to do when you reach your middle of nowhere in Canada, Ms. Andrews?" She glanced at the speedometer, even though she had no idea what it had said on the Mackinaw sign she'd just driven past. Clearing her throat, she looked at the reflection again. "I have no idea what I'm going to do. I didn't sit down and plot out a course of action before fleeing," she giggled quietly this time and then squealed as she drove by another sign. "What—ah, miles..." biting her lip a couple of times, she looked at the time. "Oh! A half hour!" Gripping the steering wheel with the very last of her energy, she focused on the road. "You did it. And the reward?" She attempted to smile, but yawned and erased what would have been the smile. "The reward is sleep."

Rayne stood, clutching the room key in her hand and looking at the car, deciding. With the way she'd stuffed the cases into the car, there was no easy way to get to the one that had the clothes she wanted, without taking everything out of the car. Did she care if she slept in something fresh? At this point, no, she would come back out later and sort out what to change into. As she started to head for the room, her brain flashed a warning. She wasn't feeling very trusting now. Turning back, she unlocked the car and reached in to grab her purse, money, camera and laptop. If anyone decided to pick up the tiny car and carry it away, she could get by with just this.

Stumbling into the dark room, she kicked the door closed. Her shoes were off in two steps, it felt glorious. Her leg smacked into the bed. Setting the precious items down on it, she shoved them to the other side and flopped down, face first. Had she asked for a wakeup call? The chances of a yes were high, but there was no way she could summon the energy to find out

KEEP READING FOR AN EXCERPT OF

CAFÉ SERENITY

By Jacqueline Paige

1

"Remi. This *guy* wants to know what's on the bacon, egg and cheese bagel…"

Remi winced and dropped the paperwork she'd been struggling with. She looked out the kitchen window to see Iris, one of her waitresses, standing in the middle of the café surrounded by customers. Every single one of them now looking at her.

"Guess we don't need to ask how her hot date went this weekend," Darien mumbled from behind her.

Betany came running through the door and slid to a stop, her eyes wide. "She didn't."

Remi glanced above the door Betany stood in to see the yellow light was glowing. The light that let the staff and patrons know that there were *normals* in the café. Normals was the term they used to describe the completely vulnerable, none-the-wiser humans.

Betany waved her hands in Remi's direction. "Stay. I've got this." Taking a deep breath, a sweet smile appeared on her face as she stepped out into the customer area.

"Well," Berk cleared his throat and glanced from Darien to her. "Happy Monday morning." With that, he turned back to the grill and flipped the French toast.

"She's been doing so well," Remi whispered as she watched Betany smile and charm the customers.

Leaning his huge body on the counter beside her, Darien nodded. "Yeah, she hasn't stunned anyone in months."

It was only seven in the morning, too early for anything but coffee as far as Remi was concerned, never mind a faerie with an attitude. "I don't think she's cut out for mornings."

"No one in our world does mornings." Darien lifted her chin and forced her to look into his chocolate brown eyes. "You, for example, look like you haven't slept."

Sighing, she pulled away from his touch. "I didn't really. I'm trying to get all the paperwork caught up before that stupid audit." Glancing out into the dining area, she almost groaned in relief to see the customers Iris had embarrassed smiling and joking with Betany. Thankfully Iris was looking after another table, a stubborn set to her chin. "How can they be so different?"

Darien chuckled. "Just because they're the same race doesn't mean they have the same personality."

Picking up her cup, she sipped her now cold coffee while thinking about everything she had to do in the next few days.

"Hey," Darien leaned closer, "why don't you get Iris to give you a hand in the office?" He shrugged. "She's got one hell of a brain in her head, and with Nadine's little one teething and keeping her up all night I'm sure she won't mind covering the dining room and not having to worry about the extra responsibilities for a while."

Remi turned to see Iris heading to the counter, her small frame was rigid, her expression clearly said she wasn't in the mood for human *or* para interaction right now. "It would solve a few issues."

Darien hissed out a sigh of relief. "Whew. I was half afraid you were going to put her back on nights." He wiped his hand down the front of his black t-shirt, over muscles she tried not to stare at. "Then I'd have to deal with Pascal and Attis PMS-ing non-stop because they had to work with her again." He shrugged. "Everyone loves Iris, she's great to work with, if she's in a good mood, otherwise we're all terrified."

Remi doubted that Darien was afraid of anything. Rolling her eyes in his direction she smirked. "I didn't know vampires got PMS."

He grinned. "They don't, but they bitch like they do."

Glancing at the time, she picked up the papers. "Order has to be put away." She glanced at the stack of boxes in the backroom. "Are you sticking around for the meeting?"

Moving around her, he reached across the counter and picked up the coffee pot and then grabbed her cup. Filling it, he handed it to her and smiled. "I've got the order and I'll do this morning's meeting, but I'll be late for this evenings." He winked at her. "If I don't grab a nap, I'll be grumpy tonight. We can't have a grumpy werewolf running Serenity After Dark." Giving her a heart-stopping grin, he sauntered out the door, grabbing a stack of boxes on his way past.

Remi watched the muscles flex in his arms and back as he lifted them with ease. Averting her eyes, she blew out a soft breath. Watching him made her flush all over her *whole* body. Turning, she noticed Berk was also watching Darien. He gave her a cheeky grin and then turned to serve up an order.

"It's not a crime to look," he wiggled his eyebrows up and down. "And I know better than to touch. I like all my appendages; attached and undamaged." He sighed dramatically. "It makes me sad though, so much man-meat and it's untouchable."

Shaking her head, Remi hugged the stack of papers into her chest and went over to lean at the end of the counter to wait for Iris to reach her.

Clipping her orders to the rack, Iris heaved a sigh and came to stand in front of her. "Sorry," she said in a somber voice. "They were so annoying asking about *every* single item on the menu. I mean if it says with cheese, they asked if it came with cheese…"

Remi could sympathize with her. Out-of-towners were so picky that way. "You could have passed them off to Betany, you know she doesn't mind."

Iris nodded, her short red hair bouncing with the motion. "I know. I just..." she sighed again.

"Listen," she gave her a hopeful smile. "I'd like you to help me get caught up in the office. With the auditors coming in two days, I need everything picture-perfect."

"Really?" Her eyes lit up.

"Yes."

She began untying her apron. "I'm all over that."

Remi looked over to where Betany was leaning, waiting for Berk to hand an order through the window. "Can you handle it for a few? Soren and the twins will be here shortly."

Betany nodded. "No problem, it's just coffee and a few orders right now."

Darien came back through the door and stopped to grin at the girls. "Disaster averted once again?"

Iris rolled her eyes and glared at him. "I wasn't going to harm them."

He chuckled. "Sure thing, Tink."

The ding of the door chime had all of them turning to see who came in. Back-up had arrived. Soren was moving quickly through the café in smooth graceful steps, like a cat, which made sense as she was a lynx shifter. Her smile was warm and friendly as she greeted the regular customers on her way past.

"Get Soren to help you if you get backed up before the girls get here." Remi told Betany as she motioned Iris to go down the hallway."

"I'll give them a hand." Darien added rubbing a reassuring hand down her back.

Remi smiled, even though she really wanted to step into his space and hug him. She'd be lost without him most days. "Thanks, Dare."

By nine thirty the breakfast customers were gone, a few regulars lingered watching the news channel while drinking their coffee. Most of them were retired or self-employed and didn't have to answer to the clock.

The elf twins, Ranae and Deanne were clearing tables and prepping for the next rush. Soren and Berk were in the kitchen preparing lunch items while singing show tunes. She didn't know how they did happy all the time, but it was better than working with grouches. Iris was content in the office entering data into the computer while Darien put the order away. Betany was helping him by restocking supplies. This left Remi time for some peace and quiet before more of the staff arrived for the meeting.,

Taking a stack of papers with her, she went outside to sit under the tree at the picnic table behind the café. It was silent out here for the moment, only a slight breeze was blowing; the sun was warm. The only sound was the gurgle of the water in the river as it moved downstream.

Flipping through the papers, she began to put them in order by date. Having to back-track into files that were five years old was an enormous task, and she was looking forward to it being done. Some of the papers in this pile went back as far as two years ago, when Doyle was still alive. She really needed to sort out the entire system he used to file and fix it.

Pausing, she looked up and stared toward the river. She still missed him. He'd been more of a father to her than any of the foster parents she'd had. Although, when she'd first met him, she thought he was insane or she might be having some sort of psychological break-down.

She'd been eighteen the first time she'd looked at the *Café Serenity* sign hanging out front, and the next seven years became a blur of edification that changed her life. Not just her life, but her mind-set and beliefs.

After leaving the foster system the second she turned eighteen, or as close as possible considering no one was one hundred percent sure of when she was born, she'd hopped on a bus with her starting-out allowance and ended up in Riverside.

On the bus she'd met a girl close to her age, Astrid. They'd hit it off right away. Astrid had invited her to stay with her, and even helped her get a job at the diner she worked at. Remi hadn't known a thing about waitressing, but with the customers demanding attention, she'd soon learned.

Things had gone well for about six months, until her life began spiraling downward, again.

Astrid's boyfriend, Carl, had tried to force himself on Remi. Thinking she was friends with her roommate had been Remi's first mistake. The second was telling Astrid about Carl, she freaked and kicked her out. Remi realized now she probably shouldn't have told her that he'd been screwing around on her for months with other girls.

Next thing Remi knew, she had no job or place to live. After sleeping in the post office for three nights, she'd gotten on the bus and headed to the other end of Riverside, setting out to find a place to live. Then she'd noticed the help wanted sign in the window of a unique-looking Café. Intrigued, she walked through the door. A café by day and a bar by night sounded interesting.

"Daydreaming?"

Remi jumped and turned to see Darien standing behind her, holding two plates.

"I brought you something to eat."

"Thanks." Setting her cup on the pages so the breeze wouldn't take them, she accepted the offered plate. "I was just thinking about Doyle," he handed her a fork, "about when I met him."

"You looked like a street rat when you came in." He took a bite of the hash browns.

"That's right; I forgot you were there that day." It was a lie; she could still remember seeing the large, muscular man unloading the delivery truck. She'd never seen someone with *that* much muscle up close before. Darien was one of those people that everyone looked at, it didn't matter whether you were a man or woman, you noticed him. He had soft understanding eyes, but his features were chiseled and hard, his body was too. All too often she'd overhear female customers calling him sexy and dangerous, in the same sentence.

He nodded slowly. "Yeah. I couldn't help wondering what Doyle was up to when he started showing you around without even knowing your name." He grinned. "Sneaky bugger that he was, placing a sign in the window only someone like *you* could see."

Remi took a few bites as she recalled. Doyle was a demon, what type she couldn't remember, there were far too many to know them all. A few days later when he sat her down and explained how he'd placed a sign in the window looking for her, and all about the para world, she'd thought he was crazy. He'd been seeking out an *almost human* to take in and train to run Serenity someday. Remi had never felt like everyone else, never quite fit in, but to be considered 'almost human', well even that was more than her off-center imagination could grasp. "You know I thought he was crazy when he told me I was almost human, but not quite."

Darien grinned. "You and me both. I thought he'd lost all sense bringing in a kid to mentor."

Pushing the plate away, she avoided the look he gave her, the one saying he wasn't happy she hadn't eaten all of it. "I was just grateful to have a place to live. I figured going along with his delusions wouldn't hurt anyone."

"Until your gifts started making an appearance..."

Stacking her half-eaten plate of food on top of his empty one, he leaned forward, his dark brown eyes moving over her face slowly.

"The first time you walked into Serenity After Dark and Pascal and Attis stopped and stared at you, I knew something was going on. I'd never seen them not be able to get inside someone's head."

Remi smiled. "Pascal is *still* trying to get inside my head."

He chuckled. "You'd think after seven years he'd give up."

Glancing down at the papers she frowned.

"You're really worried about this audit."

"I am. They're looking for something. The questions they asked were specific, not ones that you'd ask for in a random audit."

"You think someone pointed them in our direction?"

Nodding, she bit her lip. "How else would he know to examine the purchase orders?"

Darien reached across the table and squeezed her hand. "They're not going to find anything. Doyle's system keeps the unusual items in plain sight."

Closing her eyes, she exhaled slowly before looking back at him. "I hope so. Explaining bottled blood is not something even I could do."

"Remi."

Both turned to see Caitlyn leaning out the upstairs window. Caitlyn lived in the apartment at the back that Remi used to live in. She was nineteen and had been in Remi's care since she was thirteen, when her family had been killed.

Most days she was Remi's sunshine, that brightness in an otherwise dark world. Cait was a troll which, to Remi's mind before she met her, had meant big, ugly, fairy tale creature. The reality? Caitlyn was a petite, curvy beauty with snowy blonde hair, golden eyes and a smile that could thaw a glacier.

"I think you'd better come see this." She nodded to Darien. "Both of you." Her tone held a note of panic.

Remi glanced at Darien, his dark brows were drawn together in concern. Grabbing her cup and the papers, she got up and moved to the back door. She met them at the stairs, talking quickly and animated. Remi was only able to catch the main points, at least she hoped she did.

"So, Mel texted me telling me to check it out..."

Mel was one of Caitlyn's many admirers. He was a techie geek, a young werewolf that hung around whenever Cait was at work.

Cait practically danced on the spot as she turned her laptop around for them to see. Remi's stomach lurched as she looked at the gory pictures on the screen.

"Did Mel take these?" Darien asked his disapproval clear in his tone.

Cait gave him an annoyed look. "No. Mel would pass out if he'd seen this in person."

Reading the banner didn't help Remi understand. "Is this online for everyone to see?"

Cait tapped a polished nail on the screen. "No. It's only for our community, and you have to have a membership and password."

A glance at Darien's face told her this was news to him as well. Still confused, Remi looked away from the grizzly images of a shredded body to her charge. "So why are you showing us?"

Rolling her eyes, Cait leaned over the table and clicked on the screen. "Look." She enlarged photo.

Bending down, Remi focused on where she pointed. It was a picture of what was left of one blood covered arm, with a barely visible tattoo. Recognition had her straighten suddenly, her back bumping against Darien where he'd been looking over her shoulder.

"It's that inspector that was harassing us a few weeks ago." She tapped the screen. "He had this tattoo on his left arm. It's him."

Darien's hand rested on her hip as he stood close to Remi's back, the warmth from his higher body temperature didn't stop a shiver from going through her.

"Does it say what happened?" She swallowed and looked away from the screen to Cait.

Nodding, she brought up another page. "Word is he was ripped up like some crazed animal shredded him, but there's no bite marks to prove it."

"It's gruesome, honey, but what does that have to do with us?" Darien's breath brushed against the side of Remi's face, drawing her attention to the fact that he still stood close. Moving further away from him, she clutched the papers in her hand and shrugged at Cait.

Caitlyn gave a dramatic sigh. "He got all nasty and, in your face when you told him to take a hike."

Shaking her head, Remi glanced at Darien. "I didn't tell him to take a hike. I told him I had a business to run and couldn't have his minions getting in the way while they played with every wire and plug-in appliance."

"Still he was pissed and left saying he'd be back with a court order giving him the ability to do what he felt was necessary."

Darien rubbed the back of his neck. "We've scheduled the electrical updates. They'll be done in a few weeks."

Cait groaned. "They're going to look at *anyone* that had a problem with him."

"He was a pompous ass, Cait," Remi said quietly. "I'm sure a lot of others had a problem with him."

Sighing, she closed the laptop. "Okay, but don't say I didn't warn you." With that she flounced from the room, muttering under her breath.

Remi looked at the laptop.

"Hey don't worry; it has nothing to do with us." Darien's voice was soft and reassuring.

Remi glanced over her shoulder at him. "I hope you're right. With this audit I have more than I can handle."

Grinning, his eyes sparkling at her, he shrugged. "You don't give yourself enough credit, *Álainn*, you're stronger than anyone I know."

She hoped he was right.

About the Author

J. Risk is a pseudonym used by Jacqueline Paige

I wanted to write a story that would fit into new adult levels as well as adult. Something that was serious with fun elements-- paranormal / fantasy that everyone could read and enjoy.

I've decided to use J. Risk as the pen name for this to separate this series from my other writing which is definitely adult reading material.

Jacqueline Paige lives in Ontario in a small town that's part of the popular Georgian Triangle area.

She began her writing career in 2006 and since her first published works in 2009 she hasn't stopped. Jacqueline describes her writing as *all things paranormal*, which she has proven is her niche with stories of witches, ghosts, psychics and shifters now on the shelves.

When Jacqueline isn't lost in her writing, she spends time with her five children, most of whom are finally able to look after her instead of the other way around. Together they do random road trips, that usually end up with them lost, shopping trips where they push every button in the toy aisle, hiking when there's enough time to escape and bizarre things like creating new daring recipes in the kitchen. She's a grandmother to eight (so far) and looks forward to corrupting many more in the years to come.

Jacqueline loves to hear from her readers, you can find her at

http://jacquelinepaige.com/
Twitter @JacqPaige
Facebook:
https://www.facebook.com/authorjacquelinepaige

www.ingramcontent.com/pod-product-compliance
Lightning Source LLC
Chambersburg PA
CBHW031952120726
47898CB00002BA/366